Tales of the Whosawhachits

Invasion of the Realms - BOOK 3

Patricia O'Grady

authorHOUSE®

AuthorHouse™
1663 Liberty Drive
Bloomington, IN 47403
www.authorhouse.com
Phone: 1-800-839-8640

ISBN: 978-1-4634-3218-8 (sc)
ISBN: 978-1-4634-3216-4 (e)
ISBN: 978-1-4634-3217-1 (hc)

Library of Congress Control Number: 2011911300

Printed in the United States of America

Illustrations by: Diana Lynn Bell

This book is printed on acid-free paper.

Imagination is the paint brush of dreams, life is the canvas.

I dedicate this book with love to my dear friend Bobbie Conley (Lady Magick). She knows the true meaning of believing, deep down in her soul. May her garden be full of beautiful fairies to watch over all her dreams and wishes.

Back to the realms we flee,
now it's time to read book three.
More secrets of the world's mysteries unfold,
only the true believer will understand what they behold.

The adults will never comprehend,
any of this in the end.
Now we know about the men in space,
and their desire to take over the place.

Each world brings a special magic,
the loss of these would be tragic.
The realms and the humans must unite,
this time will prove to be a big fight.

The outside invaders may be green,
and now they are out in the open and clearly seen.
The realms must protect their own land,
and devise the ultimate great plan.

The fairy dust and gems just aren't enough,
help will be needed from someone they can trust.
It's a fine line to draw on what is risky,
this time it will be much more tricky.

Three worlds will collide,
someone will have to swallow their pride.
Make sure you keep an open mind,
with imagination you never know what you will find.

Welcome back to my world....again.

Always remember to keep your love of fairy tales, and then you will spend your life searching for magic doorways of opportunity and forgotten kingdoms of enlightenment.

Contents

Chapter 1
New World Invader

Today was the day that would change everything, not just the present and the future, but the past as well. Things would be different not only for the realms, but for the human world, nothing could or would ever be the same, the truth, the whole truth, would all be exposed. The realms always knew that they were responsible for many things that happened in the human world, from crop circles to earthquakes but now they came to realize that they didn't possess all the power and control, and that perhaps they never really did. There were times when unexplained things happened in the human realm, the gnomes usually just blamed the whosawhachits, who always denied it, and in turn blamed the fairies and so on, but somehow everyone just assumed it was someone in the underworld realms. Naturally there were times that they just thought the humans did these unusual things, but none of the realms inhabitants ever really thought that aliens from outer space were truly visiting the planet.

Gatsby thought about all the crazy stories he had read in the human tabloid newspapers over the years, the ones where people claimed they had seen UFO's in the sky or actually encountered aliens. Some of these people had insisted that they were even taken by the aliens onto these strange saucer shaped spaceships, but he always thought of it as utter nonsense, and no one could ever seem to produce any good credible evidence to prove their claims. He thought about all the times that the realms used these alien stories as a cover up, and implanted some of these ideas into human's heads, just to protect the realms existence from ever being discovered. Now he found himself standing and staring at this new creature which made him realize that he had been wrong about many things over the years, and this made him very sad. He had been taught things from his own predecessors, and learned from the thousands of year's experience just living his own life, which included being the Key Holder of the Realms, and one thing he was always sure of, that beings from outer space simply didn't exist. In some ways he was happy to be in the chair of second of command, he knew that he didn't have the energy or fight in him for what would come.

Jerry was determined that he would protect the realms from any and all danger, if this alien turned out to be a real problem, something that he would determine very carefully. He knew that Gatsby was just as surprised by his visit as he was, and therefore would be able to offer little or nothing as far as advice on how to handle the situation from past experience with them. They were beginning uncharted territory, a new venture, and it would change history as they all knew it. He would certainly have to step up in his brand new position as Key Holder of the Realms, he would be tested to his limits, and everyone in the realms would be not only watching his every move, but judging him step by step.

Elvin was absolutely delighted to see the alien, and just couldn't wait to befriend him. The whosawhachit thought about all the games they could play together, and couldn't wait to introduce him to all of his brother whosawhachits. His eyes almost seemed to dance in his head, with thoughts of the possibility of being able to visit other planets out in the solar system.

Elise too was impressed by the sight of this brand new creature and she wondered what, if any, kind of powers it possessed. Certainly the large antenna on its head had some kind of purpose, and it all just made her wonder, how she could use it to her own advantage. She was determined to find everything out about this alien.

Hubert stood scratching his head, not quite understanding what any of this really meant. He watched the antenna on the aliens head swing back and forth, but he was more intrigued by the white space boots he wore, and didn't understand how they could be so clean, considering the drilling he had just done to break down the realm wall.

Annastarlis and Nerby seemed shocked, maybe even a little scared. Both were still slightly curious but made sure that they stood back and observed the alien from a distance, allowing the gnomes and Elvin to take the lead, and communicate with him.

Mystic stood with her hands on her hips, looking as beautiful as usual, but her facial expression showed she was mildly annoyed by the inconvenience of it all. She really cared less about the invasion of the alien itself, and more about how and when the wall in her realm would be repaired.

Zepadoodle the little green creature from planet Kaboris was just as surprised to encounter the realm inhabitants. The alien knew nothing about gnomes, fairies, trolls, whosawhachits, or whosawhachettes, these strange beings were all new to him, and he was more than curious. The aliens thought they knew everything about planet Earth, probably because they had studied and visited for thousands of years now, watching and waiting for the proper time to step in and just take it over. They had observed the humans, understood their behaviors, wants, needs and desires. The green creatures had studied the surface of the earth so well they understood how everything worked, primitive as it all seemed to them, so beneath their own superior intelligence and technology, they thought it would be so simple. They had made one major mistake; and it would prove to be a costly one to them, the aliens had never taken the effort or the time to study under the earth's dirt ground surface, down deep, into the hidden depths of the realms, until now.

The aliens discovered the realms, by sheer accident. Zepadoodle was sent out on a scouting mission, he was to search for hidden empty pockets under the earth, a place that he could set up a base for more of his own kind to come and live, to continue their study of the planet, and of its inhabitants, the Earthlings. The aliens already had several of these camp bases set up on Earth, all well hidden, most down deep in the ocean, places the humans didn't have the technology to venture and locate, and most likely never would. They were already living in these camps for hundreds of years, making their study of the planet easy because they didn't have to constantly travel back and forth from their own planet which was many light-years away. These camps had living quarters, and full laboratories, set up for scientific experiments, testing of different chemical compounds from the Earth, and lastly, yes, the very places that they would conduct medical experiments on the few humans that they had dared to abduct.

Zepadoodle needed to ask questions, he needed to conduct a full and extensive investigation of his latest discovery. He would have to write a detailed written report of everything he found, because many questions would be asked of him, and he knew that he needed to know all of the answers or he would pay the price from his superiors. He was always prepared, extremely efficient, and entitled to the respect his position came with, his biggest flaw however was that he border lined on being outright arrogant. He would often take a full team with him on these ventures, but this time, expecting it to be a quick uneventful trip he had traveled alone. He had many questions to ask, but the one thing that he could clearly gather from pure observation, was that these beings were very different from humans, they were special, each and every one of them.

The aliens had read every book available on earth, from children's fairytales to medical textbooks, all to gain understanding of the human race. Zepadoodle knew that from these book descriptions, Annastarlis and Nerby were fairy's, and he also recognized gnomes and trolls, which were all portrayed as fictional beings, so seeing that they existed caused him great confusion and turmoil. It made him wonder if everything he had read in human books over the years could be believed and taken as complete and total fact, even if it had been published under non-fiction. The purple and pink creatures with the

4

candy striped twisted horns on their heads were something he had no concept about at all; he had never read any research that explained what they could possibly be.

"I guess the polite thing to do here, would be to say, welcome to our world," said Gatsby almost shrugging his shoulders nervously shifting his eyes from the alien over to Jerry.

"I demand to know what kind of creatures you are," said Zepadoodle directing his question towards Elvin and Elise, and completely ignoring the statement Gatsby had just made to him.

"I'm a whosawhachit, and my sister is a whosawhachette, and you came to find us in our land, so you need to just chill out with the attitude, antenna head," said Elvin sensing the authority type tone in the aliens voice.

"I already know what the rest of you are fairies, trolls, and gnomes, however we have been wrongfully informed that you were just a figment of human's overactive imaginations, written as pure fiction for children's amusement," stated Zepadoodle.

"So now you know the truth, gnomes, fairies, and trolls do exist, we are peaceful however quite secretive and plan to keep it that way, which I believe clearly gives us both something in common," said Jerry stepping forward in an attempt to show he was the one in charge, and desiring this to be a friendly encounter.

"I shall decide if we have anything in common, or what kind of a threat if any, you pose to me," said Zepadoodle.

"Let me assure you that, we can be helpful to each other, we pose no threat to anyone, and certainly hope that you aren't a threat to any of us either," said Jerry forcing a slight smile which came off strained and awkward.

"I do as I please, I make no promises or agreements until I have gathered all the information that I require," said Zepadoodle.

"Understood, but I would appreciate it if you would please give us more information about what you are, because as I'm sure you already know, we didn't believe aliens from other planets existed either," said Jerry attempting to put them on a even playing field.

"I'm asking the questions here, allow me to continue with my investigation," said Zepadoodle removing a glowing neon red writing tablet and strange looking pen instrument from his pocket, as if he had planned to scribble down notes.

"Excuse me, but you are an uninvited invader, here in our home land, therefore I believe I am the one who should be calling the shots," said Jerry strongly.

"Yes, and just look at the damage you have done to my realm, this is a mess, and you haven't even apologized for it," huffed Mystic, still clearly upset about the disarray of her realm.

"I make no apologies, not ever, I'm on a mission. If you sustained damage, that is not my problem," said Zepadoodle.

"Well, that isn't very nice, green man," said Elvin clearly disappointed that the alien was not going to be much fun, and wanted to be everyone's boss.

"Please, everyone be quiet, this isn't helping matters. Zepadoodle, I believe it would be best if you came along with me, over to the gnome realm. Let me properly introduce myself, my name is Jerry, and I'm the Key Holder of the Realms, the ruler here. We can sit and talk at the Great Hall of Justice, exchange thoughts, information and ideas. There is no reason for either of us to make this hostile," said Jerry attempting to calm the situation down, and make sense of everything that had happened.

"If you are the leader here, then I will talk to you. I have no desire to speak with anyone that offers me useless data," said Zepadoodle shooting a look at Elvin as if to say, don't waste my time.

Chapter 2
Golden Rule Days

It was the first day of school, and once again Kyle and Eric were in the same class. It was truly a surprise to everyone, including Eric that he had managed to graduate from the 4th grade, because he had struggled so much last year in Mrs. Edwina's classroom. She had passed him with the bare minimum grade point needed to the 5th grade, and many toyed with the idea that she simply pushed him thru just because she couldn't handle even the thought of having him in her classroom for another school year. Although, this theory was suggested by several people, anyone that seriously knew Mrs. Edwina, understood, she had deep seeded principles, and would have only put the boy thru to the next grade if he indeed had passed her class on his own merit.

The boys entered the brightly lit classroom together, to find their new teacher Mr. Burt Koza eagerly waiting for them. He announced that they should take the seat of their own choosing and Kyle and Eric picked two desks sitting side by side towards the back of the room. Eric thought this position would be perfect for cheating, something he always needed to consider. Location was everything, especially if it was out of the eyeshot of the teacher. Scribbled on the blackboard in large chalk letters were the words, "Mr. Burt Koza" and "Welcome

7

Back". The classroom was decorated with the typical school learning posters, a flag, and a world globe but it did have a few unusual things that sparked the kid's attention. One of the front corners of the room was decorated in a space theme, with pictures of the moon and such, but above that poster board hung something very different. From the ceiling suspended on clear fishing line was a large plastic model spacecraft of the Starship Enterprise from the old television show Star Trek, which seemed odd and out of place. Mr. Koza often spoke of this TV show and the newer ones that had spun off from it. He was a self proclaimed "Trekkie" or maybe just a "Trekker". There is significant dispute on this point. Some trekkers believe that a trekkie is someone so obsessed with the series that he has "no life," while a trekker is simply a big fan, perhaps Koza was somewhere in between.

Eric took his time sizing the new teacher up. The man seemed to be lost in the time of the hippie years of the 60's, and one had the feeling he could just hear the Beatles music playing in his own head. He was dressed in faded jeans, button down shirt, and a wide tie loosely hung around his chubby neck, haphazardly knotted. He was slightly stout, and wore a short trimmed beard and mustache with wire framed glasses, and a large unmistakable pleasant smile on his face.

It was clear to everyone that it would be more of a relaxed type atmosphere this year in the classroom, from the way their new teacher casually sat on the outside corner of his desk as he spoke to his students. Last year in Mrs. Edwina's class it was stiff and all about education, work, structure and discipline. The bell rang signaling the official beginning of the day and Mr. Koza began to address his new students, first by doing the usual roll call of attendance. As he went thru the names, he would stop and ask a few of the kids if they had an older brother or sister that maybe would have been a student of his a previous year or so based on a last name he recognized. Then he would make a pleasant comment about their relative as if he was returning down memory lane via the yellow brick road.

When the man talked about history his eyes almost glistened and twinkled. His entire face seemed to light up as the words passed his lips, making it all sound like they would be going on a fun adventure instead of learning schoolwork. He talked about everything from the importance of debates, voting, protests, and boycotts to the founding of the nation of the United States. Koza was a diehard Liberal Democrat and he would have more influence on his student's future political views then he even possibly knew.

The kids all seemed to really like this new teacher, but not Eric. Eric didn't like the man one bit mainly because he represented the one thing he disliked the most, authority. No matter how jolly and friendly the man was, he could still dish out homework assignments, and Eric was determined to give him a hard time.

The man continued to talk to his class, teaching them, and allowing them to ask questions freely, in fact he encouraged class participation as much as possible. He cracked several jokes and all the kids laughed, except for Eric. Mr. Koza seemed oblivious to this fact, or that he had the troubled kid of the school placed into his care for the year. Eric wondered if this teacher had been warned about him, which really didn't make any difference, because the man would soon find out that he had big problems on his hands. Mrs. Edwina did in fact take the time to speak with Mr. Koza, she felt it was her duty to tell him of all the things the child was capable of, but the man didn't seem ruffled by any of it.

Koza opened the floor to question from the kids, they could ask him anything they wanted, it was his way of getting to know them, and for them to get to know a little bit about him.

"Do you give a lot of homework," asked a pretty brunette girl wearing a short ponytail from the back of the room.

"I don't really believe in homework, if I do my job here in the classroom, then taking work home shouldn't be necessary. I may give you one project during the year, but you will be given plenty of time to complete it, and it will be something you'll enjoy for the Social Studies fair," said Koza.

This was a great question indeed, and Eric certainly liked the answer that the teacher gave, however he still had many reservations about the man. He looked at the spacecraft hovering from the ceiling in the corner, and decided to give the teacher his very first test. He quickly raised his hand, hoping he would be called on next to ask his question.

"So, what's the deal with the Starship, do you believe in aliens and UFO's and stuff or do you just like to still play with toys?" asked Eric stiffly, secretly hoping he could embarrass the man.

Koza didn't answer the question immediately. He stroked his beard and thought for a second. He picked up two Star Trek action figures that sat prominently on his desk, gifts from students of years past and held them in his hand. He looked at them, placed them back down on his desk, stood up and then answered the question.

"There are many possibilities, and my mind is open to all of them. It's a big universe, and I think it's small minded to think we could be the only intelligent life force. As for me still playing with toys, video games seem to be one of my favorites," answered the teacher with a smile and a wink.

Most of the kids enjoyed how he answered the toy part of the question, and even the teacher himself seemed pleased. He didn't allow Eric to faze him, and most likely never would. Score one for the teacher, zero for Eric, and now the boy was only more determined.

"Do you think aliens are here on Earth posing as human beings, because sometimes I think the teacher I had last year was an alien," said Eric looking towards his fellow students for some kind of a laugh.

"It has long been a debate that extraterrestrials pose as humanoids, and I would have to say that anything is possible. I doubt nothing, in fact, I think I have had a few students in my class over the years that made me wonder the very same thing," replied Koza.

Score two for the teacher, zero for Eric, and all the kids laughed. The remainder of the school day went about fairly normal, to Eric's complete frustration. It had become very clear to him, that it would take a lot to make this man angry, but he would somehow find a way. He would think about it tonight, and tomorrow the man would be in for it. He resented the fact that the other children seemed to be enjoying school, and that they truly liked this teacher.

Kyle went straight home after school. He found his mother Sarah sitting in the living room sharing a glass of milk and homemade cookies with his little sister Aimee Lynn. It was also her first day at school. The little girl started the first grade, and had been properly placed into a special needs class, because she still refused to speak.

Sarah was patient with the girl, chatting away, in hopes that someday she would receive a few muttered answers from her conversation. While it was true, that on the very rare occasion Aimee Lynn would manage one or two words, she seemed to reserve them for very special occasions. When she did so, Sarah was delighted.

Kyle told his mother about his first day, grabbed a few cookies, a glass of milk, and off he went into his bedroom to change out of his school clothes. He needed to head out to baseball practice. He would be playing on the same team that he was on last year, and was happy in his own way, that Eric didn't want to join. As much as he had finally become friends with this other boy, he still enjoyed time away from him, because Eric could be very taxing to be around all the time. Plus he was never really able to give Eric his complete trust, because he knew all too well, that the boy could turn on him any second, although as time went by, he seemed to do it to Kyle less and less.

Kyle was just about to leave his bedroom when Annastarlis and Nerby popped in to see how he was doing. They would make a point of stopping in to see Kyle a few times a week.

"You aren't going to believe who Jerry is having a meeting with right now," said Nerby excited to share all of the realm news.

"I don't think we should be talking about that," snapped Annastarlis.

"Why, it's just Kyle, we don't have to hide anything from him," said Nerby in a defensive manner.

"Fine, go ahead, but if we get into trouble for it, you are the one who is going to take all the blame, don't say I didn't warn you," said Annastarlis flipping her hair.

"Don't I usually get all the blame anyways," said Nerby.

"Well, you are usually the one who causes all the problems, and drags me into all of the messes" said Annastarlis with attitude.

11

"Ok, stop fighting and just tell me who Jerry is having a meeting with," said Kyle impatiently, and looking at his wristwatch to make sure he wasn't going to be late.

"Zepadoodle, he's a alien creature from the planet Kaboris," blurted out Nerby in excitement.

"Oh, come on, you're pulling my leg," said Kyle doubting what he was hearing.

"No, he's not kidding you, he's a real live space alien," added Annastarlis, now excited that the cat was out of the bag, and she was free to talk about it.

"What's he look like?" asked Kyle.

"Green skin, with an antenna on his head," said Nerby.

"Now, you're just messing with me," said Kyle disbelieving them.

"No, we're totally serious. He drilled thru a wall from a volcano here on earth, right into the fairy realm," insisted Nerby.

"I thought it was the realms that implanted all the ideas of aliens and stuff, and that they didn't really exist," said Kyle.

"Well...we have certainly done that in the past, but the truth of it is, we didn't think that beings from outer space existed either, until now. Even Gatsby and Jerry were in a complete state of shock," said Annastarlis.

So, what's the deal with him...does he seem friendly?" asked Kyle.

"We don't really know yet, but he kinda has an attitude," said Nerby.

"Yeah, that he does," added Annastarlis.

Chapter 3
Meeting of the Minds

Jerry and Gatsby led Zepadoodle to the Great Hall of Justice. Zepadoodle took everything in as they walked thru the fairy realm, into the astral plane, and then finally the gnome realm, missing nothing.. His brain was similar to that of a computer, and he seemed to be recording everything he saw, for future reference. Zepadoodle was amazed at the gem lined streets in the gnome realm, mostly because he was already well aware of the powers that gemstones held. The aliens had mined many gemstones from the planet earth, thousands of years ago, and tapped into their great natural resource of power. He wondered if the gnomes were aware of what they had, and he knew that when he left this place, he would need to take all of these stones along with him.

The three took seats at the long table inside of the hall, and wasted no time starting their conversation. It was Jerry's hope that he would manage to get as much information as he could about the new invader and his true intentions. He had already decided that he himself would offer as little information about the realms, its inhabitants, and their abilities as he could possibly get away with, he needed to be vague. He hoped that the aliens would believe that the realms possessed more magical powers than they really did, because deep down inside, he was afraid that they didn't have enough.

Zepadoodle immediately took out his glowing neon tablet and what first appeared to be some kind of writing instrument and placed it on the table in front of him. It was clear that he would be using this item, to somehow record or document their conversation. The gnomes were shocked when the alien took what they originally thought was something of a pen or pencil, and placed it into a compartment that opened on top of his head , and made it slide down into the antenna. As soon as he did so, the board seemed to glow even brighter, and Jerry and Gatsby looked at each other puzzled.

"What did you just put into your head..ah...antenna and can you tell us what is that glowing board in front of you?" asked Jerry in a non-threatening manner.

"Something you wouldn't understand, your brains just aren't advanced enough, but let me assure you that it is not a weapon," replied Zepadoodle slightly annoyed.

"I didn't think it was a weapon, I was merely asking from curiosity purposes, so that we may learn from each other," said Jerry sincerely hoping that he could manage to make some kind of a connection with this being.

"If you must know, it is...in terms that you would be able to understand...a transmitter, that beams direct impressions of what is happening here to the other members of my group. It allows them to read my direct thoughts, and for them to hear and see everything that is happening to me," said the alien.

"So you are saying that it gives you and them telepathy abilities," asked Gatsby attempting to show that gnomes were far from stupid.

"That is correct, very good that you knew that, but you will find that we are a far more advanced culture than you or the other human inhabitants of this planet. We have no need for such outdated things like cell phones, recorders or satellite because we are capable of communicating directly from our own minds, believe me you are no match for us," sneering Zepadoodle.

"You would be very surprised by the magical abilities we possess here in the hidden realms, don't make the mistake of underestimating us either," said Jerry insulted yet still very much intimated, and hoping that he wasn't showing that on his face.

Zepadoodle let out a low sounding laugh, he seemed more amused by the statement than threatened by it. While he was already aware that the gnomes were very different from the humans, and that they most likely did possess some kinds of magical qualities, he was already able to decipher that they didn't have his own intelligence level.

The beings from Kaboris had large oval egg shaped heads for a reason. As they evolved over the years, they used more and more of their brain, which made each generation smarter, with more natural born abilities, that they were able to tap into. Once their society reached the point of using their entire brain, the next generation was born with a larger brain, that gave them more possibilities, therefore it seemed that the younger aliens had even bigger heads to harness their own brains out of necessity.

Zepadoodle already knew that humans only used a portion of their brain. They failed to tap into the remainder of its use and therefore had only managed to excel in silly things like electronic technology, and building gadgets. Humans had failed to ever change or better their own bodies even over many centuries of time, they had just stopped evolving. The Earthlings had worried about the world around them, and how they could alter it for their own comforts or pleasures rather than how they could change themselves. From what he had already gathered over all the years of abducting humans, one of the only changes he could see is that they had grown taller, had bigger feet, and seemed to be getting fatter, all of which seemed pointless and without proper reason. He wasn't quite sure about the realm inhabitants, so they would need to be studied more carefully. He already analyzed that realm inhabitants showed emotion, and portrayed that they were soft at heart and he took these things as signs of their weaknesses. He was well aware that he needed to take the upper hand now, and because this meeting really had little to do with getting to know each other, but more about exactly how much of a threat one was to the other. They had already begun a mental power struggle, and he was certainly the one on top for the moment and he planned to keep it that way.

"Let's waste no more time, and just get down to business. We have been visiting this planet for thousands of years. We need a new residence, planet Kaboris has problems that are now out of our control. We have estimated that our entire planet will experience a catastrophic collision with other planetary embryos currently in orbit, which will shatter our planet into hot dust particles causing the ultimate extinction event. We already know that can't be changed, therefore we must evacuate, and have been preparing to do so for several years now," said Zepadoodle somberly.

"I'm very sorry to hear that, I do understand your dire need," said Jerry concerned about what all of this would mean for the realms and the humans. He shot a quick look over to Gatsby who shared the same concerned expression on his old face.

"We haven't spent all of our time and energy coming here for nothing. We have been aware that this situation was coming, and have planned accordingly. We need this planet, and therefore will be seizing it for our own use," said Zepadoodle non-chantingly.

"What do you mean exactly by the word seizing it? Certainly you understand that everyone could live here peacefully and share this planet," said Gatsby.

Once again Zepadoodle laughed, he found the gnomes pure nature amusing in a way, as they had already showed him they were not aggressive. He did however feel that on some level they could manage to be useful, at least temporarily until the full takeover was completed. He seemed to take a minute of silence, as if halfway in a trance, however in truth, he was really busy speaking mentally to other aliens set up in the Earth camps, and a few higher level officials still living on Planet Kaboris.

"As soon as the simpleminded humanoids are aware of our presence they will certainly panic and start a war, a war that they couldn't even begin to win. This war would only cause major damage to this planet, and we would prefer to avoid it. We don't want any more of this planet's natural resources destroyed by their pure ignorance.

They have already managed to do enough damage from their lack of understanding of how their backwards technology is ruining things that can't be reversed," said Zepadoodle.

"I understand that, we don't like war either, nor do we want to see any damage done to the lands," said Jerry.

"Then I expect that you will cooperate with us fully, and not get in our way during this time of transition. My superiors have just informed me that if you give us your full assistance, we will spare you, and your kind," said Zepadoodle in an official tone, which almost sounded like someone else's voice speaking thru him.

"Well, clearly before we could enter into any type of an agreement, we would have to understand what your exact plans are, and what terms you expect from us. Also, just to set the record straight, we represent all the inhabitants of the realms, the gnomes, fairies, trolls, whosawhachits, and whosawhachettes," said Jerry merely attempting to gather as much information as he could about what the aliens had planned.

"You will accept our terms, or you will not be, it is very simple, we are not in negotiations," stated Zepadoodle smugly.

"I have to wonder, with so many other planets out there, why you must pick planet Earth," requested Gatsby.

Before the alien could answer, there was a large knock at the door, and Jerry got up from his chair to see who would be interrupting this meeting. Everyone in the realms knew that they had an invader and that an interrogation of sorts was being conducted, although clearly it wasn't going as originally planned. Jerry was not the one in charge of this meeting, so in a way, he welcomed a small break to hopefully regroup. He did think that if someone was at the door, it had to be important, and he couldn't imagine what else could have happened, although, nothing at this point would have certainly surprised him.

"I so thought that our new friend Zepadoodle might be hungry, and so I made him a beautiful, tasty welcome cake," said Elise attempting to look past Jerry to have another look at the alien sitting at the table.

"Elise, I appreciate your thoughtfulness, however we are in the middle of something very serious, and don't want to be interrupted," said Jerry annoyed.

"Fine, be like that, I so tried to do something nice, no wonder my brother so doesn't like you," said Elise angry, now focusing her full attention on the glowing red neon board sitting on the table in front of the alien.

"Please allow this creature to enter, I have questions I want answered," demanded Zepadoodle. He thought her statement was very telling, clearly the realms weren't as united as the gnomes would have liked for it to appear.

"I would prefer to finish this conversation privately, just between the three of us, the gnome council rules the realms, without any outside input. We make the rules, all the decisions AND we enforce them," said Jerry loudly as he motioned for Elise to leave.

"Well, I don't wish to continue privately. Bring this pink colored creature to me NOW," said Zepadoodle rising from his chair in such a strange way, that he almost appeared to be levitating.

Elise needed no more encouragement, and pushed past Jerry, practically running towards the large table, balancing the large white and pink frosted cake in her hands. She had her own agenda, she not only wanted to be the first to get any information about this new visitor, but she wanted to see what he could do for her. She had long ago decided that it was always best to keep her friends close, but her enemies even closer, especially if she could manipulate them for her own selfish needs.

Chapter 4
Secrets Kept

Kyle walked quietly home from his baseball practice, he was a little frustrated that his new coach put him in the spot of playing left field. This year he had high hopes of pitching, but his tryout for the position didn't go as well has he had hoped. It was going to be another boring year for him, standing in "left out" field, daydreaming about being on the mound. He was doing much better batting, and that was just going to have to be enough for now, until he could prove his value to the team. He was never going to be the star hitter, but at least this year with his weight loss, he would manage to at least get on base.

When he rounded the corner of his block, he could see his stepfather Joe pacing around outside in the driveway on the telephone. This meant one thing, that he was talking official FBI business, and was seeking privacy for his conversation. Normally Kyle paid little attention to these secretive phone calls. Mostly because he had no interest in them, and understood little about what was being said from just hearing one side of it, but also because it had been drilled into his head by Joe, and his mother, that he should never eavesdrop on them. Although it was never really said out loud, he gathered that there would be some kind of repercussions from doing so. Joe always acted his role of the FBI agent, and maybe in his own subconscious Kyle even feared that Joe would have him arrested for breaking the law of listening to his top-secret government conversations. He knew that was paranoid thinking on his own part, surely Joe wouldn't really have him put into jail. He knew that his own fears were due to the intimidation he felt from Joe, and it started to make him angry that the man had that much of an effect on him and his own security, especially inside of his own house.

Today was different, and for whatever reason, Kyle found that he was curious about Joe's conversation, or maybe he just felt the need to rebel. Kyle had learned some things from Eric, to be stronger, stand up for himself, stop allowing people to walk all over him and every once in a while, just try to throw caution to the wind and enjoy life. Kyle was starting to become a little more assertive, and he would take risks he thought would have a decent payoff.

Perhaps it was the way that Joe paced nervously around the driveway, or how he seemed to be waving his arms wildly in the air as he spoke, that really got Kyle's full attention. When Joe was stressed out with work, he showed it in the way he walked and talked, Mr. Cool wasn't always so cool. Something important seemed to be going on, and Kyle couldn't help but wonder if it had anything to do with the information that Annastarlis and Nerby had just told him about their new alien visitor from some other planet showing up in the realms. Was it possible that Joe knew about the alien? Had his UFO been seen landing inside of the volcano? Had Joe somehow even discovered the secret of the realms existence? Kyle knew that he would just make himself crazy guessing, because Joe could be talking about just about anything.

Kyle cautiously continued down the street towards his house, taking the opportunity to duck behind cars, a hedge of bushes, trees, and anything else that he thought would provide him cover. The sun was on its way down, it was almost dusk, and would be dark within the next half hour, and Kyle wished that time would go faster. Kyle needed to use the darkness to hide because he didn't know how close he could get before the ever observant Joe would spot him trying to sneak up on him. To his advantage Joe had been completely engrossed in his conversation, and paid no attention to anything going on around him, which was truly out of character for him, he almost seemed emotional. This told Kyle that the phone call was of great importance, and now he wanted to hear what was being said even more.

Once Joe turned his back, Kyle took the chance to run from his hiding spot behind the next door neighbor's car, and thru the grass to the side of his own house. He pressed his body up against the wall, where he would not be seen, but should be able to hear everything his stepfather was saying, it was the perfect spy position he thought.

Kyle listened carefully; he could hear Joe saying something about Aimee Lynn. He heard Joe say that something wasn't ever going to happen, and that he would do whatever he had to do to put a stop to it. Then he said something about some people being insane, and getting them the help that they needed. There seemed to be a long pause in the conversation, where Joe was just listening to the other party talk, which Kyle found frustrating. Finally Joe finished up his conversation by saying something about how well Aimee Lynn was adjusting, and how Sarah was bringing her back from the damage of an unstable environment, and that he would contact his attorney if necessary.

Joe hung up the phone and went back into the house. Clearly since his phone call wasn't regarding work, he would talk to Sarah about it. Kyle waited a minute and then ran around the house to the front door, hoping that he hadn't already missed what Joe would have said to Sarah. He was shocked to find that Joe was just sitting in the living room watching the evening news on television. He did see that Joe was nervously tapping his foot on the floor, as if he were restless. Joe called out a "Hi" to Kyle as he closed the door behind him, and the boy was relieved to know he had gotten away with listening to his phone conversation.

Aimee Lynn was in her usual spot, sitting on the floor pushing a few dolls around in a toy car. Although, she didn't say hello to him, she did look up and smile when he came in the door, they were starting to make some kind of a connection.

Kyle headed into the kitchen, he wanted to observe his mother.

She was like an open book and always showed when she was upset; his mother never hid anything from him. Sarah seemed to be in a pleasant mood, she was just taking a meatloaf out of the oven, and he could see that the table had already been set.

"Can I do anything for you, Ma?" asked Kyle attempting to be helpful, and to judge if she was truly doing well.

"I'm just about set, but if you want to grab the salad out of the refrigerator and put it on the table, I would appreciate it," said Sarah happy.

"You got it," said Kyle opening up the refrigerator.

"Then if you would go call Joe, and your sister, we can sit down to eat," said Sarah happy.

During dinner Kyle kept a watchful eye between his mother and Joe. He was determined to pick up on any signs or clues between them, that there was a problem going on, but he saw nothing. Sarah seemed to be in a very good mood relaxed and smiling, just enjoying a family meal.

Aimee Lynn sat quietly eating, but she was making progress, Joe was right about that. When Sarah went to cut her meat for her, the child pulled the plate towards her, and motioned with her hand, letting her mother know that she wanted to do it herself. This was a sign that she was adjusting and showing some kind of independence.

Kyle focused his attention on Joe, he was crankier than usual, and he could see the stress showing on his face. Joe never really talked that much at the dinner table, it was always Sarah who started and ended most of the conversations, and tonight was no different. Kyle noticed that Joe looked over at Aimee Lynn several times during dinner and smiled at her, in fact, once Kyle even saw him give the child a wink. Joe wasn't really a bad guy, and he was becoming a decent father, he could be abrupt, and maybe a little cold, but it was becoming more evident, that underneath his tough FBI exterior, he really did care.

Joe normally ate quite a bit, he loved Sarah's cooking, and the ten pounds he had put on since they were married showed it. Tonight Joe only ate half the food on his plate, something was bothering him, and Sarah had started to pick up on it.

"Anything wrong....did it taste alright, you hardly ate anything," asked Sarah disappointed.

"No, no, dinner was delicious, as usual. I guess I'm just not that hungry", said Joe.

"You, not hungry, that's a first," said Sarah concerned.

"It was a rough day, I'm just tired, work stuff, but nothing for you to worry about," said Joe.

Sarah seemed to accept his explanation, and began clearing the table without a second thought. Kyle was very surprised that something was going on with Aimee Lynn and that Joe was withholding the information from Sarah. While Kyle even had to admit to himself, that he wasn't really overjoyed when Sarah and Joe adopted the girl, she had been there for several months now, and he had finally accepted the fact that she was his sister. He felt responsible for her in a way, and he really didn't want to see her leave, especially if it meant that she wouldn't be living in a good situation. Joe never really talked about what happened to her, but Sarah had mentioned something once about her parents just abandoning her, but only after Kyle had pressed her for information.

Kyle went into his bedroom, and like he often did on nights he needed to just talk to someone, he picked up his stone to call Annastarlis and Nerby. Tonight he was after information about the alien situation and he knew that they would tell him everything that they knew. He also thought that perhaps since they could be invisible that maybe they would be willing to spy on Joe and find out exactly what was going on with his sister.

Annastarlis and Nerby finally popped into his room.

"I didn't think you were coming, I called you like an hour ago," said Kyle slightly stressed.

"Sorry, we had to take care of some other things for Jerry, things are a little crazy right now," said Annastarlis.

"What's going on with the alien guy?" asked Kyle.

"Oh, it's not good at all; they want to completely take over the planet. Zepadoodle had a meeting with Jerry, there are lots of them, they are already here, and living somewhere down deep in the ocean," said Nerby.

"Where in the ocean?" asked Kyle surprised.

"He was kinda vague, somewhere around Puerto Rico, Florida or Bermuda from what he said," declared Annastarlis.

"What are they doing there?" asked Kyle shocked.

"We don't know all the information yet, but Zepadoodle said they have been in a base camp there for three hundred years," said Nerby.

"How could they be living in the ocean, and no one knew about it, this is insane," said Kyle nervously.

Kyle thought about Joe and it made him wonder. How would he officially handle the existence of gnomes, trolls, fairies, whosawhachits, whosawhachettes, and now aliens from another planet? It was times like this that he wished he could confide in Joe, but he knew that would probably never happen.

"Jerry and Gatsby are doing everything they can to find out more about it," said Annastarlis.

"I wonder what they are doing there," said Kyle.

"We don't know much about it yet, except that they do different kinds of experiments, testing on minerals, and gravitation pull and stuff like that there," said Nerby.

"Yeah, they have labs set up there, and hundreds of aliens from the planet Kaboris live there, while they are studying this planet," added Annastarlis.

"Did he tell you anything else about this hidden camp," asked Kyle.

"No, he really didn't say very much, but he called the place "The Triangle Camp", said Nerby.

"The Triangle Camp, that's a strange name....I wonder," said Kyle.

"Wonder what?" asked Nerby.

"Could this have anything to do with the Bermuda Triangle,

the place where it's claimed that boats, and planes and stuff just disappear," said Kyle.

"It might...I think Jerry suspects that too, because Zepadoodle did admit that they abduct humans from time to time, and do medical experiments on them," said Annastarlis concerned.

Chapter 5
Down Under

Zepadoodle returned to his home base, the Triangle Camp, where he had been working and living for the last 48 years. The place was located in the heart of the Bermuda Triangle, in one of the deepest marine trenches in the world. The temperature was slightly cold there, just the way the aliens liked it. He had wanted to take along a member from each of the realms; one gnome, one troll, one fairy, one whosawhachit and one whosawhachette, but Jerry refused his request. He could have taken a specimen of each of them, by force, but had decided it wasn't necessary at this point in time. He knew that he would have the opportunity to get them back to his camp to study them better when the time was right, and he was ordered to do so.

There was a reason why the place had been given its name, "Triangle Camp", because the hidden base was shaped exactly like a large triangle. The aliens preferred this shape over any other, because they had learned to harvest great power by its very design flow.

Zepadoodle had been requested to file his report, in person, directly to his superiors regarding everything that he learned in the realms. The other aliens had listened in when he had his meeting with Jerry and Gatsby, but they would want his input on what he had observed first hand. He could tell them things that perhaps weren't clear enough on the video transport his brain was sending over to them via his antenna.

On his way to the main office, Zepadoodle walked past the human experiment laboratory, and glanced thru the observation glass window. He noted that they were currently conducting tests on two human adults, both males. The men seemed to be in a lower stage of consciousness, clearly in a calm fog like state, both were wearing pajamas. One of the men had a large belly that hung out of the bottom of his sleeping garment, and it made Zepadoodle nauseas looking at it. He secretly hoped they were doing an experiment that would remove the man's belly. He had no concept of fat, but did understand that people were guilty of eating more food than their bodies really needed. He took notice of the chocolate ice cream stain on the front of the man's pajama top, which told him the story of why he looked like he did.

The men would be returned to their own beds later that night, and neither would remember anything about being here. This had been done so many times, it had just become routine, and usually went quite smoothly. From time to time they would experience a problem, but it was always handled swiftly by the Kaboris security department.

While many people have believed over the years that aliens were directly abducting humans when they passed thru the Bermuda Triangle, it really isn't true, or at least it has never really been intentional. Most of these boats and planes have disappeared simply because of the thunderstorms and water spouts, especially with the interaction of the strong currents that just spell disaster in that area. Add to that human error, and panic making many of these marine accidents simply just that, nothing more than accidents.

In the few cases of the disappearances that the aliens are truly responsible for in the triangle, the ships or planes just became trapped in-between time dimensions and had no way out, which the aliens never really intended. When this happens, it really is just a case of being at the wrong place at the wrong time for the humans. The aliens much preferred to choose and pick their human test subjects, depending on the need of the experiments they wanted to perform, rather than get them randomly or accidently. Sometimes these tests require just males or females of the species, or they have a specific need for a human of a certain age or even illness.

The Bermuda Triangle is one of two portals, used by the Kaboris aliens, to travel from their planet to ours. The area, when it is "in-phase" is constantly in motion and intensity. The aliens knew that every once in a while a human boat or a plane had gotten caught in the center or within the first two outward radiating rings. This would cause it to disappear from its own earthly dimension. The aliens really weren't happy about having these unannounced visitors that instantly showed up in their base camp and saw them as more of an intrusion than a gift. It was work for them to deprogram these people, and set them back into place, on a boat out in the ocean, therefore most of the time, the aliens would just transport these "lost people" out into space, sending them back up to planet Kaboris. The aliens deemed this punishment reasonable considering the inconvenience the people bestowed upon them.

Many Earth people were living on planet Kaboris, none by their own choice, most due to being caught up in either one of the portals of travel or some others because they had strong minds. The stronger minded people were very tough to de-program, and the Kaboris aliens refused to waste time working on them. These kinds of humans could not be hypnotized, and were considered to be stubborn, therefore being the cause of their very own fate. If a human wasn't properly de-programmed before being returned to their home after abduction, it was risky that they would remember being taken and speak about it. It was certainly helpful that most Earthlings didn't believe in aliens or UFO's, and felt that people who made these types of claims, were suffering from mental problems, or overactive imaginations. This was something that the aliens had in common with the realms. They both knew that humans didn't think "outside of the box", they tended to be self-absorbed and didn't want to believe in anything that was new, strange or out of this world, especially if their beliefs made them seem odd to others.

As for the time travel portal, it is not opened all of the time, it can only open and close 25 times a year and lasts for just 28 minutes that is for Camp Triangle. The "Pacific Triangle," the site of the Kaboris aliens Camp 2, has it take place only 3 times a year, therefore the humans don't seem to get caught up into it nearly as much.

The "Bermuda and the Pacific Triangles" are linked to other triangles that exist throughout the universe, and the aliens learned how to use them all. The Kaboris alien's technology enables them to use time compression, solar power and the ability to reduce friction, for travelling across vast distances.

The aliens from Kaboris found the human's vehicles of travel amusing, because they are so far behind in technology. Humans might think that they have come a long way developing cars, trains and planes to go faster, but what they have accomplished is nothing compared to the aliens method of travel. As for how this time travel hole works, it is a little complicated. When the time hole is compressed, the alien spacecraft enters one end and when the time hole expands itself, the craft is at the opposite end exiting one time hole and entering another. The aliens know exactly which time hole is compressed, at any given time, and therefore are able to use them at will, when the timing is right. They have these time tables memorized in their heads, just like a human might do with a train or bus schedule.

Traveling thru these time holes, can sometimes cause side effects, which some of the aliens considered embarrassing. Zepadoodle, unfortunately was suffering from one of them right now, and he wasn't happy that he would have to see his superiors in this kind of condition. He always tried to hide himself until he returned to normal when this situation occurred. Due to the lack of moisture, he had lost much of his natural skin pigmentation. He appeared a whitest, almost a pale blue grey in color, instead of his usual bright green. His normal deep blue eyes also appeared to now be deep pools of black. It would be about an hour before he would return to normal, and he somehow felt this was a direct reflection of his own capabilities, or lack thereof and that he would be deemed weak by the others. Why this happened to some of the aliens and not to others was still yet to be determined, but somehow Zepadoodle thought it had to do with being weak of mind. Anytime he traveled he attempted to keep his thought patterns strong, but was always disappointed when he arrived at his destination and examined himself. He desired to be promoted to the security department, and knew he needed to work harder, if he was ever going to have the job he wanted.

Zepadoodle was considered to be somewhat of an expert at traveling these time holes, because he would make several trips a year back to his home planet of Kaboris. Each time he returned home, he knew that time was growing short, and that soon the entire planet would be completely evacuated. Well, evacuated by the resident aliens, they would leave the Earthlings behind; at least that was the current plan. It was a rule that when one alien would make a return flight, that they returned back to Earth with more residents from Kaboris, that needed to be relocated in one of the camp bases.

The Earth camp bases were becoming overcrowded, and work and living conditions were getting harder. This was one of the reasons that Zepadoodle had been drilling down in the volcano. He desperately needed to locate valuable real estate, hidden places that more of his own kind could live in, without the earthlings knowing that they were there, yet.

Zepadoodle finally reached the main office, he didn't like to go there, it was stressful for him to meet with the bigwigs. Inside the two head generals of their army were waiting for him, and he was mortified when one mentioned his color.

"I see you have turned into a grey," stated Zoop one of the generals.

"Ah….I….have my report prepared for you," said Zepadoodle ignoring the comment, almost feeling slightly flushed in his face. He now worried that his cheeks would turn pink, causing him further embarrassment.

"Do you believe that any of these beings could pose a threat to us?" asked Krempie the other general.

"The trolls are complete idiots, far worse than the humans," said Zepadoodle.

"We gathered that from observation, tell us something we don't already know," said Zoop.

"The fairies need to be studied and evaluated. They are capable of traveling by wishing where they want to go, and pop in an instant they are there. One of them spoke about mushroom rings, complete and utter nonsense. When I requested the data on how this scientific process is being performed, they insisted on toying with me. They kept giving me the foolish answer that it is magic," said Zepadoodle firmly.

"That is quite sophisticated travel, and it makes me wonder what else they are able to do. Ha, magic, do these fools think we would believe that? We must keep an eye on them. What else do you have to report?" said Krempie.

Zepadoodle reached into his pocket to remove the beautiful gemstones that he had stolen from the gnome realm. He knew that once he presented them the generals would be proud of him, and maybe even offer him a job promotion on the spot. He was flabbergasted that his pocket was now empty. He continued to dig in his pocket, and wondered how he had lost the stones. What the alien failed to realize is that, long ago, the gnomes had put spells on the gemstones, making it impossible for anyone to remove them from the realms, without direct permission from the Key Holder himself.

"Stop fumbling with your pocket, and complete your report," snapped Zoop growing impatient.

"The gnomes are intelligent, and claim to have powers. I do know that they have discovered at least some of the power that gemstones hold, however, I have yet to be able to tell to what extent," said Zepadoodle.

"Well, perhaps, it would have been helpful if you would have brought some of these stones back with you," said Zoop slamming his fist down on the table in front of him.

"I also have concerns about these purple and pink creatures. They each have large curly ram type horns on their heads, as you can see from what I transmitted. When I questioned their purpose, I was cleverly told they had none," said Zepadoodle.

"The purple creature they call Elvin, seemed childlike, yet wise. I do believe he would be uncooperative, and irritating to deal with. However, there is a point of weakness in these realms. They are not as united as they would like to appear. This pink Elise whosawhachette has a need to rebel, she desires power, and we can use her," said Krempie.

"Yes, I agree. I want you to go back there, and bring this creature Elise back with you. Do not take her by force. Get her confidence, and bargain with her, she will be our source of information," said Zoop.

"As you wish," said Zepadoodle.

Chapter 6

Damage Control

Mystic was still quite annoyed about the damaged wall in her realm. The large crack had been scary enough, but then to see a huge gaping hole, well, it almost made her faint. Jerry ordered six trolls to be sent over to the fairy realm and they worked to repair the wall for several hours. Mystic just couldn't stand hearing the noise or seeing the mess any longer. Plus the distinct odor of the trolls was really starting to get to her, and she wanted everything sprayed with disinfectant when they were finished. She knew that manual labor was the best way to fix it, because this time magic wasn't going to be the answer. Once the repair was completed, then she would sprinkle the entire exterior walls of her realm, placing a spell on them using fairy dust, so that no one would ever be able to breech her realm security again.

The head fairy was also having a difficult time with the new rules that Jerry had put into place. She really didn't like the other realm inhabits coming and going inside of her beautiful realm. She couldn't help but notice that Elise had been spending much time around the singing flowers, and the fairy dust trees. She knew that the whosawhachette couldn't do anything with them, because of the spells that had been placed on them, but still it made her very uncomfortable, and in a way she almost saw it as trespassing. Everyone else insisted that Elise was simply exploring, and learning all about the other realms, but Mystic thought it all just came down to plain old snooping.

Annastarlis and Nerby came to see Mystic, they needed to ask permission to follow out a few things that Kyle had requested from them, namely to spy on his stepfather Joe. Before they could take on any mission, they needed to have it approved, although they didn't always follow direct orders, both were trying. Mystic denied their request, stating that it was meddling in human government business affairs, and said that she saw no emergency need or reason to do so. Both of the young fairies plead their case, insisting that this was very personal, and family oriented but Mystic would not reconsider. She had enough things to worry about without having her fairies, attempting to spy on someone from the FBI; the risk far outweighed any gain.

Mystic knew that she would need all of her fairies on call and available, in case the gnome council decided that the aliens were going to be a problem. She had been called to a meeting at the Great Hall of Justice, along with the heads of all the other realms. This was going to be a different meeting than most of the ones she was used to, and it would be a change that she was going to have to accept. Usually the gnomes and fairies did most of the talking, and the trolls just sat and nodded their heads. At this meeting, a member from the whosawhachits and whosawhachette realms would also be attending. She knew that most likely it would be Elvin and Elise, and having them give input on important issues was certainly going to alter the balance of things to come in the future. She shuttered to even think about any ideas that Elvin would have to offer, much less Elise. It was a new era for the realms, and this meeting was only the beginning of it.

Jerry sat in his rightful position at the table, in the Key Holder's chair. He called the meeting to order. Seated at the table were, Jerry, Gatsby, Optical, Mystic, Annastarlis, Nerby, Hubert, Bernie, Elvin and Elise.

"This is an informal gathering, more so than an official meeting, so everyone please just relax," said Jerry trying to set the tone for things to come, as he sat back casually in his own chair.

"Ok, so why is it that we have 3 gnomes, 3 fairies, and two trolls, but only one whosawhachit and one whosawhachette in attendance, that so doesn't really seem fair to me," said Elise already creating problems.

"Elise we have called just a brief meeting here, but in the future if you desire that your realm be represented with another member or two, then we can arrange for that." said Jerry attempting to hold the peace.

"Well, I so do, because my realm is just as important as the other ones," snapped Elise annoyed.

"I agree, my realm is important too, Dude" said Elvin towards Jerry. Elvin was proud that his sister picked up on this fact and he turned and nodded at her in approval.

"I want everyone to be happy, so please, let's just start things off on the right note," said Jerry.

"That's fine, I have made a note of this for the next meeting, shall we move on now," said Optical taking the official minutes for the meeting.

"Yes, please let's move on to important business, like this alien," said Mystic already annoyed at the disruption that Elise created.

"What does this alien green dude want," said Elvin impatiently.

"He wasn't as candid as I would have hoped. I had the impression that he held back much information," said Jerry.

"I could so get him to talk, men find me irresistible," said Elise batting her long eyelashes.

"Oh, give me a break, I guess what you really mean is that you think your stupid love stones will make him fall for you," said Annastarlis upset.

"I don't know what you are talking about, so sorry that you are jealous of me," said Elise adjusting the tiara on her head.

"Jealous!! Me jealous....of you? Why does she still have that retarded tiara on her head? I thought she wasn't allowed to have gemstones," cried Annastarlis towards Jerry.

"Girls, please we have no time for fighting, we all must be on the same side. As for Elise's tiara, I did make the decision to allow her to keep it, only because it helps her with her eyesight." said Jerry.

"Well, I don't think it's fair that she has a tiara with stones in it," said Annastarlis, truly feeling threatened and a little bit jealous.

"Annastarlis, you have plenty of rings and necklaces that contain stones," said Gatsby with a small smile.

In a way Gatsby was attempting to tell Annastarlis something. She hadn't really thought about all the jewelry she had obtained over the years, beautiful necklaces, bracelets and rings. Certainly all of these stones held powers, especially when used together. Annastarlis relaxed, because she now knew that she most likely had far more gemstone powers than Elise did. Plus the little fairy had magical fairy dust, something Elise would never get her hands on, and so the meeting continued.

"The aliens have strong scientific advancements. They have travelled far from their planet of Kaboris. What Zepadoodle did share with us, is that they have problems on their own planet, and want to live on this planet," said Jerry concerned.

"Yes, they already have base camps set up in several places around the globe. Some of them have been secretly living here for hundreds of years already. He was out scouting other areas for more of them to live in, and came across the realms by mere accident," added Gatsby.

"Well, now that he knows this area is already occupied, does that mean he will just go away?" asked Mystic concerned.

"We don't believe so. I think that they are in a more dire position than he had wished to tell us," said Jerry.

"So what are we going to do," said Elise in almost a panic.

"We must make them believe that we are capable of great things. In this case, since we honestly don't know what we are up against, we must put them in that same position, not knowing our intentions and being afraid," said Jerry.

"Yes, I agree. Most beings are more afraid of what they don't know, usually making it far worse in their own heads than what it really is. If we create the impression that we are extremely powerful, then we have a better chance of taking the upper hand, and making them go away. Always remember that we possess the power of magic," said Gatsby.

"Do you believe that the aliens will go after the human realm soon?" asked Nerby.

"I do believe that they will do just that," said Jerry.

"We can't let that happen, we have to stop them," said Annastarlis.

"Why do we so have to do that, we just need to worry about ourselves," said Elise.

"The realms have always watched out for the human and their animals. We have peacefully, secretly co-existed, and this will never change. We have protected them for centuries, and in many ways, they have protected us, even though they are unaware of our presence," said Gatsby strongly.

"How are we going to have further communications with this alien, because I hope that he doesn't think he will be able to just come crashing into my realm anytime he feels like it," said Mystic, tapping her long fingernails on the table.

"Gatsby and I have made arrangements with Zepadoodle to give him temporary access, just into the astral plane, he will then have to knock on the green door, to gain any entrance into the realms," said Jerry.

"What should we do if he comes knocking on the fairy realm door?" asked Annastarlis slightly afraid.

"We do not want the aliens getting into any of the other realms. I'm giving strict orders right now, that if anyone receives a knock on their door, you should not answer it," said Jerry.

"I wouldn't mind talking and hanging out with the little green guy, but if you don't want me to, I will do as you say," said Elvin shrugging his purple shoulders and thinking about how much fun it would have been to play with the alien on the roller coast and water slide.

"How do you even know that he will ever come back?" asked Optical.

"Ohhhh, he will come back, I don't doubt that for one minute. He didn't learn enough about us, and believe me, he has a need to know," said Jerry.

"Do you have a plan for how we are going to deal with the aliens?" asked Nerby.

"Gatsby and I have put together a very good plan. First we want to keep Zepadoodle contained to just one realm. Since we all know that there is strength in numbers before we gave Zepadoodle astral plane access we made him agree to come here alone. Also we can close off this entrance anytime we want. He can communicate with his people using the antenna on his head; therefore he has no real need to bring any others along with him." said Jerry.

"I knew that antenna did something," said Elvin excited.

"We will have a better way to control the situation with just one of them here, plus it will be easier to create the illusion," said Jerry.

"The illusion?" asked Elise curious.

"Not just any illusion, a grand one," said Gatsby with a smile.

Chapter 7
A Lesson in Space

Kyle and Eric walked thru the school parking lot together towards the double door front entrance. Their teacher Mr. Koza wheeled in behind them driving his fancy new sports car. The wind was blowing in his hair, and the sound of Beach Boys music was heard blaring from the man's car stereo. The teacher pulled into his assigned spot and quickly parked his car. He was running a little behind this morning, having overslept by just a few minutes.

"Nice car, huh," said Kyle.

"It's ok, I guess….ah….you go ahead inside and I will catch up with you in class, I have something I need to do," said Eric smugly.

"What do you have to do, the bell is going to ring in a minute, you'll be late," said Kyle innocently.

"Don't worry about it, just go," said Eric firmly.

Kyle shrugged his shoulders, and had a confused look on his face, but continued on inside, leaving Eric behind. He had no idea what his friend was going to do, but he already gathered enough to know that it was probably best that he didn't.

Eric casually stooped down and untied his sneaker lace, and then re-tied it tightly, while he watched the teacher get out of his car. Koza grabbed his briefcase from the passenger side seat, and finally entered the building, via the side door. Eric was thrilled to know which car the man drove, it was a great opportunity, and he planned on taking advantage of it.

Eric shot his eyes around the parking lot, the coast was clear, no one else was left in sight. He seized his chance, grabbing his pencil sharpener from his backpack; he placed it on the ground, and stomped on it hard with his sneaker, smashing the plastic case into pieces. Satisfied, he picked up the razor that had been safely contained inside of it, and casually walked over to his teachers car. Once again, he stopped and looked around the area, and saw no one. Next he knelt down by the driver's side door, and began carving words into the beautiful shiny paint.

The boy could hear the sound of the bell ringing in the distance, signaling the beginning of a new school day. He hurried up and finished, just as his friend had predicted, he was going to be late, but he really wasn't worried about it. Being late would just be one more thing that could possibly annoy his teacher, and he could think of nothing better than to start his day by doing that.

Eric stood up and took a few steps back, admiring his handiwork. The razor was the perfect tool, and he managed to get the letters in nice and deep. He smiled just seeing the words carved into the door in bold etched letters, "HAS BEEN BEAMED UP". He just knew that this would cause some kind of a reaction from the man later on that afternoon when school was over. Eric was also smart enough to realize that his teacher would certainly suspect him as the culprit, but that didn't bother him, besides he would be hard pressed to prove it.

Eric entered the classroom just as Koza was finishing up roll call. The man didn't really seem bothered by his tardiness or at least he managed not to show it. The teacher wasted no time beginning the lesson plan for the day. He sat casually once again on the corner of his desk, talking passionately about the different branches of government and what each one did. You could tell from the way he spoke that he just loved social studies and everything that went along with it.

Eric watched his classmates, they were all giving this man their full and total attention, they seemed interested in what he had to say. Granted the man did have a knack for speaking, and he had a way of getting the kids to listen, not because they were forced to, but because they wanted to. Eric had to even admit to himself that he much preferred to hear the teacher talk rather than to sit and read a chapter in his history book. He had a problem remembering what he had read, he just saw the words, read them, but nothing ever really seemed to stay in his brain. He once heard Dr. Melanie Hammer talk to his mother, and she called it something like "poor reading comprehension", which naturally he didn't like hearing. The boy started to realize that some of the things Koza said had managed to get into his brain,, and that he actually was learning something. He knew that the first test would be given soon, and just maybe this time he would know some of the answers, and not have to cheat on it. The boy raised his hand high in the air, to show Koza that he had a question, and hoped he would get called on.

"Yes, Eric, do you have a question?" asked Koza curious.

"Well, you are talking about The Senate and Congress and stuff, but what about all the other parts of the government?" asked Eric intelligently.

"The United States government is made up of many departments and agencies, which of them are you the most interested in?" asked Koza.

"Well....what about....like.....the CIA...what exactly do they do?" asked Eric.

"The Central Intelligence Agency, known as the CIA is responsible for providing national security," replied Koza.

"So, then if the world was getting attacked by aliens, it would be their job to keep us safe?" asked Eric.

"Well, certainly the CIA would have involvement as well as the FBI and I'm sure the United States military forces," replied Mr. Koza.

"That's confusing that they all seem to do some of the same stuff, sooooo, if I see an alien who should I call then," asked Eric wisely, attempting to egg the man on, in hopes of backing him into a corner.

"Most people would probably just call 911 Eric, but in your case, it would most likely be best for you to just call your doctor," said the teacher.

The entire class laughed loudly. Eric's face flushed red, and now he felt embarrassed. Clearly the man really believed in aliens, and the boy tried to make a fool out of him, but it didn't work, not this time. He decided not to allow this comment to upset him, after all, he knew what he had done to Koza's car, and just the thought of that made him happy. If the teacher got in a cheap shot at him once in a while, so be it, because Eric felt that in the end, he would be the one who came out on top, he always did. Part of the reason for this was that there were no lines the boy wouldn't cross, and the teacher had his own set of rules he would have to follow, set up by the school board. The school didn't allow corporal punishment, so what could the teacher ever really do to him?

The conversation that Eric had opened up in the classroom made Kyle think. If aliens were really going to take over planet earth, Joe would be the best person to go to, because he worked for the FBI. He toyed with the idea of speaking to his stepfather, but decided that it would most likely be a complete waste of time. If Joe did know something about the aliens from Kaboris, it would be official government business, and he would never discuss it with Kyle. He hadn't slept very well the last few nights, and even had a nightmare about green creatures climbing thru his bedroom window. Last night he went to sleep with his calling stone under his pillow, thinking that in the case of an emergency he would be able to call his friends for help if needed. Kyle's thoughts were consumed with aliens, and he naturally feared what their intentions would be, and hoped that Annastarlis and Nerby would have something new to tell him tonight. He kept thinking about the Bermuda Triangle, and this base camp the fairies spoke about. Deep down inside he knew that he would eventually get involved with the aliens and the realms fight, but this time he was truly afraid.

Kyle then realized he may just have another option. He always knew he could talk to his mother about anything, and she would certainly believe him, but she wouldn't really know what to do in the case of an outright alien attack, but he wondered about Mr. Koza. Was this teacher someone he could trust if it came to getting help for the realms? With all of his experience watching alien TV shows, wouldn't he know what should be done? The only problem Kyle could possibly see was that he had a connection and friendship with Eric. Perhaps Mr. Koza would think he was playing a game with him, and wouldn't believe what he had to say because of Eric's constant alien taunting. He decided that he needed to start to disassociate himself from Eric, at least when Koza was around.

When the bell rang declaring the school day was over, Kyle stayed behind in class. He made a lame excuse for Eric to go ahead, and casually rummaged thru his desk, until his friend lost patience and went on ahead. Kyle wanted to take the opportunity to have a private conversation with Mr. Koza. He needed to build a relationship with him, and soon.

"Ah, all that was pretty interesting, about...you know, the government and stuff," said Kyle awkward, not really sure how to start his conversation up.

"I'm glad you enjoyed learning about it, what did you like the most?" quizzed the teacher.

"Well, to be honest, my stepfather works for the FBI, although, I'm not really supposed to tell many people that," said the Kyle coyly.

"Yes, I actually did already know that, I'm sure he is a fascinating gentleman," said Koza.

"Well...not really, he's kinda boring," said Kyle looking down at the floor.

Koza laughed at the boy's honest statement. He could sense that something was bothering him, and the boy wanted to talk.

"You seem like you have something on your mind, something troubling you?" asked the man as he packed up his briefcase.

"Ah...well....no...not really, I mean, I guess I just wanted to say... that...I errr...I'm not really friends with Eric. I mean...I...well...I just pretend to be his friend, because otherwise....he....well...it's just easier that way. I don't want you to think that I have anything to do with him harassing you and stuff," stammered Kyle nervously.

"A man should pick his friends, not the other way around. I can tell you're a good kid, don't be afraid to stand up for your own principles. You have the makings of a leader, not a follower, make Eric follow you, not the other way around," said Koza giving advice.

"Yeah…ah…I know you're right. I don't follow him when he's doing bad stuff, I don't want to get into trouble or anything," said Kyle attempting to slightly defend his situation.

"I'm glad to hear that," said Koza giving the boy a smile.

Kyle hesitated before exiting the classroom, he really wanted to ask the man a few more questions, but he knew it wasn't the time to just start talking about aliens.

"Mr. Koza….what do you think is the real truth behind the Bermuda Triangle?" asked Kyle.

"Hard to say, the world is made up of many mysteries, science explains only some of them. The Bermuda Triangle doesn't truly officially exist on maps, but certainly something is going on there," said Koza stroking his beard deep in thought.

Koza left the building and walked to his car. The usually calm and happy man was angry when he spotted the damage to his prized vehicle. He instantly knew that Eric most likely defaced his property, and he hoped he could prove it. The teacher briskly walked back into the building and down the long hallway towards the main offices. Koza thought about the conversation he just had with Kyle. The boy seemed upset about something, and he wondered if Kyle knew what had happened to his car, and perhaps was letting him know that he was aware of the incident but wasn't a willing participant. The more he thought about the brief chat, he realized Kyle was nervous, and hesitant, as if he were holding something back. He had the distinct feeling the boy wanted to tell him something else, but chickened out. The thought had even occurred to him that perhaps, it was his job to keep the teacher in the classroom, while Eric went into the parking lot and engraved the car door. The truth would come out because now it would just be the matter of having the school principle review, the hidden surveillance videos from the cameras on top of the school that overlooked the parking lot.

Chapter 8
When One Door Closes

Zepadoodle did exactly as his superiors ordered, he returned back to the realms, determined to find out more information about the realm inhabitants. This time he did not make entrance using a mining drill thru the volcano wall; instead he entered thru the tree trunk Jerry set up in the woods for him which allowed him access to the astral plane.

He walked thru the misty plane, and carefully studied the doors. He had been told that each door would take him to a different place. Jerry was clear with him that only the green door which led to the gnomes would open to him. He knew that he needed to get inside of all the other realms, each and every one of them would have to be studied more carefully. He wasn't very impressed with the fairy realm when he had originally entered it. The alien thought that the tiny little fairy houses and sparkly trees were just freakish looking. Needless to say, at this point, he had no knowledge of fairy dust and its purpose. His superiors were curious about the fairy's themselves, therefore he had been ordered to get another look at them and their realm for future study.

He assumed correctly that the brown door was for the trolls, and knew that they would offer him little or no useful information. The trolls were no threat to the aliens, because of their limited mental capabilities and the aliens had already decided not to waste any time on them.

Zepadoodle knew it was most important that he gain entrance into either the whosawhachit's or whosawhachette realms. He walked over to the purple door, and turned the knob, it was locked, which he knew it most likely would be. Next he went over to the fuchsia colored door and gave it a try, again locked tightly. He decided he had nothing to lose by pounding on both of the doors, if he was lucky one of them would make the mistake and open up for him. He already knew that these were the two groups that would be the weak link in the chain of command. These creatures were childlike, yet smart, impish in a way, yet both showed they didn't care very much for following orders and seemed to have minds of their own.

Zepadoodle had his antenna tuned up and was aware that his leaders were watching every move he made. They were depending on him to do a good job, and he wasn't going to disappoint them. He knocked loudly on the fuchsia pink door several times but got nothing in response. Then he received a telepathic message in his head from Krempie the general demanding that he get inside the one of the doors immediately. Zepadoodle tried to remain calm, and not panic, because he was aware that all of his thoughts and fears could be transmitted directly to everyone at base, just one of the reasons he always disliked having his antenna on, nothing was ever personal or private. He had times in the past when this was a major problem, and managed to turn off his communication with the others by disconnecting his transmitter, and insisted that it had malfunctioned when he was later questioned about it.

The alien rapped loudly on the purple door and was quite pleased when Elvin promptly opened it. Elvin could really care less about the alien, or what powers he had or didn't have, he didn't really even have a desire to learn anything about him. He couldn't help himself when a chance to tease someone different came along.

"Hey, well, if it isn't Zepa Dude," said Elvin with a large grin.

"My name is Zepadoodle," said the alien serious, missing the whosawhachit's sense of humor.

"You have the wrong door Space Boy, you want the green one, that will take you to see the gnome dudes," said Elvin.

"My mistake, however, since I am already here, perhaps I can come in and we can talk, and you can show me around your home," said Zepadoodle in an attempt to be friendly.

"Ah, no can do, doodlehead," said Elvin with a jeer and then a laugh.

Zepadoodle was confused by Elvin, he couldn't quite make up his mind if he was dealing with a child or an adult.

Meanwhile Elise had her ear pressed up against her door, she could hear Elvin and Zepadoodle chatting, but wasn't able to make out exactly what was being said. She was slightly annoyed and angry that Elvin opened up his door to the alien. They had been given strict instructions to keep their realm doors locked and not to have any contact with the aliens. She wanted to talk to Zepadoodle more than Elvin did, yet he was the one that broke the rule, even after he warned her not to do so, after the meeting with Jerry. It made her angry that Elvin could break rules, but he demanded that she follow them. This didn't seem fair to her, especially since she was supposed to be co-leader of the purple and pink realms.

Zepadoodle was able to get a small peek inside the whosawhachit realm, he noted the large purple roller coaster, purple pathway, purple sky and even trees which seemed quite strange to him. His large eyes, which were more like those of a camera lens, snapped images, and video which was sent directly back to his headquarters for examination.

Elvin refused to let the alien into his realm, instead he just taunted him with name calling, and then finally stuck out his tongue and slammed the door in his face. Elvin laughed loudly behind the safety of his door, and then ran off to play with the others, forgetting all about the incident.

Slowly and quietly Elise opened her door, just a small crack. She could see Zepadoodle in the astral plane heading towards the gnome realm, and decided to call out to him.

"So who is out there knocking on my door?" asked Elise barely above a whisper.

"Oh, hello, that was me," said Zepadoodle as kindly as he could.

"So what do you want?" asked Elise innocently.

"I just thought that maybe we could talk for a few minutes," said Zepadoodle.

Elise opened her door halfway, and studied the green creature. She noticed that the antenna on his head almost seemed to be glowing, something she hadn't remembered the last time they had met. She knew that if her conversation continued any longer with the alien, she was risking Elvin or someone else hearing it. Elise tried to quickly decide if she should chance inviting the alien into her realm where they could speak in private. She wondered if Elvin could have his ear pressed to his own realm door listening, just like she had done just a few minutes before. She knew the alien was testing her, and in a way, she was doing the very same thing to him.

"Sure, we could so talk, but you have to keep your voice down," whispered Elise still slightly weary about inviting him into her realm.

"Okay...what is the purpose of the horns on your head, and what powers do you possess?" quizzed Zepadoodle in a lower voice.

"Oh, you would be so surprised by all the powers I possess," said Elise smiling, as she turned the astral plane mist pink.

Zepadoodle was shocked at the color change and this certainly concerned him, but the whosawhachette was clearly holding back much information and he pressed forward with his interrogation.

"You can make things change color, but what else are you capable of?" asked Zepadoodle.

Elise changed the astral plane mist back to its usual color, before anyone else saw it, and then she dared to step out of the safety of her own realm, closing the door behind her. Zepadoodle had already gotten just a small peek into her realm, and once again his eyes had snapped pictures of what he saw and sent them back to his base. He studied the gemstone tiara on her head, and assumed that the creature was aware of the powers the stones contained, and he decided it would be best to keep some distance between them. He took a step back, almost startled that she dared to come closer to him, and knew that he could not risk her ever touching him. He instantly heard a message in his head from Krempie the general, yelling that his body language had just showed a sign of weakness, and that he needed to take the upper hand. He mentally sent the message back to his leaders warning about the love stones, but they insisted that her tiara didn't contain enough of them to have an effect on him, and therefore ordered him to go closer to her.

Elise had in fact noticed the alien's fear of her, and that he had pulled back, and this made her happy. She decided at that point, that if the alien truly believed she was powerful, she would be the one in control. Elise didn't have many powers, but the alien didn't know this, at least not yet, therefore she decided to lie.

"I am so the most powerful of all here. If you have something to offer me, perhaps we could so make a deal," said Elise lying.

"We are not against making a deal, but first you must tell me what you have to offer," said Zepadoodle.

Before Elise or Zepadoodle could say another word, the gnome realm door flew open and out came Jerry, and Optical. Elise could tell from the look on Jerry's face that he wasn't happy to find her standing and speaking with the alien and she quickly offered up an explanation.

"I was so going over to the fairy realm, and I just happened to so run into this alien out here in the astral plane, I was going to report this to you immediately," said Elise batting her long eyelashes and acting innocent.

"I believe you were given strict instructions to have no contact with the aliens. I would like you to return back to your own realm, lock the door and stay there, we will talk later," said Jerry firmly.

Elise did as she was told, but did so in a way that made it look like she really didn't care one way or another. She had a way of doing things to seem like she did them because she just wanted to, rather than having been ordered to. She casually adjusted her tiara, and slowly strolled back to her own realm, as if she had every intention of doing so.

Jerry had put an alarm into the tree trunk that he set up for the alien to use, that way he would know immediately that the alien had entered the astral plane. The gnome was already aware that Elvin and Elise had opened their realm doors to the extraterrestrial, and Jerry was quite disappointed in both of them. The gnomes turned their attention to the visitor standing before them.

"I see you were able to use the tree trunk I set up for you, what is the nature of your visit today?" asked Jerry hoping to sound strong and official.

"I think you need to understand more about our intentions. We are going to take over this planet, sooner than you think. The situation is now critical, therefore I must give you full warning about some of the things you can expect," said Zepadoodle from the direct orders he was given.

"We never agreed to allow you to just do that. I don't understand why you need to take it from the humans. Can't you just come here to live, and the share the planet with them?" asked Jerry.

"We tried many, many years ago, to share this planet with the humans, and at the time it worked, but it will not now," said Zepadoodle.

"What are you talking about, I know nothing about aliens inhabiting this planet, and we have lived here for thousands of years," said Jerry.

"Have you ever heard of Atlantis which was near Bermuda by the island of Bimini?" asked Zepadoodle.

"I vaguely remember it, although I can't say I ever visited," said Jerry confused.

"We once lived there, and had built quite the community. People just believed it had been inhabited by a more advanced civilization of humans, but that was us," said Zepadoodle.

"What happened there that made it...well... just sink and vanish?" asked Optical.

"We brought our supremely powerful fire crystals from Planet Kaboris. These crystals allowed us to harness energy, but a terrible disaster that caused the fire crystals to go out of control ended up sinking us. This was a newer technology to us then, but now we have perfected it. We will not make that mistake again, however I must warn that the human's are bordering on something similar with their own nuclear energies, and we will stop that. This is just part of the reason we refuse to share the planet with them, because eventually they will just blow it up. The humans must be completely eliminated to save Earth. All that is left now is for us to decide if we can share this planet with you, or if you have to go too," said Zepadoodle repeating what he was told to say directly by Zoop via transmission.

Chapter 9
The Magic of Illusion

Zepadoodle followed Jerry and Optical into the gnome realm, he had no idea what he would be in for. The gnomes and fairies had planned for his return visit and they were determined that he would not be disappointed. Jerry was well aware of how long the alien had been in the astral plane and he allowed him to stay there for a few minutes on purpose. Actually he did so for two reasons, one they needed more time to prepare their illusion, and second he felt it would be a good time to test the whosawhachits and whosawhachettes. Needless to say he was concerned that both of them had failed their first test of realm freedom. He knew that they would never be able to be trusted, and would continue to defy direct orders. If the world was going to be saved, it would have to be done by the fairies and gnomes.

The alien took everything in; he carefully studied the landscaping of the gnome realm, paying extra attention to all the details, snapping picture images with his eyes. He noticed many gnomes walking around the different gardens, but saw none of the other realms inhabitants. He had hoped to be able to observe all of them, intermingling together. It was becoming clear to him that while the realms were a unit together, they were very separate communities governed under the gnomes.

Zepadoodle was determined that this time he would leave here with a few of the gemstones which lined the sides of all the streets and pathways. He was still confused on why the ones he had stolen the last time simply disappeared in his pocket, therefore he would safeguard them much more carefully once he was able to grab them. He couldn't afford to make any mistakes, and followed all the commands he was being given by his superiors exactly. At their request, he started the conversation.

"I believe it is time that you showed me exactly what you are capable of, otherwise we see no reason to keep you around," said Zepadoodle.

"I completely agree with you. I was thinking that we would give you a little demonstration of our powers today," said Jerry in an arrogant way.

"I'm glad that you are willing to cooperate, because I have been given direct orders to exterminate you if you do not," said Zepadoodle.

"Once you see what we are able to do, I believe your tone will completely change, and you will realize that although we are usually peaceful, it is you that will have something to fear," said Jerry.

"Prove it," snapped Zepadoodle.

They all reached the Great Hall of Justice, and stopped outside the large doors. The gnomes and fairies had decided the perfect place for their show would be to hold it on the front steps. Gatsby was standing outside waiting for them, with a slight smile on his face, he seemed pleased with Jerry's plan. He had taken the time to set up several chairs, so that each of them could sit back and enjoy what was going to happen.

"Please, have a seat and relax," said Gatsby to Zepadoodle, as he motioned towards the chairs lined up neatly in a row, as if it were an outside theater.

"Before we begin, I would like to ask that for each thing we show you, we'd like you to do something for us in return. A display exchange of powers, which seems fair," said Jerry.

"I have no problems in exchanging demonstrations of power, and that way you will understand that we are far more advanced than you are, and these silly games can stop," said Zepadoodle.

"Great, would you like to begin or should we?" asked Jerry.

"I will, and when I'm done, if you are intimated and don't want to continue, you can just say so," said Zepadoodle with confidence.

"Then, please, go ahead and show us something," said Gatsby.

"Do you know what telekinesis is?" asked the alien.

"Yes, the power to move objects with one's mind," said Jerry.

"Well, allow me to demonstrate it for you," said Zepadoodle proudly.

The alien got up from his seat, and walked over to a small, light weight gemstone sitting on the ground. He concentrated hard, staring at the stone, willing it to move. Everyone there, waited and watched, and within a few minutes, the gemstone finally moved, but very slightly, perhaps an inch. Zepadoodle was proud of his accomplishment, it had taken him several years to learn this skill, and although he wasn't fully able to make the stone move by a great distance, he did show the brain wave power he possessed.

"Ok, well, I can't really say that I'm all that impressed. Allow me to show you how I move objects with just my mind," said Jerry.

Jerry stepped up and Zepadoodle sat back down, the alien doubted the claims that the gnomes made, but he was willing to let them entertain him. He expected the gnome to stare at the gemstone for a long time, and then make a lame excuse about why it didn't move. Jerry barely looked at the gemstone or any of the others around it. He raised his hands, as if he were conducting an orchestra playing music, and on cue, ten gemstones rose from the ground and danced wildly in the air. Then the stones formed into a pattern of a midair circle, as if someone were juggling them.

Zepadoodle was shocked but managed to hide his fear at the sight of this spectacular sight. His superiors ordered him to walk over to the gemstones to make sure that this was not some kind of trick. He was instructed to look for any hidden wires or strings, but clearly none were there. He waited for the stones to fall to the ground after Jerry ordered that they do so. The alien quickly picked up on the stones and rolled several of them thru his long green fingers, studying every side of them, for a clue that he was being tricked, and saw nothing. He finally dropped some of the stones back down to the ground, and then casually tucked two of them into his pocket. The gnomes didn't have any telekinesis type powers, but they had something even better, invisible fairies all around them, working together to create any illusion needed.

"Well...that was...sufficient, but let me show you the power of levitation, certainly you will be impressed with this, and I know that you can't do it," snapped Zepadoodle.

Zepadoodle closed his large eyes, and concentrated hard, he almost seemed to be in some kind of a trance. Everyone waited and watched him to see if he was able to do what he had claimed. After waiting almost ten minutes, the alien finally managed to lift from the ground, he hovered about 6 inches above it for a few minutes. He finally opened his eyes, breaking his concentration, and his feet hit the ground hard.

Jerry didn't wait even one minute, he leapt from his seat and stepped forward, eager to show up the alien. He knew that it was going to take all the strength the fairies had working together to lift him off the ground, and he hoped that they could do it.

"I don't even need to think about it, or close my eyes to concentrate, just watch me rise," said Jerry lifting his arms straight up in the air, hoping this would help the fairies pick him up.

The fairies all worked together, and Jerry rose from the ground. Annastarlis used some of her fairy dust to make the gnome lighter, and the fairies flew together to lift him 30 feet up into the air. They held him there for a few minutes, and made it seem like he was just slowly floating. Jerry's heart was pounding, in truth the gnome was a little bit afraid of heights, but he put on a brave face. He felt relief when his feet touched the ground again, after his friends gently placed him back down.

Zepadoodle was surprised by what he had seen; he was no longer listening or paying any attention to the gnomes. He was now busy having a telepathic conversation with Zoop and Krempie. It really wasn't a full conversation with mental dialog on both sides, because his superiors were doing most of the talking, which was truly more yelling. They weren't happy that the gnomes were showing up Zepadoodle, and ordered him to stop making them look stupid.

"Well, you can't communicate with each other just using your minds like we can. You have to use the spoken word, and different kinds of electronic communications, like the simple humans do," said Zepadoodle.

"Oh, we can do something even better than that. We can talk to animals using telepathy, and make them do anything we ask," piped up Gatsby.

"Oh, please, that's impossible, I demand that you show me this right now," said Zepadoodle.

"Do you see that deer way out there in the field, I will call it over to me right now, using just my mind," said Gatsby.

Gatsby did exactly as he said, he called the deer over to him, gnomes were truly able to do this. The deer quickly followed the gnome's request, and walked from the field directly over to the gnome.

"That proves nothing. How do I know that the deer didn't just want to walk over here," snapped Zepadoodle.

"What would you like me to ask the deer to do, so that I can prove to you he is listening to me?" asked Gatsby.

"Make him run around in a circle," demanded the alien.

Gatsby requested that the deer run around in circles promptly following his command. The deer performed making 10 perfect circles, and then stopped and looked at the gnome, waiting for further instructions. Zepadoodle was ordered to examine the deer in order to confirm that the animal was live and not a silly computerized toy. Upon his close up inspection, the deer bit the alien's hand, and dark olive green blood began to drip from it. Seeing what had happened Gatsby immediately stepped up to touch and heal the injury, something gnomes did automatically. The alien pulled back, and held his hand; he wasn't sure what the gnome's intention was.

"Please, just allow me to touch you, and I will instantly heal your injury," said Gatsby.

"Seriously, are you now claiming that you possess healing powers?" asked the alien.

"Yes, gnomes have healing powers, with all the realms inhabitants, human realm animals, and humans as well. I'm not quite sure if I can heal you, but it's certainly worth a try," said Gatsby.

Zepadoodle reluctantly placed his hand towards Gatsby, just to see if the gnome was telling the truth. He really didn't want to test this healing power, but was once again ordered to do so by Zoop. Aliens already had the power to heal themselves from just about any injury, especially from something like a minor bite from a human animal, so if the gnome was unable to heal him, Zepadoodle would quickly do it himself.

Gatsby held the aliens cold green hand and it took him longer than he had expected, but he managed to heal the wound. He was surprised to see that the bite left a noticeable scar on the alien's skin, but at least he was no longer bleeding. Zepadoodle immediately laughed, and placed his other hand over the scar, and it disappeared.

"There, that is the proper way to fix an injury," said Zepadoodle with an arrogant smirk.

Elvin arrived on the scene, curious as to what was going on. He sensed that he had been missing out on something. He walked with a bounce in his step, excited at the very idea of being able to taunt the alien.

"Yo, Gnome Dudes and Greenie, what's going on?" asked Elvin.

"I believe that I asked you to stay in your realm, what are you doing here," snapped Jerry annoyed.

"I got bored, and I want to go to the human realm," said Elvin.

"You are going to have to wait, please return back to your own realm now," said Jerry angry.

"Okay, but did you know that Ifffer is hiding over there by the tree's watching you?" asked Elvin with a smile, and pointing towards a garden out in the distance.

Chapter 10
A Lesson Never Learned

Evelyn received a phone call from the school principal early in the morning requesting that she attend a school conference before school began. The principal refused to discuss any reason for the emergency parent conference on the phone. The woman did say she wanted Eric in attendance as well, and that he should not report to his classroom.

Evelyn asked Eric several times on the way to school, if he had any idea why she would be called down, and he pleaded innocence to any knowledge at all, insisting that he had been on his very best behavior. Evelyn and Eric sat in the cold plain office waiting, and finally the principal Mrs. Veronica and Mr. Koza entered the room and took their seats. Eric sat quietly in the principal's office listening to the adults talking as they all viewed the surveillance video together that showed him damaging his teacher's car. He wasn't nervous at all, and almost seemed to find the entire situation amusing.

"What do you have to say for yourself young man," demanded Mrs. Veronica.

"Ah...well...someone that kinda looks like me set me up, I guess," said Eric.

"Oh, please, Eric, are you really going to just sit there and try to claim that isn't you on the video?" asked Mr. Koza disgusted.

"I admit the kid looks a little bit like me, but I didn't do it," said Eric.

"We are going to have to suspend Eric from school for a week," said Mrs. Veronica.

"Yes, I certainly understand that, and I can tell you that he will be punished severely at home as well," said Evelyn.

"I don't want to have to call the police into this matter and officially press criminal charges against the child; therefore I would just like to request from you that restitution for my car be paid directly to me," said Mr. Koza sadly.

"I really appreciate it that you aren't going to have my son arrested, I certainly would like to avoid that as well. If you could please just take your car to a repair shop, and give me the bill, I will pay it immediately," said Evelyn.

"I must tell you that although I have just suspended your son for only one week, I was very tempted to expel him permanently from our school. Mr. Koza argued with me against expulsion because he believes he can have a positive impact on Eric, and that he has hope and promise. I'm not entirely sure that I would agree, but out of respect for his wishes, I have agreed to do it this way," said Mrs. Veronica.

"Yes, I understand, and I thank you allowing Eric to have another chance. I will call his doctor immediately and make an appointment for him to see a therapist today. I will let them know that he is "acting out" again by doing destructive behaviors," said Evelyn embarrassed.

Eric was taken directly to the hospital, the place he had stayed at so many other times, and he wondered if they would admit him again. He really didn't care if his latest antics bought him a short stay in the mental ward, it was better than having to attend school. Evelyn requested an emergency visit with one of the doctor's on the phone, and had been instructed to bring him in and they would find someone available to see him.

The hospital had been short on staff during Dr. Melanie Hammer's departure, but she was now back, and in full swing. Although she had preferred not to take Eric on as a patient, she was the only attending doctor that had a available time slot at the moment. She didn't refuse to see the child, he was in need of medical help, but deep inside she certainly resented it on a personal level. She tried hard not to allow her own feelings for the boy to show on the outside, and acted as professional as she possibly could under the circumstances.

Eric sat in the doctor's office with a broad smile on his face. He had truly missed seeing Dr. Hammer and harassing her. He knew that he had a way of getting under her skin, and enjoyed that.

"Well, Eric, I see that nothing much has changed with you since our last visit. Still getting into trouble, and destroying others property, this is a serious situation you have gotten yourself into this time," said Dr. Hammer.

"I didn't do anything," replied Eric.

"I have been told that you damaged your teacher's car, and the incident was captured on video tape," said Dr. Hammer.

"Well, it might have been on tape, but I didn't do it," said Eric.

"Then how would you explain the video tape showing you doing it," asked Dr. Hammer.

"The eyes can play tricks on people, as you know; sometimes things you see aren't really real or even happening....or are they? I mean, I guess it could be possible that a ghost made himself look like me, and then did it," said Eric with a large smirk on his face.

"Eric, I'm not going to sit here and play games with you. I am admitting you to the hospital, and I will make arrangements for you to see a new doctor. As I told you in our last appointment, I don't believe that I am the doctor to help you. I will be starting you on some new medications. Enjoy your stay with us," said Dr. Hammer as she rose from her chair and walked out of the room.

Eric was taken down the hall, and shown a room which contained two beds, his roommate was out at the time, so he would have to wait to meet him, but that really didn't matter to him. He would manage to find other ways to amuse himself while he was waiting. He was happy that he was out of school for at least a week and now since he was in the hospital perhaps even longer. He decided to go thru his new roommates personal items, rummaging thru dresser draws, nightstand, and then finally the closet. He discovered a comic book about aliens that the other boy had, and borrowed it. He flopped on the bed, and casually flipped thru it, scanning the different colored illustrations of flying saucers and aliens.

Mr. Koza taught his class for the day, and managed to put thoughts about his car damage out of his mind. He was a dedicated teacher, loved most of his students, and knew that the other kids in his class needed him. He paid special attention to Kyle, who he now knew had nothing to do with the car incident, perhaps because he felt slightly guilty having originally thought he could have been involved. It became clear to him that Kyle was intelligent, and a good student, and that he seemed more relaxed in class with Eric being gone. The day went by with no interruptions, and everyone quietly did their school work, a day without Eric seemed to be a good one for everybody.

None of the other students were told what had happened, it was confidential information, but several had seen Eric walking into the principal's office with his mother early that morning. Therefore they had surmised that he must have been in some kind of trouble. Naturally a low buzz went on around especially at lunchtime, with each of the kids suggesting different things that Eric could have possibly done. All of the speculation and guesses got so far out of hand that; one child even went as far to suggest that Eric had murdered a teacher who had called out sick that day. All the kids laughed and giggled but none of them truly believed such a thing. Each had a different theory, but most likely only one would find out the real truth about what had really happened, Kyle. He knew that certainly his mother would have spoken with Eric's mom, and he couldn't wait to get home to find out.

Sarah had in fact talked with her friend Evelyn, and she was saddened to know that Eric had done such a thing, and was back in the hospital. In some ways it made her remember all the time's that her own son spoke about not wanting to be friends with the boy, even pleading with her to keep Eric away from him. The things Kyle had said about the boy were not over exaggerated, because he clearly was not a good influence on her own son, and this would put her in a tough position. She had been enjoying her friendship with the boy's mother, and certainly didn't want it to end, but now she would be more careful about how much time their son's spent together, avoiding it whenever possible. She had a long talk with Kyle when he got home from school, but was very careful to explain to him that anything they said could not be repeated at school.

Aimee Lynn was in her bedroom, doing what she liked the most, playing with her dolls. She was shocked and delighted when Elvin popped into her room. This time he wasn't alone, he had Annastarlis and Nerby with him. She smiled at the sight of seeing a fairy and pixie, but it was Elvin that she seemed the most interested in.

Elvin had been begging Jerry to allow him to go to the human realm, he truly just wanted to see the little girl. Many things about her fascinated him, and Jerry had to agree that the child was certainly in need of realm help. Elvin, naturally couldn't be trusted to go to the human realm without the fairies, because even though he was trying to show that he had good intentions, he somehow always seemed to manage to find trouble one way or another, even if he wasn't really looking for it. Elvin had limited knowledge and understanding of the human world and the gnomes knew that he had much to learn about it. Jerry also felt that in a way, having the fairies take Elvin to the human world, was also getting him away from the things that were going on in the gnome realm with the alien situation.

Annastarlis and Nerby were instructed not to let Elvin out of their sight. They were told to assist him in speaking with the child, and then they should all promptly return back to the realms when finished. He would expect a full report from the fairies about how Elvin conducted himself, so that he could decide if he would be allowed to venture into the human realm in the future, supervised of course. Annastarlis was also given a special stone to call for help, just in case Elvin decided he wasn't going to listen to them, and run around causing any problems there.

Elvin wasted no time once he got there, he immediately started interacting with the little girl. She was sitting on the floor with her dolls, and he knelt down beside her, picking up some of the doll furniture and rearranging it.

"Do you remember me? I'm Elvin, we talked and played?" asked Elvin in a very sweet manner.

The little girl didn't respond to him verbally, but shook her head yes, and then smiled at him. She then turned her attention to Annastarlis and Nerby who just stood there watching. Finally she pointed her tiny finger at them, almost questioning what they were with her eyes.

"I'm Annastarlis, I'm a fairy, and this is Nerby, he's a pixie. We are friends of Elvin," said Annastarlis.

"How come she doesn't talk?" asked Nerby.

"Don't be rude, if she wanted to talk she would," snapped Elvin afraid that Nerby could offend her.

Aimee Lynn leaned over and gave Elvin a hug, something about him made her feel safe, perhaps it was the way he had just defended her.

"I have a little sister, her name is Elise, you would really like her," said Elvin continuing to establish some kind of meaningful relationship.

The child listened to every word that the whosawhachit said, and she also took in the conversation between him and the fairies. She had started to speak once in a while with Sarah, just short one or two word answers to her mother's questions, but nothing more. She never uttered a single word at school or to anyone else, except for Elvin. She was making progress, but didn't really have any desire or need to talk with people, but something about Elvin really made her want to talk, made her want to communicate.

"You are purple," said the child reaching out to touch the whosawhachits skin.

"Yes, I'm purple. I remember when I tried to get you to say purple, but you said green," laughed Elvin.

"Do you know the green men?" asked Aimee Lynn.

Annastarlis, Nerby and Elvin all looked at each other shocked. The little girl instantly knew that they did know.

"You mean the aliens, yes, we know one of them," said Elvin surprised.

"They are bad, they took my mommy and daddy, can you find them for me?" asked the child.

Chapter 11
A Turn of Events

Zepadoodle left the gnome realm to go back to his Earth base in the Bermuda Triangle. He was completely stunned at everything he had witnessed, and knew that Zoop would not be happy. He was dreading going back, because he knew that he didn't display nearly as much power as the gnomes did, and didn't manage to make the strong impression on them that he was directed to do. He tried very hard to keep his own thoughts to himself, because he knew everything he thought would be transmitted back to his leaders. He forced himself to think things like, I did the best I could, and they have more power then all of us aliens, what else could I have done. As he entered the astral plane he hesitated wondering if he should make yet another attempt to speak with Elise, and maybe even get the opportunity to abduct her. If the gnomes were able to do so many things, what could the purple and pink creatures do? He worried that the realms might just be more than they had first appeared, and could cause problems when it was time to take the planet over. His thoughts went back to headquarters and he was quickly answered with a reply from Zoop himself, go knock on the pink door and get us more information, now. If you can manage to bring one of these beings back with you, do it, but make sure she comes along on her own. If you risk taking her against her will, she may pose dangers that we aren't yet prepared to handle, because we don't yet know what she is able to do. Zepadoodle listened to them carefully, he wanted to follow the orders he was given exactly. He hesitated for a few minutes, to think about what he would say to the pink being. Then the alien walked towards the pink door with confidence and a plan in mind but before he could knock on it, he ran straight into another gnome. He had never spoken with this one before, but quickly realized that something about him was different from the others he had met. Aside from the obvious hat color difference, he wasn't quite sure why this gnome seemed different from the others, and he began to study him. Perhaps what made him odd was the way he presented himself, as if he were hiding, or at least that was the impression he gave, and not so much from the aliens but more so from the other realm inhabitants. The gnome just seemed to be sneaky, his eyes shifted nervously back and forth, as if he was afraid that someone would find him out in the astral plane but yet he managed to show other signs of authority with his body language, a very confusing message.

"I don't know where you think you are going, but perhaps I could assist you," said Ifffer.

"I was just looking for the exit, and I will be on my way home," said Zepadoodle slightly panicking.

"No, you weren't. I believe you were heading towards the whosawhachette's realm, something there that you find interesting?" asked Ifffer.

"Well...I admit I'm intrigued by these pink creatures, and I would just like to know a little more about them," said Zepadoodle pressing the issue, since his true intentions were already out.

"I will tell you everything you want to know, but understand that...information doesn't come without reward," said Ifffer.

"You aren't like the others....but what kind of reward are you seeking?" asked the alien.

"I was like the others, until all of them betrayed me, and made a fool out of me. I speak only for myself, not for the others. Let me assure you that I can be of great help to you," said Ifffer.

"I already gathered that…but you didn't answer me, what do you want from me?" asked Zepadoodle.

"I want the realms. I want the others to kneel or bow at the very sight of me. I will rule this place one way or another, and if you help me succeed, I will give you all the info you need to take over planet Earth," said Ifffer.

"Come back with me to our base camp, and I will let you speak directly with my superiors. They are telling me that it is possible we can work out some kind of an arrangement with you," said Zepadoodle.

Zepadoodle and Ifffer started towards the exit of the astral plane when the gnome door flew open. Jerry and Gatsby stepped out from the doorway. You could see how angry both of them appeared, not at the alien but at the traitor in their own realm.

"Ifffer I knew that you were capable of just about anything, but this time you have gone too far," said Jerry.

"Have I….well, hold on to your hats boys, because I have only just begun," snickered Ifffer.

"I'm giving you a direct command as Key Holder of the Realms to return immediately to your home in the gnome realm," said Jerry.

"You will be taking orders from me, I am the rightful Key Holder of the Realms, and you will listen to me starting right now," said Ifffer winking at his newfound friend.

Zepadoodle reached out and touched the gnomes hand and within seconds the alien and Ifffer made the transformation from the astral plane directly into the alien's home base. The alien wasn't quite sure what he had just witnessed, but he knew the realms had problems, and this could be the chance he needed. He needed to bring at least one realm inhabitant back with him, and now he had a gnome that was ready and willing to go.

Ifffer felt slightly ill when they arrived, he had never experienced such a trip, and it took his breath away. He needed to sit for a few minutes before he was able to even stand on his own two feet. He finally looked up and noticed that Zepadoodle's skin color had changed to grey; then he saw that the aliens blue eyes were now deep pools of black, and he was scared. He doubted his decision for a few minutes, and hoped that he didn't just seal his own fate in a bad way. He knew he had to make this new friendship work; he needed to make a deal, because it was too late. There would be no going back to the realms now; they would never forgive him, not for anything in the past, and certainly not for this. He defied a direct order from Jerry, he sold them all out, but in his own bitter heart, he felt that they all truly deserved it for doing what they had done to him. None of the gnomes would ever respect him anyways; he had lived the last few weeks in hiding, wearing the common gnome hat ashamed and embarrassed. As each day went by, he became angrier, and just a little more bitter. He didn't want to live his life as a total recluse, and knew deep down that he had destroyed any minor friendships he had made over the years. While he had been hiding in his house, locked up from the rest of the realms by his own choosing, no one, not even Gatsby or Optical even stopped by to visit, or to offer any words of encouragement or hope. Everyone was angry at him, and it was foolish of him to ever think that they would ever forgive and forget. The only choice he felt he had was to become even more evil since that was exactly how everyone already viewed him now. If he couldn't have friends, visitors or associates, then he would have prisoners that would follow his orders, but being alone wasn't going to be an option for him.

Zepadoodle led Ifffer down a long cold plain hallway towards Zoop's office. The gnome wasn't used to being in underwater buildings, and he could feel the pressure pushing against the walls, it was a very strange environment for him, and he didn't like it. Ifffer already missed the deep green grass, lush tree's and beautiful gardens, and he hoped that he would be able to return back to his home soon....as the realm leader. Gnomes loved nature, and desired to be outdoors most of the time, which is why they are commonly located in gardens. The gnome shuddered to think that this cold dull place could be his home, even temporarily, because he would probably hate that even more than living the way he had been, locked up in his own tree house, peering out the windows watching everyone else happy.

As they neared the main office, Ifffer showed no fear, he truly wasn't afraid to speak with the other aliens. He had already devised his very own plan, and he would stick with it.. Gatsby and Jerry did a fine job of displaying gnome power, even if it was all made up, and now he could use all of that to his own advantage.

Just as they reached the office door, Zepadoodle reached proudly into his pocket, but once again the two stones he had managed to steal were gone. In his frustration he turned to the gnome and blurted out his question.

"I took gemstones from the realms, not once but twice, why do they just vanish when I arrive here?" said Zepadoodle loudly as he was opening up the door.

"The old Key Holder of the Realms Gatsby had placed a spell on all the gemstones so that they could never be removed from the realms," answered Ifffer as he stepped into the office. He answered loud enough for everyone inside to hear his response; he wanted to show them immediately that he could be valuable to them by providing answers to their questions.

Just as Zepadoodle had expected Zoop and Krempie were eagerly awaiting. They had naturally listened in on Zepadoodle's conversation with the gnome, and had more questions about these gemstones in the gnome realm.

"Please come in and sit down," said Zoop in a commanding way, and not as friendly as Ifffer had hope, but he quickly took a seat anyway.

"I took gemstones again, but they disappeared, and I have proof that it wasn't my fault, I did my job, I'm not careless, and you can depend on me," sniffed Zepadoodle.

"Yes...yes...so we already heard, but we will speak privately later on about how you have handled things," said Krempie annoyed.

It was already clear to Zepadoodle that his leaders were far from pleased with him. He turned off his transmitter antenna, so that his own thoughts would no longer be heard. He sat quietly in the office listening to the conversation between the gnome and his leaders, pouting. Within a few minutes, his pale grey skin turned back to his usual shade of green, and he was feeling a little bit better.

"What are all the gemstones the realms possess, and what kind of powers have they managed to unleash from them?" demanded Zoop.

"We have opals, rubies, sapphires, diamonds, amethyst, jade, emeralds, topaz, pearls, alexandrite, aquamarine, amber, garnet, onyx, and turquoise," answered Ifffer.

"And....what can you do with them?" asked Krempie.

"Well...I have already answered two questions about gemstones. Before I give you any more information, I would like to know what you can do for me in exchange for my answers," said Ifffer.

"It is my understanding that you wish to rule the realms, however, at this point in time, we haven't even decided if we are going to allow the realms and its inhabitants to continue to even exist. Can you tell me why we shouldn't wipe all of you out?" asked Krempie.

"Yes...because of magic, and I will make sure that it is all used to not only serve me, but to serve you as well," said Ifffer.

"If you are talking about releasing power from gemstones, we are already well aware of that, and can use them without you," said Zoop firmly.

"Perhaps our gems are of no use to you....but what about if you had friends that would follow your orders, and they possessed the power of invisibility? Do you have any of that, and do you even realize what can be done with that?" asked Ifffer confident.

Chapter 12
Say it so you believe it

Eric was starting to settle back into his life at the hospital. He already knew some of the other children staying there, and they remembered him from his previous admissions. He couldn't exactly call any of them friends, because they certainly never forgot how he would taunt them, and manage to get them into trouble any chance he got. He met his new roommate, a twelve year old boy named Paul, that didn't speak very much. The boy was large for his age, and Eric had already made the determination that he would be best not to mess with him; therefore he avoided the boy whenever possible. While Eric was more into playing mind games and harassing, his roommate had the ability to use his fists, and he had no desire to have that kind of exchange with him. He had overheard the fat nurse talking earlier that morning, and she said something about his roommate going home soon, which would leave Eric in the room alone, and he was happy about that. Being alone was never a problem for him, it gave him more opportunity to sneak off and do things, without having a tattletale or witness to worry about. He thought his roommate was strange, just from having gone thru all of the boy's personal belongings. He knew the kid had made claims about being abducted by aliens, and found that quite interesting, although he desired more details, he reframed

71

from asking any questions. He always enjoyed taking on the traits, symptoms and problems the other kids claimed and decided this one could be fun.

Eric had a private appointment with his brand new doctor. This time his doctor was a man, his name was Dr. William Booker. The boy sat in his office, sizing up the gentlemen. The doctor appeared to be in his late fifties, slightly overweight, and sported salt and pepper colored hair. The man smiled and tried to come across immediately as the boy's friend, hoping that they would make some kind of a connection. This always annoyed Eric when his doctor's attempted this approach with him; he found it way too familiar, and almost an insult to his mental capabilities. He found it amusing in a way that these doctors thought they could trick him by being friendly. Naturally he knew that his new doctor had not only completely read all of his previous mental records, he was quite sure that the man had a formal talk with Dr. Melanie Hammer, so she could fill him in on his case file. She certainly would have told him that Eric was difficult and warned him that the boy would be a problem. This didn't bother him either; in fact, he pictured what he thought their conversation would have been like in his own head, and rather enjoyed it. He knew that the real reason Dr. Hammer no longer wanted him as a patient; it was because he had beaten her, and outsmarted her, and they both knew it. The fact was, Dr. Hammer simply couldn't handle Eric, and she had made no headway with him at all, accomplished nothing and only frustrated herself trying.

"Eric, please sit down son, and let's just chat and get to know each other," said Dr. Booker.

"Yeah, ok, but my name is Eric, and I'm not your son," said Eric already showing is annoyance.

"I didn't mean to offend you, please just relax Eric," said Dr. Booker.

"I'm relaxed just fine, so what do you want to talk to me about," said Eric innocently.

"Well…I would like to discuss what YOU think the reason is as to why you did this damage to your teachers car", said the doctor.

Eric hesitated before answering, so much for small talk and just getting to know each other. Clearly this doctor was going to just jump and get right down to business. The boy didn't have a problem with that; he was already well prepared for his appointment. This time he wasn't going to deny what he had done, he now had a much better story, at least more entertaining. The doctors always thought that they controlled these kinds of appointments, swaying the conversation to what needed to be discussed, but with Eric this wasn't always the case. The boy always managed to take these visits exactly in the direction he desired to go, usually quite a calculated one. He mentally prepared for his appointments, plotting the stories he would tell, and even planned on how he would act during all of it. He was such a good actor; he often thought he could be in the movies.

"Ah...well....I know why I did it, but I'm afraid to tell you," said Eric coyly.

"You have no reason to be afraid. You can tell me anything, this is a safe place for you," said Dr. Booker.

"Well, I was....told to do it...really I was forced to do it against my own will," said Eric as sincere as he possibly could be considering that he was outright lying.

"Forced? Who made you do this?" asked the doctor concerned.

"You're not going to believe me," said Eric looking down at the floor as if he were going to cry.

"Eric, I assure you that I will believe you, please just tell me what happened," said Dr. Booker unaware of what the boy would say next.

"Ok....it was...well...it was....the aliens. They don't like my teacher Mr. Koza, because he has little dolls of them on his desk," said Eric.

"So are you saying that the alien dolls told you to do this?" asked the doctor, preparing to write the boy's answer down on his clipboard which he held on his lap.

"NO...that would just be stupid, dolls don't talk, I'm not a mental person," said Eric.

"I don't think I quite understand what you are saying then, please explain," said the doctor.

73

"Real aliens told me to do it. They visit me from time to time, and threaten to abduct me if I don't do things they want me to do," said Eric.

"How often does this happen," said the doctor entertaining the story.

"When they feel like coming to see me. They visit lots of people," said Eric.

"And...explain again to me why they don't like your teacher?" asked Dr. Booker.

"Ugh!!! Aren't you even listening to what I am telling you? Mr. Koza has these little plastic dolls of them on his desk. I think the aliens feel like he is mocking them or something," said Eric.

"What does your teacher do with the dolls?" asked Dr. Booker.

"I don't know, probably plays with them or something, the guy is a little weird, thinks he's like a hippie or something," said Eric.

"Well, from what I have been told, your teacher is a very nice man. I understand that he refused to press charges against you and so you wouldn't get arrested and have a criminal record," said Dr. Booker.

"Yeah, yeah, that's probably because he is afraid of the aliens too. He has a plastic spaceship of theirs hanging in our classroom. The dude is totally obsessed with aliens and talks about them all the time," said Eric.

"What has he told you about aliens?" asked Dr. Booker.

"He is always talking about these stupid TV shows he watches about them," said Eric.

"Well...if you believe that you are in contact with aliens, and have been visited by them, why didn't you speak to your teacher about it? It seems to me like he would have been a safe person to have that kind of discussion with," said Dr. Booker.

"I'm in school to learn, and this guy is wasting my important educational time on alien stuff. I want to make something of myself one day," said Eric sternly.

Dr. Booker managed to contain the laugh at the back of his throat, and somehow kept a straight face. Eric certainly wasn't fooling him one bit. The boy was clearly quite intelligent for his age, and the way he attempted to manipulate every conversation to covey his own innocence and advantage was indeed amazing. Booker even thought that this kid had the future makings of a great politician.

"Okay, well let's just put aside what happened at school and your feelings about your teacher for the moment. Tell me more about the aliens you think are visiting you, and the things they have to say to you," said Dr. Booker.

"I don't like the way you said that. It's not that I THINK aliens are coming to visit me, they ARE visiting me," said Eric angry.

"I'm sorry if I have offended you with my statement that was not my intention. Please just tell me where and how the aliens come to see you," said Dr. Booker.

"Fine, I will, but you said this was a safe place, and I'm not feeling very safe right now," said Eric folding his arms across his chest.

"Please....just continue....you can say anything to me," said Dr. Booker sincerely.

"Ok...well...it always happens at night. I'm sleeping and then I wake up and a few of them are standing in my bedroom, just kinda staring at me," said Eric.

"Then what happens?" asked Dr. Booker.

"They...threaten me. They tell me they are going to take me far, far, away to another planet...unless...I do stuff for them," insisted Eric.

"What kinds of things do they ask you to do?" asked Dr. Booker.

"All kinds of stuff, things that will get me into trouble...like...my teacher's car....and....they always tell me not to do my homework, even though I really want to do it," said Eric sweetly.

"Yes...I'm quite sure you always want to do your school work. I see here in your chart, that you have told Dr. Hammer in the past that you were being visited by fairies, gnomes, and even ghosts at night, is that still going on?" asked Dr. Booker.

"Well...not so much...they don't like the aliens either, so they don't come around as much anymore," said Eric.

"I see, so are you seeing anything else that I should know about, or hearing any other voices telling you to do things?" asked the doctor.

"NO...I knew it...you don't believe me! I had a feeling that I couldn't trust you. Aliens are real, and one day you are going to find that out. When you do, they might eat your brains and then you're going to really owe me a big apology," said Eric defensive.

"I just have to wonder what you will see next, Leprechauns?" asked Dr. Booker.

Eric's appointment was over and he walked down the hall towards the room he was staying in. He knew that his new doctor was going to be a little harder to work over, but he would find out his weak point and then go for it, it was only a matter of time. He stopped in the public bathroom on the way back to his room. With precision, he stuffed both sinks with paper towels, and turned the water faucets on full blast, and then he waited until they began to overflow onto the floor. Pleased with the mess he created, he opened the door to the hallway quietly, peered out to make sure no one would see him exit, and bolted for his own room.

Chapter 13
It's all mapped out

Jerry and Gatsby returned back home after witnessing Ifffer disappear along with the alien. The two spoke about what could be done, and decided that Ifffer would be the first gnome in history banned from the realms. They placed spells on all the realms entrances including the one in the astral plane. Should the old gnome ever return from life with the aliens in the underwater camp, his only option would be to live in the human world, hiding in gardens and from humans. This was a severe punishment, and one that they didn't take lightly, but Ifffer had given them no choice this time. He had proven more than once that he put himself before all the realm inhabitants, and would stop at nothing. Ifffer was now considered to be an enemy of the realms and it truly saddened them, to know that one of their own had turned against them to this degree.

All of this had to be recorded in the official law books, and the full details about why the old gnome had been banned. Although Jerry and Gatsby both knew all the reasons and rules that had been broken, it needed to be recorded for the future generations who didn't witness it. The only person that would ever be able to open the realms back up again for Ifffer to make entrance would be the current ruling Key Holder of the Realm. Most likely a new realm ruler wouldn't take office until thousands of years from now, but since gnomes lived so long, they couldn't risk Ifffer ever being able to gain entrance to the realms ever again. Knowing what they already knew about him, made them believe that he would spend the rest of his years, planning and plotting his revenge.

The two speculated about what Ifffer's true intentions were with the aliens. They feared that he would tell them about the tricks they performed for Zepadoodle, and now they needed to take action. Before they could do anything to stop the aliens from taking over planet Earth, they needed to protect the realms. Jerry decided to call an emergency council meeting, all ten members would have to weigh in on what could be done next. They also called in Mystic, Annastarlis, Nerby, Elvin, Elise and Hubert, so that each realm division would be represented.

The Great Hall of Justice's main meeting room was brimming with sounds of everyone talking as they all gathered together. Jerry hadn't called the meeting to order just yet, he was still in his office speaking with Gatsby.

Both of the gnomes spoke about several things they each felt must be addressed at the meeting. Gatsby had spent the night pouring thru old law, gnome history and record books, searching for any reference to aliens that would have been documented by past generations, but found none. The old gnome looked exhausted from the stress and lack of sleep; therefore he was happy that Jerry was now in charge, and the full responsibility of it all wasn't on his own shoulders. Finally the two exited the office and entered the main room.

"Please everyone take your seats, we have much to talk about today," said Jerry taking command.

Hubert seemed confused by the rush of everyone to sit at the long table, and then realized that this meant the meeting was going to begin. Hubert lumbered over and finally took the last seat at the table. His odor today seemed to be exceptionally foul, and Annastarlis wrinkled her nose when he sat in the empty chair behind her. She shot a quick glance at Nerby, who clearly was having problems keeping his smirk under wraps. The two would most likely argue later on about the position she had been in, as she saw no humor in the situation whatsoever. She gave him a light kick under the table, which told him that he was in trouble, and he bit his lip, putting a serious look on his face.

"Ewww, what smells so bad in here?" squealed Elise.

"It's the troll, remember I told you about that," said Elvin honestly.

"Elise and Elvin that isn't polite, please let's just get down to business," said Jerry, trying to ignore the stench that seemed to linger in the room.

"We would like to inform everyone that Ifffer has been permanently banned from the realms," asked Gatsby.

"It needed to be done, and now I'm quite sure that the news will spread quickly, you have everyone's full support in this matter," said Mystic sadly.

"We need to put that situation behind us, and move forward. It saddens me that it came to that. I had hoped that he would live his life out here, peacefully and quietly in seclusion. Right now, my concern is that Ifffer is with the aliens, and I don't really know how much information he will give them," said Jerry.

"I guess that all the work we did tricking Zepadoodle has probably been exposed, and now they know you don't have the power to move objects with your mind, or to levitate," said Mystic.

"That would be my guess as well," said Jerry.

"I don't know about that....I know Ifffer a little better than some of you. If you want my opinion, I believe that he will go along with all of that, so that they think he is more powerful than he really is," said Optical.

"That is a possibility, and it does seem more to fit his personality," said Gatsby agreeing.

"Well, we need to be prepared either way, and we can't sit here and speculate about it one way or another, because we are only guessing, and wasting time on it," added Jerry.

"Why don't we just so go to this underwater space station, and just blow it up," said Elise batting her long eyelashes.

"We don't have any bombs or weapons like that, and I could never justify taking the life of any being or creature. Magic can never be used to maim or harm, it's simply forbidden," said Jerry annoyed at the whosawhachette's time wasting suggestion.

"Yes, the realms have never resorted to any kind of violence," said Annastarlis after shooting Elise a dirty look for shocking statement.

"I think we should just break into their camp, and show them that we can invade them too," said Nerby smartly.

"We have no way of getting into their triangle camps. As far as I know they have two of them, both are deep in the ocean, and we need air to breath. We couldn't possibly swim that deep, nor do I believe it would be safe for us, even with diving equipment," said Gatsby.

"Do you think we fairies could just pop inside one of them, I mean we can do that in the human realm?" asked Annastarlis.

"I don't know how they have been built or if that is even possible. It would be risky, because if you gain entrance, we wouldn't know if the environment there would allow you to even survive," said Jerry.

"It must be safe, otherwise Ifffer wouldn't be there right now," said Nerby trying to make a point, plus he wanted to show support for the statement Annastarlis just made, hoping it would help to get him out of trouble with her later.

"We have no confirmation to even know that Ifffer is still alive. We are assuming his body was able to adapt, but we don't know that for sure, and perhaps we never will," said Jerry somberly.

"Then why don't we just go into the huge camp that the aliens have under the Great Pyramids in Egypt? That's not under the water," asked Elvin with his usual grin.

"What camp in Egypt? I know nothing about any camp there. Where are you coming up with this idea?" asked Jerry confused.

"Well, I know all about it, in fact, you will be proud that I'm on your side now, because I've got a map of the joint," said Elvin.

"A map...but how?" asked Gatsby.

"I have been practicing the art of pick pocketing, just for fun and stuff. You know, like a magic trick. Zepadoodle knocked on my door, and yes Dudes, I did answer it for him, even though you said I shouldn't. Since he was there, I went ahead and checked out the Space Creep's pockets," said Elvin proudly.

"Why didn't you come directly to us immediately with this?" exclaimed Jerry.

"Well...I kinda forgot about it, because I was in the middle of playing a game when he came knocking...and then...I thought maybe you gnome dudes would get mad that I kinda stole it," said Elvin.

"Normally stealing is very wrong, but in this case, you did well, please let us have a look at this map," said Jerry.

Elvin proudly pulled the tattered old map from his pocket and placed it in the middle of the long table. Everyone rose from their seats, and leaned over the piece of parchment paper attempting to get a good look at it. In a struggle for the best position, heads bumped into each other, and Elise's horns tangled with Gatsby's tall gnome hat, finally knocking it off his head.

It was indeed an entire map showing the Pyramids in Giza, and directions on how to use them to gain entrance into the alien city contained below it. The room buzzed with excitement, as each one of them still continued to jockey for a better view to inspect the document.

"In a way this doesn't truly surprise me. When I was reading thru our history library last night for any references made about aliens, I found a notation about the pyramids. Our forefathers were questioning the appearance of these huge structures, and looking for an explanation as to how the humans built them. Apparently, they were built over a course of many years, but none of the realms inhabitants ever saw any humans physically working on them," said Gatsby.

"Are you saying our records state that these were just appearing out of nowhere, being built and worked on each day or night, but no one was ever seen doing it," said Jerry.

"That seems to be the case, and it was a concern many years ago. Apparently the Key Holder at the time, kept a close eye on it. After hundreds of years of seeing nothing worthwhile, he finally just dropped it," said Gatsby.

"Did you find any other facts that our elders noted about this?" asked Jerry.

"Well, they did note that the three main pyramids are lined up with the Belt of Orion in the sky, and that the structures appear to be located at the exact center of the land mass of earth which is quite interesting," said Gatsby.

"You know, I remember reading something in the old fairy files about the Great Pyramids. It seems that when some of the fairies took flight high up in the human realm one evening, they discovered that the polished surfaces on the pyramids seemed to reflect light like a beacon into the sky. They wrote that it could most likely be seen as far as the moon. I myself have never really flown quite that high, but for them to document this fact is quite curious, and I think they were trying to tell us something," said Mystic.

"It does seem that the Pyramids have everything to do with our visitors from the sky, and even though our record books don't state this fact, I think our ancestors suspected it. The map we have here finally gives us the proof we all needed," said Jerry nodding his head in approval at Elvin.

"Yes, I believe it does. A copy of this must be preserved for future generations, and duly noted in all the record books," said Gatsby.

"And...it should be recorded that Elvin the Great King of the Whosawhachits was the one to discover it," said Elvin with a broad smile.

"I will see that it does," said Jerry.

Several copies of the map were made, and handed out to each of them who attended the meeting, and the original was officially filed. They spent the afternoon discussing how they would evade this underground camp, and what needed to be done to save the realms from extermination.

After the meeting Elvin requested permission to go into the human realm to visit the little girl Aimee Lynn. He told the gnomes about the statements the child made, about the green men taking her parents. When his request was denied he argued that he should be given some kind of finder's fee or reward for turning the discovery of the map over to the council. He begged and pleaded, and even pouted like a small child attempting to get his way. He kept insisting and arguing to enter the human realm, just briefly for a visit, because it was reasonable, and finally Jerry agreed to it.

Chapter 14
A Promise of Hope

Elvin went into the human realm along with Annastarlis and Nerby. He located Aimee Lynn playing outside in her backyard with a large kickball. Kyle was swimming in the pool and Sarah busy in the house. In order for him to speak with the child, he needed to show himself, and therefore he had to be careful, not to be spotted by any other humans. Annastarlis was strict about enforcing all the rules she was given and Elvin was starting to get annoyed with her. He was used to being a ruler, at least in his own realm, and didn't like having to take orders from the fairy; in fact he truly resented it. Elvin stood behind a large tree trunk, and scoped out his position, he looked around carefully in all directions just to make sure that no one would be able to see him, and finally he appeared.

"Pssst...Aimee Lynn, it's me, Elvin, come and talk to me," Elvin whispered.

The small child immediately responded to his call, and ran over to the tree excited to see her purple friend. Annastarlis and Nerby both stayed invisible, each one taking a post of lookout, to make sure that no other humans would be able to see the whosawhachit. Elvin's purple color was difficult to camouflage, especially against the brown tree trunk and green grass. His purple skin color almost seemed to glisten and sparkle in the sunlight.

"I wanted to come and see you, but I can only stay for a few minutes, ok" said Elvin.

"Play ball," said Aimee Lynn throwing a kick ball directly to him.

Elvin was careful to stay in his place hidden behind the tree. He caught the white ball in his hands, turned it a light shade of purple, and then thru it back to her. The child's eyes gleamed when she retrieved the ball back from him, with its new vivid color. Elvin's playful demeanor delighted the child and she wished that she could play with him all the time.

"I'm going to look for your parents. We are going to go into one of the alien's underground camps in Egypt and maybe they will be there. I promise you that I'm going to do everything I can for you. If your parents are there, I will bring them back," said Elvin attempting to help the child.

Annastarlis instantly popped out of her invisibility and stood in front of Elvin annoyed. She was so upset that she forgot about being in the middle of a human backyard.

"Don't go making any promises that you can't keep. That is one of the very first rules when helping humans. You don't even know for sure that you will be going on that exploration," snapped Annastarlis as her cheeks started to flush a bright shade of red.

"Oh...I will be going, dude-ette because it was MY map," said Elvin proudly.

"You don't have full security clearance," said Annastarlis annoyed, and now with her hands on her hips to further show her aggravation.

"Doesn't matter, I will get it. I bet they even put me in charge of the group that goes," said Elvin, and then sticking his tongue out at the fairy. This made Aimee Lynn giggle.

"Ha, I doubt that, especially when I tell them that you just broke another rule," said Annastarlis being bossy.

"Geez, what rule did I break now?" asked Elvin overwhelmed with all the rules.

"You told a human official realm business. You should not have said anything about the alien base camp or the map. All of that is confidential information, and the only ones that should know about it, were in the meeting. You will be in big trouble for that, and I'm reporting it when we get back," said Annastarlis.

"Oh yeah, well think about it wing girl, the girl is only 6 years old, and she doesn't talk to anybody. C'mon….give me a break, I'm trying to do something good here," said Elvin throwing his arms up in the air.

Nerby decided it was time to pop out and join into the conversation. The three seemed to forget where they were standing and began to argue. Aimee Lynn stood watching all of it, as if she were viewing a tennis match on television, turning her head back and forth as each took a turn speaking. Nerby understood Elvin's point, and thought that Annastarlis was being too hard on him, which only made her even madder. She felt ganged up on, as if now it were the boys against the girl, but the real truth was, sometimes she allowed a little bit of power to go to her head. Nerby no longer broke rules, but he still tended to bend some of them slightly. He understood that Elvin's heart was in the right place, and he hoped that Annastarlis would see that and cut the guy a little bit of slack, as far as the rules and tattle tailing on him.

Kyle had been relaxing in the pool floating on his back, lost in watching the different cloud formations above in the blue sky, He had almost forgotten that he had been given strict instructions from his mother to keep an eye on his little sister. She was always so quiet, and for that reason, it was very easy for him to just put her out of his mind. He had very little companionship with her, because she still refused to talk with him, and only communicated by using a few hand or head motions.

Kyle heard something, a noise or maybe it was someone talking, and he popped up out of the water. He looked around for its source and then noticed Aimee Lynn standing with a confused look on her face, watching something, or someone. He quickly swam to the side of the pool, exited up the ladder, and grabbed a towel off the lounge chair to dry off, so that he could investigate. Then he spotted Annastarlis and Nerby in the grass standing near his little sister. He was surprised to see his friends from the realm, especially because they were visual to Aimee Lynn.

"Hey, what are you guys doing here?" asked Kyle.

"Elvin wanted to visit your sister, they kind of made friends," answered Nerby.

Kyle walked up to the tree and saw Elvin standing behind it, and almost jumped back startled, but was able to hold his ground. Was it true that Elvin had become friends with Aimee Lynn? He was still very much afraid of the whosawhachit, and the sight of him standing in his own backyard shocked him. The whosawhachit just made the boy uncomfortable, and seeing him in the human realm again, made him nervous. He had been told that Elvin was now a good guy, but still could this purple, chocolate cake eating creature that held him as a hostage not that long ago, really be trusted?

"Friends...but how?" asked Kyle confused.

"Long story...but we are keeping a close eye on things," said Nerby casually.

"So what's going on with the aliens, anything I can do?" asked Kyle.

"Oh, you wouldn't even believe it. We found out that they have a huge camp underneath the Pyramids in Egypt," answered Annastarlis.

"Whoa...you just broke a rule. How come you just told him about the base camp, which...by the way...you should know I am personally responsible for discovering," said Elvin directing the second part of his statement towards Kyle.

"He is different, Kyle is a friend to the realms, and someone that we entrust with information," said Annastarlis.

"Well, so is his sister," demanded Elvin, trying to justify the rules he had broken.

"How many aliens are living there?" asked Kyle ignoring Elvin's statement, and turning towards Annastarlis and Nerby.

"We don't really know yet, but the plan is to go inside of it in the next day or two. Jerry and Gatsby are working on all the details of it right now," said Nerby excited, and looking forward to the adventure.

"I know you have a lot going on right now, and not that I really want to talk in front of....you know who...but remember I asked you if you could....ah...watch Joe and find anything out for me..." said Kyle.

"Gatsby wouldn't allow us to do that....but we have found out some information. Aimee Lynn's parents were abducted by the aliens, she must have witnessed the whole event," said Annastarlis.

"How do you know this?" asked Kyle.

"She told Elvin all about the green men and what happened," answered Nerby.

"What....but she doesn't talk," said Kyle confused.

"She talks to me Dude," said Elvin smirking.

Kyle looked at his little sister, she smiled from ear to ear and then shrugged her shoulders, as if to say, yes, I do talk, but only to Elvin. She began to bounce her ball, and finally thru it to Elvin. He caught it, balanced it between his horns making it spin, and then finally threw it back to her. The child giggled, missed catching it, and ran after the ball when it bounced to the back fence of the yard.

"Why doesn't she just talk to me?" asked Kyle.

"I don't know, but at least you know she can speak," answered Annastarlis.

"She likes me," said Elvin attempting to annoy Kyle even further, if that were even possible.

Kyle watched Aimee Lynn as she returned with her purple ball; she didn't seem shocked or afraid of any of the realm visitors. In fact, she seemed quite relaxed, content and happy. He remembered the first day he met his friends in the woods, that day changed his life forever. He hoped that her relationships with them would only help her, but he still felt a need to be protective when it came to Elvin. He stared at the purple kickball she held in her hands, and knew that it had been originally a white color. Kyle decided he needed to try and get his sister to speak to him, they had to bond if he was ever going to be able to help her.

"Did the green alien men take your real parents?" asked Kyle directly to her.

Aimee Lynn looked at her brother and shook her head yes, but didn't answer him verbally.

"You don't have to be afraid, I'm your big brother, and you can talk to me. Did you see the aliens?" asked Kyle.

Aimee Lynn ran over to Elvin, he had knelt down on the ground and was waving her over to him, and she ran into his arms. She whispered something in his ear, and then he whispered something back to her and the two of them giggled together. Kyle was highly aggravated that Elvin managed to form this kind of a relationship with her, and that she still refused to speak to him or anyone else, he found it frustrating and embarrassing on some level.

"Maybe you can just tell Jerry that Elvin should just stay in his own realm again. I think it was better when he was locked up in there," said Kyle resentful.

Chapter 15
Information Exchange

Ifffer had been in the alien underwater camp, deep down in the Bermuda Triangle for two days now. He had spent much time with Zoop and Krempie, seeing very little of Zepadoodle. The aliens had been quite good hosts to him, assigning him his own private room, which consisted of nothing more than a small bed and a simple plain wood table and chair. The room offered no warmth or color, the walls made of cold metal. Still it was clear that they tried to make his stay as comfortable as possible, offering him anything they thought would please him. They weren't quite sure about the truth behind the things the gnome told them, and the powers he claimed to possess. They were listening, taking notes, and then scrutinizing all the data before making their final determination about the gnome's possible usefulness to them.

Aliens lived on mostly a plant diet, but they were strange plants, ones that they were actively growing down deep in the ocean. The plants were harvested and processed to the extent that they weren't truly food but more like a liquid fuel providing all the nourishment to make their bodies run efficiently. They fed the gnome the plain harvested plant, as if it were a salad. Although, Ifffer didn't find the taste of these seawater plants unpleasant, they didn't seem to fit into his own natural plant, grain, and nuts diet, and it was starting to have some effects on his body, at least this was his thinking. He wasn't feeling quite himself, his joints were starting to ache, more so than usual for his age, and he starting to notice that his hands were trembling slightly. His accommodations had no mirrors, but with his hands he could feel bags and puffiness below his eyes, which he related to being just overtired.

Ifffer was in his room taking a nap, he felt exhausted from just talking earlier this morning with the alien leaders. He tried to stay extremely sharp, taking extra care with all of his answers to their questions. Attempting to stay one step ahead of them, it was like being in a mental chess game, and it had started to drain him. Early this morning they spoke in depth about gemstones, and exchanged information about what each had discovered, and how they each used them. Ifffer had been fairly honest with them, about the different spells the gnomes could place on gemstones, however, he didn't give them all of the details on how the process completely worked using their gnome magic. The aliens talked about a gemstone they had hidden deep in the ocean, and said that it was dangerous, and the very downfall to Isle of Atlantis, and that it should never be used or discovered by anyone or it would be the end of Planet Earth. They claimed that it they could unleash this gemstone anytime they wanted to, but hadn't done so yet, because they had decided the planet was worth saving for their own use. They even showed the gnome pictures of this glowing red/yellow gemstone, as further proof of its very existence. The gem in the picture had been encased in a granite stone that was crafted and carved so that its very shape was the design of a perfect pyramid.

Zoop wanted to sit and talk again in the afternoon, after the gnome insisted that he needed to take a break. They could see the gnome was sweating, his color seemed to be pale, and they decided that it would probably be best that he take a brief rest. They would summon him later on that day for another round of information exchange.

A grey alien knocked on Ifffer's door, awaking him from his nap.

The gnome had fallen into a deep sleep, and his snoring could be heard several rooms away. Ifffer willingly went along with the grey alien back to the main offices to meet with the alien leaders again. He didn't feel quite right, but the nap did do him some good. He was slightly annoyed that they disturbed him from his slumber, because he thought he had only been sleeping for about an hour. In truth, the aliens had allowed the old gnome to sleep for almost 5 hours, and finally grew impatient waiting for him to rise.

"We hope that you are feeling better," said Zoop insincerely.

"I believe that I am...I think perhaps I'm not feeling well because I'm not eating my normal food," said Ifffer.

"You are most likely wrong; if anything our nutrients would help you. We believe you are having some side effects from being down deep in the ocean, due to the extreme water pressure. Most of the humans we bring here suffer greatly from that, therefore we either return them quickly or take them to one of our underground camps, which they seem to tolerate better," said Krempie in a know it all type tone of voice.

"So you have other camps on this planet?" asked Ifffer.

"We have several, only two are deep underwater in the oceans. This evening we are going to move you to one that is under the Great Pyramids of Egypt. That one has quite an extensive natural oxygen ventilating system built into its construction, and we think you will feel much better," said Zoop.

"Why do you take humans? What use can they possibly be to you?" asked Ifffer.

"We do many different kinds of experiments on them, so that we may learn from their mistakes," said Zoop.

Zoop spoke about the human experiments they had been conducting in their labs all around the world. The gnome was amazed by all the information they had shared with him, regarding how they felt about humans. The aliens truly believed that the human civilization wouldn't make it and evidently would fail, becoming extinct because of the human's own brutality and stupidity.

"Our job has been to gather information and store it in a collective network that is shared throughout the universe" said Zoop.

"So you mean that there are other alien races, group....ah civilizations besides yours that we don't know about?" asked Ifffer shocked.

"Ha...oh yes, many. Lucky for us, all of them have travelled here to this planet, and none have the slightest bit of interest in it," said Krempie.

"Then if they aren't interested in it, why are you?" asked Ifffer.

"We have the need for another planet, they do not. While it is true, that these stupid humanoids have done much damage to it, we believe we can reverse some of that. At the very least, we can stop anymore from happening, if we act quickly," said Zoop.

"What kind of damage have the humans really done?" asked Ifffer.

"They are responsible for most of all of their own sickness and diseases. They have brought it all upon themselves because of the conditions of their own environment, and one that they have stripped of natural useful resources," said Zoop.

"We study the humanoids bodies, their skin, hair, tissue cells, and blood to see what chemicals they have exposed themselves to by living here. They have contaminated this planet with toxic waste in their garbage dumps, changed the air quality with smoke and fog. We must know and understand what they are suffering from so that we don't inherit their fate," said Krempie.

"If you have been watching them for so many years, why haven't you stopped them from doing all of this damage?" asked Ifffer.

"In the beginning it was kind of like an experiment. We watched them to see how far they would progress. We also wondered how long it would take for them to continue their foolish technology until it was the end of their own demise. You must understand that we didn't want to get involved, and at the time we didn't realize we would have a need for this planet," said Zoop.

"Are you claiming that you have never interfered with the humans," asked Ifffer exhausted from all the thinking.

"No, we admit that we have. If we didn't step in during their World War 2, this planet would no longer be here, and it could have caused problems in the solar system for some of us. We have manipulated some of their situations for the better, not only for them, but for the survival of other planets," said Krempie.

"Like what?" asked.

"I'm not going to give you all of that data, Universal law would not allow me to do so," said Zoop.

"How many other aliens are out there?" asked Ifffer.

"There are twenty other alien nations. All different species some look nearly identical to humans, others more like us. We are peaceful together, have worked, and ruled as a unit for thousands of years," said Zoop.

"Amazing that none of you knew about the existence of the realms, doesn't that say something about us?" said Ifffer arrogantly.

"Not really, you hide, buried under the ground like rodents. We may not have discovered you sooner, but you didn't know about us either, and there have been times that we have flown directly in plain view," said Krempie.

"Let's just get right down to the reason I really came here. If you want the planet and to rid it of humans, I will not stop you, but in return, I want the realms to be left as they are, with me as the ruler there," sniffed Ifffer.

"We want to know more about this invisibility that you briefly spoke of, please demonstrate it for us," demanded Krempie.

"Well...I cannot. Gnomes don't have that power, but one of the other realm inhabitants does. If I'm the Key Holder of the Realms, I will make them do as you request," said Ifffer.

"Is it those pink or purple little creatures with the horns on their heads?" asked Zoop.

"I will not divulge which realm inhabitant or inhabitants have this power until we have an agreement," said Ifffer strongly.

"Invisibility isn't enough, we need more than that to make it worth it to us," pushed Krempie.

"What if I told you that the realms contain a....special...substance?

The only place this substance will grow is there, so you will not want to destroy it. All the user has to do is wish for something and it will appear by using it," said Ifffer.

Ifffer didn't want to tell them about the fairy dust, he chose the word substance on purpose, hoping that they would believe it could be any item in the realm. He wasn't feeling well, and the constant questioning was taking a toll on him. When he made his last statement, he thought he had been clever but because of his extreme fatigue, he made a large error.

"Substance?....So it grows there....well, the only strange thing I saw there that was growing were those strange tree's in the fairy realm, with all the fluffy stuff on them," said Zoop remembering the images that Zepadoodle sent back to them.

Ifffer looked down at the floor, he was angry with himself for having given up so much information. He had hardly anything left to use as a bargaining tool. He noticed that his grey beard appeared to be snow white in color, as if he had aged hundreds and hundreds of years in just a few days. He forced himself to stand from his chair, and began pacing the room. Every bone in his body ached, and he knew that he needed to get out of the underwater camp as soon as possible.

"Show us again how you levitate and hover in the air," said Krempie sensing that something was wrong with the gnome and suspicious that the gnome really didn't have this kind of magical power.

"I cannot....I mean....I can...but not now, feeling ill, must get out of here, soon," said Ifffer ashamed that he had to admit any weakness.

It was at that point that Ifffer finally realized what was wrong with him. It wasn't the alien plants that were making him ill. It wasn't the pressure from being so deep in the ocean. It wasn't the piped in oxygen either. The plants he normally ate weren't special, most if not all of them could be found growing up above in the ground that people ate. What made the realms plants special was the water. All the plants were watered with the very same water that all the realm inhabitants drank. It came directly from The Fountain of Youth, which is the very reason they all lived so long.

Chapter 16
Unexpected Visitor

Eric was called to Dr. Booker's office, the doctor had quite the surprise for the boy. It was his feeling that Eric got away with things, because he was never really forced to confront the people or situations that he made statements about, this was about to change. The doctor was going to take a stronger approach with handling his patients care. Dr. Booker had seen many children over the course of his career, several just like Eric, and he knew what direction to take in his treatment. The boy would no longer get away with pointing the finger at others for things that he did, and his lame excuses were going to be called out, front and center.

Now while it was impossible for the doctor to call in aliens to his office, he thought long and hard about the reason Eric claimed he did the car damage. The boy said that his teacher wasn't liked by the aliens, because he mocked them, and believed that they all truly existed. It seemed reasonable to him to request that this teacher come in for a visit with the boy, so that they could get it all straightened out. Eric needed to learn how to communicate, not only with other children but with adults, especially with those that were in authority. If he never learned to do this, he would never be able to keep a job, because he wouldn't get along with his boss or co-workers. The doctor wanted to show him that any and all misunderstandings could be easily straightened out, by just talking about them. The doctor also assumed that Eric had never really truly given his teacher a proper apology for what he did, and that was something he also needed to be taught to do.

Eric casually walked down the long hallway towards his new doctor's office. He already had several things in his mind that he would entertain the doctor with today. One of which, was to claim that the aliens had come into his room last night for a visit, informing him that the doctor was in serious danger. He planned and plotted what he would say, and actually was quite excited to begin his next appointment.

Eric was surprised when he opened the office door and saw his teacher Mr. Koza sitting in a chair casually chatting with his doctor. He wondered why the man was here, and instantly knew that this wasn't a friendly visit; it had been planned by his new stupid doctor. He never had a teacher visit him in the hospital; none truly ever cared about his mental health. They only wished and hoped that his stay would be long, so that he wouldn't be returning back to their classroom. Something about this new teacher was different, he really did seem to care, enjoy and like his students and it only annoyed Eric.

"Eric, come on in and sit down. Your teacher Mr. Koza will be joining us briefly for the first part of your session with me today," said Dr. Booker smiling.

"Whatever," said Eric.

"That isn't the proper way to greet someone that has come to see you. Show some manners, and say hello," pushed the doctor.

"Hello," said Eric rolling his eyes and taking a seat next to his teacher.

"Hello Eric, it's good to see you, we have missed you in class," said Mr. Koza with his usual bright smile.

"Yeah, sure," said Eric.

Having his teacher here had completely changed his plans on how this appointment was going to go. Eric liked to direct these sessions from start to finish, but the doctor managed to throw him off course, and he wasn't very happy. He would need to take a new direction, think fast, so he could come out on top.

Just as the doctor had suspected, putting the boy in a small enclosed room with his teacher, having to face the situation and talk about things that he had lied about made him noticeably uncomfortable.

"Eric, this is a safe space, we are all going to openly talk, get everything out, and when you leave here, I believe you will feel better," said Dr. Booker.

"I feel fine now," said Eric.

"I asked your teacher to come in today, and I was very happy that he accepted my invitation. I think there are several things that should be talked about," said Dr. Booker.

"I don't have anything I need to talk about," said Eric.

"Well…I thought that maybe we could discuss aliens, since this seems to be a subject that you both have a common interest in," said Dr. Booker.

Eric wasn't unhappy about this subject, in fact, he thought for a second or two, and decided that just maybe he would be able to go back to his original plan for the visit today. He really thought the doctor would just jump right in and want to talk about the car, so this was a real treat for him. The doctor had opened the door of opportunity and Eric was going to grab for it.

"That would be good, because the aliens came to see me last night," said Eric.

"We will get to that later. Right now, let's just stay on the subject of whether or not aliens truly exist," said Dr. Booker cleverly taking control of the direction of their conversation.

"Well, they do, and I have seen and talked to them. I'm in the middle of trying to tell you that, if you would just let me finish," said Eric defensively.

"Don't be defensive about it. Let's take a minute and hear what your teacher's opinion is about aliens," said Dr. Booker.

"Whatever," said Eric annoyed.

"Mr. Koza, I understand that you have alien dolls in your classroom.

Eric feels that you perhaps use them to taunt, or mock real aliens," said Dr. Booker.

"Yes, I do have several alien figures. They have been gifts from past students I have had over the years. Almost everyone knows that I'm a Star Trek fan, and so they purchase me collectibles from that series," said Koza.

"See Eric, now we have one misunderstanding cleared up," said Dr. Booker.

"However, since Eric has direct contact with these beings, and he says they don't like me, perhaps he could let them know that I'm not mocking them, so that I can avoid anymore damages in the future," said Koza teasing.

Dr. Booker saw the humor made in the man's statement and the child side that he possessed. He completely understood why kids would mesh with his personality. The doctor carefully thought about what the teacher had just said, and decided that maybe he too should take the lighter approach with the boy.

"See, now he's mocking me. What does that statement mean," snapped Eric.

"Eric, you have said time and again that you are in contact with the aliens. You claim to be upset that no one believes you. Yet, here you sit with two adults that are really listening to you, keeping an open mind to the things you claim, and you are getting angry," said Dr. Booker.

"Yeah, well....ask him...if he believes in real life aliens, he told the whole class that he does," sneered Eric.

"That is not exactly what I said, I believe you are misquoting me. What I said was, I believe it is POSSIBLE that other life forms exist that we don't know about," said Mr. Koza.

"Ah, no, I'm not misquoting you, I think you have been beamed up too many times," said Eric.

"Keep in mind that when you are speaking to an adult, although you are free to voice your opinion, it must be done in a respectful manner," said Dr. Booker.

"Oh, excuse me...I believe in my opinion that Mr. Koza has been respectfully beamed up too many times," said Eric.

"Eric, if the aliens don't like Mr. Koza and asked you to damage his car, I have to wonder why you would listen. You seem very strong willed and only do what you want to do. I guess I find it hard to believe that you would follow directions," said Dr. Booker.

"Because...they threaten me...with stuff," said Eric.

"What kind of things do they threaten you with?" asked Dr. Booker.

"Stuff like....well...that they will take me up to their planet," said Eric scampering for words.

"Well, as someone who has been beamed up many times, I have to tell you it's really quite an experience," said Mr. Koza joking.

"I'm not going to just sit here and take this," screamed Eric.

The boy rose from his seat in anger, opened the office door, and exited, making sure that he slammed the solid wood door behind him, so that the sound would echo down the hallway.

He wasn't happy that his new doctor had now joined forces with his teacher. The two men did give the boy a taste of his own medicine, and Eric was determined that there would be hell to pay for it. Yes, the boy could dish it out just fine, but couldn't take it back.

It was almost lunchtime, and Eric went straight to the cafeteria. He paced the room nervously, watching the two women that worked there, getting things prepared and ready. They each wore white uniforms, typical hair nets on their heads, with clear plastic gloves on their hands. He thought about everything that just happened. He didn't really know why he couldn't just admit, that he damaged the teacher's car, because, well, he really didn't even know why, he just felt like it. Why did he have to make up a story about aliens telling him to do it, saying the aliens didn't like the man? The boy knew deep down that something was clearly wrong with him, other kids didn't go around making up stories, and they didn't damage other people's things either. He really didn't want to be this way, but he was. Maybe what the doctor's had said in the past was true, perhaps he did have some kind of chemical imbalance. Maybe he just enjoyed misbehaving, whatever the case, for the first time, he was starting to come to terms with it himself. He was finally admitting that he did really have a problem.

For the very first time, Eric started to analyze himself, his own thoughts and ideas. He couldn't really help it that he always seemed to have ideas, he was creative. Could he control his impulsive behaviors, and stop himself from doing things that he knew caused problems for other people. He looked around the cafeteria again, but this time, he did it, looking for something to do, just to see if he could stop himself.

He saw the ladies putting lunch out in metal trays, stacking and lining them up neatly for everyone to eat. He saw stacks of green food trays waiting for people to take them. He wanted to run over and knock the stacks of trays down, but he didn't. He wanted to dump all the food on the floor, but didn't. He sat with his hands tightly wrapped around the seat of his chair, almost daring himself to do something or maybe to stop him from doing something. He was in the middle of an inner struggle, and he didn't really like it. The boy got up out of his chair and walked around the room, truly he was pacing, because he had nervous energy and needed to find an outlet for it. What did other kids do when they were bored? Why did being bad make him happy? He had a need to entertain himself, he had to be occupied doing something or else. He noticed several magazines on a small table in the corner, he grabbed a few of them and sat down and began flipping thru them. If he could just keep himself busy for a few more minutes, lunch would be out, and other kids would be coming in, he could do this, he needed to prove it to himself.

Chris, a younger boy Eric knew entered the room; he stood frozen for a few seconds, as if he were afraid to be alone with Eric. In the past Eric had done a few mean things to him. He told everyone that the boy was a bed wetter, and teased and taunted the child every opportunity he had gotten. Eric was determined that he wouldn't do this today.

"Hey Chris, c'mon in, almost time for lunch," said Eric attempting to be sincere.

"Yeah…ah…ok," said the Chris hesitantly.

"You should sit with me during lunch," said Eric motioning towards the chair next to him.

"Why, what are you going to do to me?" asked Chris.

"Nothing, why does everyone always think I'm going to do something," said Eric annoyed.

"Because you usually do," said Chris.

"Well, not today, today, I'm not going to do anything," said Eric defensively.

"Yeah, ok," said Chris not sure if he should trust Eric.

"By the way...don't eat the meatloaf. I have been watching these two women make lunch, and it has boogers in it," said Eric.

"Ewww, really," said Chris.

"Yup, it does, big green ones," said Eric happy.

Eric tried, and considering everything that he could have done, lying about booger meatloaf was nothing. He told himself; just take baby steps; because even he knew that he would certainly never become an angel.

Chapter 17
Treasure Map Voyage

The group was ready to leave on their journey to investigate the alien's camp hidden deep below the pyramids in Egypt. Annastarlis, Nerby and Optical would be the chosen small group sent to take a peek into the camp. They were ordered not to do anything except, make entrance into the place, and remember as many details as they could about it. The gnomes needed to know certain things about the place, such as how many aliens were there, and if human's were also being held against their will at this location. Since the fairies always had the power of invisibility they would be able to easily investigate without being discovered. Gnomes did not have the luxury of this power; therefore, Jerry had to place a spell on a red ruby, which would allow Optical to be invisible in the human realm only, but only while he carried it in his pocket. The gnome would have to be extra careful not to drop or misplace this stone; otherwise, he could be seen by not only the aliens, but by humans as well.

Elise was having a fit that no one on the council offered her a position within this special group. She not only wanted to investigate the alien's camp, she was very curious to have a look into the human realm. The whosawhachette, had never been in the human realm before, and began huffing and puffing in anger. Elise wasn't the silent type, if something was bothering her, she had no problems expressing it, no matter to who it was, even the Key Holder of the Realms.

"I so don't think this is fair, at all. Why do the fairies get to go on all of these missions, but I don't get to ever go," demanded Elise.

"We automatically send fairies because they can be invisible everywhere," said Jerry.

"Gnomes can't be invisible, but you are so allowing Optical to go, and you gave him a special stone and stuff," said Elise.

"I can be invisible in the human realm, and I think you also have that power," said Elvin directly to his sister.

"Is this so true? I can so be invisible, can I?" gushed Elise with excitement.

"Well, actually, yes, you can be invisible in the human realm only, all you have to do is think it and it will happen," said Gatsby.

"Then I want to go on this mission, oh, please, pretty please," said Elise as sweetly as she possible could.

Jerry looked at Gatsby as he thought about the whosawhachette's request. He agreed to open her realm, and give her free roam of the realms, but sending her into the human realm could be quite risky. She had already shown that she couldn't be completely trusted, and seemed to always have her very own agenda, and put herself first. He knew that this first mission into the alien camp was just a scouting mission, and therefore it would be less of a risk if he sent her in now, rather than later on. Still, he realized that this was putting a burden on Annastarlis, Nerby and Optical, because not only would they be expected to take in everything they could once inside of the place, they would also have to keep an watchful eye on Elise as well. He found that he couldn't offer any solid argument to give Elise as to why she couldn't go, not unless he was truthful and told her that he simply didn't trust her, and he already knew that wouldn't be a good idea.

"Well...this is what I can offer you right now; you can take it or leave it. I will allow you to go on this mission; however, you must follow any and all directions given to you by the others. If I hear from any of them upon their return that you refused, I will never again allow you to go into the human realm," said Jerry.

"Ok....so fine I will take it, but just for the record, since I so control my own realm as leader, and none of the others have that kind of position, I do so think I should be in charge of this mission...I mean... I'm just saying," said Elise.

"The others all have much experience in the human realm, you must understand that there are things you will not even understand, that is the reason they are in charge," said Jerry as gently as he could, so that he wouldn't offend her.

"Yeah, but what kind of experience do they all so have inside an alien underground camp, huh," said Elise still not completely satisfied with the gnomes answer.

"That is hardly the point. Perhaps I should put this way for you. I'm the key holder of the realms, I call all the shots. What I say goes... period, if you don't want to go under the rules I have stated, then perhaps you should just stay behind," said Jerry annoyed.

"I will so go, I was just....asking a few questions," said Elise quickly.

"Well, if my sister is going, I want to go too," piped in Elvin with his usual large grin.

"Elvin, I can't seriously risk sending in two realm leaders at the same time. Who would run your realms in the event that something happened to the both of you? Let your sister go this time, while you look after her realm and your own, and on the next mission, I will send you in," said Jerry.

Jerry had anticipated that Elvin would also ask to go, which worked perfectly. He knew that Elvin could be trusted more than his sister, and would pose less risk to the realms on the next mission. Now he had the perfect excuse to use when Elise demanded to go the next time.

Annastarlis, Nerby, Optical and Elise set out for the human realm. Once inside Annastarlis had the four hold hands in a circle, and using just her thoughts she was able to pop them directly into Egypt in front of the pyramids.

Elise was already confused, as she stared at her brand new surroundings. When they had first entered the human realm, she saw green grass, tree's, blue sky, houses and cars, and now she stood sinking into hot beige colored sand. Jerry was truthful; there would be many things in the human realm that Elise and Elvin would have to learn about.

"Help…I'm so sinking, the ground here is eating me, I'm going to so die," shrieked Elise fearful of the sand.

"The ground isn't eating you, Sand isn't solid like other areas, you will only sink down an inch at the most," said Annastarlis already annoyed.

"Well, you could have so warned me," said Elise now embarrassed.

The four entered the pyramid and opened the alien map. They studied the instructions and started to follow the directions given, hoping they would eventually end up in the alien camp underneath them. The map stated clearly that each step needed to be followed in order, or they could find themselves trapped in a dead end passage of a sealed chamber and possibly never escape from it.

"So, like if we all end up in the wrong place, you can just pop us out of there, like a genie right," asked Elise.

"Well, usually anywhere in the human world, all I have to do is think about where I want to go and it happens, but this might be a different situation. We are inside the pyramids, which are said to hold magical properties. We honestly don't know how things will work inside," said Annastarlis.

"Ok, so like I can see myself and all of you, why aren't we invisible right now?" asked Elise.

"We are invisible to all the humans and the aliens, but we can see each other because we are invisible together," snapped Annastarlis annoyed at the whosawhachette already.

They group entered the pyramid and followed the path into the Ascending Passage, which lead them into the Grand Gallery and finally into the King's Chamber. Annastarlis took the lead and the other three followed. She took her job as leader seriously, and carried a copy of the map in her hands, making sure she read each direction loudly to the others, as they encountered the next step of their journey. It was a long walk to the King's Chamber, and they were tired on arrival. Elise insisted that they sit and rest for a few minutes and Annastarlis took this opportunity to quietly study the map in detail, she knew that they couldn't afford to make any mistakes. The map showed several things that she found quite curious. They would be heading into the Queen's Chamber next, and the map marked that the intersection of the Queen's Chamber floor and the floor of the Ascending Passage at it's opening into the Grand Gallery created a triangle shape. That would be the place where they would need to remove their first key stone. The group finally reached the Queens Chamber and stood in the middle counting the stones, until they located the seventh one. The stone didn't look any different from the others, but did move when they pushed on it at the correct point just as the instructions stated it would. To their complete amazement, a wall slid open in the Queen's Chamber, which had a smaller chamber room on the other side. The room seemed to be a dead end, having no other visible hallways or doorways leading to or from it. Annastarlis directed them to enter this secret room and Elise began to complain.

"So, wait a minute, what if this room is a trick. Doesn't the map warn of these trap rooms. What if we so can't get out of there," cried Elise.

"Stop being a baby, the map directions said this is the right way to go, and if Annastarlis is telling us to go this way, then we are following," said Nerby.

Annastarlis warned the others before entering the room that it had been noted on the map to be aware of something the aliens had referred to as the Bottomless Pit located on the dark right side of the room. They would need to completely avoid and stay away from that area; therefore they all walked to the left side of this room. Once they walked into the chamber, the sliding wall, slammed behind them, and Elise gasped loudly.

"Maybe you shouldn't have warned Elise about the bottomless pit, seems like that would be a good place for her to end up," whispered Nerby to Annastarlis.

"Are you so whispering about me?" demanded Elise.

"No, I didn't say anything about you," insisted Nerby, before he could see the large smile on Annastarlis's face.

"What does the map say to do next," asked Optical.

"We are looking for a trap door on the ground, it should be in the left side back corner," said Annastarlis with complete confidence.

The group located the trap door which was shaped like a triangle exactly where the fairy had said it would be. This secret chamber sat directly to the left of the lower Descending Passage which lined up with the Pole Star, clearly something of importance to the aliens; otherwise they would not have bothered to make reference to this fact on the map.

Under the trap door they discovered a long ladder, and took turns going down it, one by one. They found themselves in a room which looked very different from all the others. It was lined with what appeared to be some kind of strange metal, and it almost seemed to glow. In the center of this room was a large stone pyramid. Annastarlis walked over to the stone pyramid made a fist and tapped in a rhythm pattern around it. She knocked seven times on each side, and finally the three sides collapsed and flipped down. The pyramid opened to reveal that it contained one large glowing amber colored stone.

Elise nearly pushed Annastarlis off her feet and out of the way to reach in and grab the stone, but right before she touched it the fairy screamed out to her.

"Noooooooo, don't touch it, DANGER," shrieked Annastarlis.

"What danger, it's so just a stone," replied Elise.

"Not according to this map. It says right here. Don't touch this stone, or risk death, danger," said Annastarlis pointing to that spot on the map.

"You wanted to come along, but you must listen and take directions, otherwise we will not be responsible for your safety," said Optical now also annoyed with the whosawhachette.

"So, what do we do next," asked Elise innocently.

"We just wait, something else will happen," said Annastarlis looking around the room slightly nervous.

Chapter 18

Fighting for Love

Joe arrived home late from work, he seemed more stressed than his usual self. He did eat decently, but he made no attempt to join into any of the conversation. His wife even noticed that he seemed to fail to make any eye contact with her, which told her that this time something was seriously bothering him, and for some reason, she knew it wasn't work related. When dinner was finished Sarah discreetly asked Kyle to go into his room, and take along Aimee Lynn, so that she could have some quiet time to speak with her husband.

Kyle took his sister into his room, and opened up a board game, hoping that he would be able to entertain her for a few minutes. He could faintly hear his mother talking to Joe, and although he knew it was wrong to eavesdrop, he couldn't help himself. Aimee Lynn didn't seem to notice the conversation or even realize that her brother was keeping her occupied while the adults talked, she played with the game board pieces happy and contently. She really never played any of the games correctly, or followed any of the playing rules. She seemed happier to just push the game pieces around on the board, sometimes making them even dance on it. Naturally, whatever game they played, Kyle would always allow his little sister to win, especially since she was the only one of the two that ever understood how her game was even played. He had come to understand that when his sister's game piece was on the last spot of the board, and she stood up and danced, that meant she had won the game, and he accepted it. Kyle wasn't truly interested in even playing a game, he just wanted to press his ear against the door to hear better, but knew that would get the attention of his little sister. Even though, she really didn't talk much, and therefore wouldn't or couldn't tattletale on him, he decided it probably wouldn't be a good idea. He tried to focus on keeping her occupied, but all of his attention was really on the voices that softly carried from the living room.

"Ok, Joe, I have had enough. I'm your wife, and I know when something is really bothering you. I understand your job is all confidential stuff, but sometimes you just need to talk and let things out. What is going on?" asked Sarah determined.

"It is work, but it also has to do with home....us...our family," said Joe.

"Ok, well if it involves our family, then start talking," insisted Sarah with a slightly softer tone to her voice.

"It's time.... I don't even think that I can hold it in any longer. I haven't said anything about it, because I just didn't want to worry you," said Joe.

"Well, seeing you like this worries me. Just tell me what is bothering you," said Sarah.

"It has to do with Aimee Lynn," said Joe sadly.

"Ok...tell me, we can handle anything...together," said Sarah.

"Her biological parents have shown up, they want their daughter back," said Joe.

"What? You told me when we adopted her that her parents were unfit, and would never come back for her. I just don't understand," said Sarah upset.

"Please calm down. They did abandon her...in a field, I told you that. We really didn't know all the circumstances, because they just disappeared. They never looked for her, claimed her, or even filed a missing person's report. The child seemed traumatized, dirty, and in shock when she was found. We assumed it was a drug deal that went bad, something criminal, but in any event it certainly had to be considered outright child neglect and abandonment," said Joe.

"Yes, I know all of that, so what happens now," said Sarah upset.

"The parents are claiming some insane story about having been beamed up by aliens into a spaceship, They insist that is the reason they couldn't look for their child, because they were kidnapped, and held against their will," said Joe.

"Ok, let's put their story aside, what are the chances that we will lose Aimee Lynn?" asked Sarah.

"I think we have a 50/50 chance, it's still too early to say. The parents hired a hotshot attorney and have filed petitions with the court, to overturn our adoption of her. Then they will have to explain to a judge where they have been all of this time…with aliens. Certainly no judge in his right mind is going to believe them, and just hand them over custody of a child," said Joe.

"Well, stranger things have happened," said Sarah.

"What worries me the most is that both of them have taken lie detector tests…and both of them passed," said Joe scratching his head.

"How can someone pass a lie detector test, if they are lying," asked Sarah.

"It's not impossible to do, but I must say, that two of them getting away with it is…well….curious to say the least, and it would be much harder. I don't know that I have ever seen that done before," said Joe.

"Have you met the parents? What are they like? Are they better than us?" fired Sarah rapidly.

"I have spoken with both of them. I hate to say it, but they seem… nice, sincere, like loving parents. I'm sure they are just putting up a good front. They have probably cleaned themselves off of drugs, and now they are sorry. All I can think of is that, they both truly believe all of this happened to them, because they went on a drug trip together, and think their hallucinations were real," said Joe.

"If you are right, then that would explain how they could both pass the lie detector tests," said Sarah.

"That is the only thing that really makes any sense. I mean, can you seriously imagine anyone sane claiming that aliens took them away," said Joe with a slight mocking type amused laugh.

Sarah didn't say a word, she was thinking. She knew that gnomes, fairies, trolls, whosawhachits, and whosawhachettes all existed, but aliens? Something deep inside of her just had to question the existence of aliens. Did she wrongfully take some else's child? She knew the pain firsthand of having a missing child; she would never forget when Kyle was missing for so many days. Then the crop circle appeared, and she did all the research on the internet, completely convinced that aliens had him. She learned that sometimes you had to believe in things that you couldn't see, because sometimes they really did exist.

"Joe...what if...what if...," said Sarah.

"Don't say it, please don't say it," said Joe.

"I have to...what if aliens really do exist. What if these people really were abducted by them? What if they are good parents, and hurting because they want their little girl back?" blurted out Sarah.

"What if both of these people are suffering from schizophrenia like Kyle, and just think they visited alien lands," snapped Joe angry.

"Why do you keep throwing that up in my face? Maybe my son doesn't even have schizophrenia, maybe he is just a normal boy, who is just afraid to tell the truth to you, just like I am," screamed Sarah.

Kyle heard the voices from the living room getting louder and louder. He no longer needed to strain to hear what was being said. He peeked at his sister, who seemed to pay no attention to the conversation, even though, it was now clear that every word was being screamed instead of spoken. He didn't want Aimee Lynn to get upset, and remembered what Elvin had told him about the green men. Being a protective brother, he jumped up and clicked on the TV in his room, making sure that he put the sound on louder than normal. He quickly clicked thru the channels until he found cartoons, something he knew his sister would watch. Once he was sure that she would sit in front of the television, he opened his bedroom door and slipped out into the living room.

"Kyle, please go back into your bedroom, your mother and I are having a difference of words," said Joe.

"A difference of words, seriously? Is that what you would like to call it? Kyle, stay right here, in fact, come sit down on the couch with us," said Sarah.

Kyle stood frozen for a minute, he looked back and forth between Joe and his mother. This was the first time he had ever really witnessed the two of them fighting. They had minor disagreements from time to time, but nothing like this. He now wasn't sure if he had made the right decision by leaving his bedroom.

"I'm sure you have managed to overhear some of our conversation," said Sarah.

"Well...I...heard...a few things," said Kyle quietly not quite sure how much he really wanted to admit to.

"Why are you bringing him into this, it's between you and I," said Joe annoyed.

"He is a member of this family, and Aimee Lynn is his sister, besides I have a feeling that he will know something about some of this," said Sarah.

"What do you mean," said Joe.

"Kyle, I want you to tell the truth, we are no longer going to hide anything. I want you to ask your friends, if aliens from other planets visit here, and if they take humans," said Sarah.

"I...well....I...," scampered Kyle not sure on if he should truly tell everything that he knew in front of Joe.

"You want him to ask his friends from school about aliens?" asked Joe completely confused about what was going on.

"No, I want him to ask his friends from the realms. The fairies, trolls, gnomes, and whosawhachits," said Sarah annoyed.

"Oh boy, here we go again," said Joe.

"Tell him Kyle, I want you to tell him, tell him everything," said Sarah.

"Mom.....don't...please," said Kyle.

"You probably don't remember this, but when you were a little boy you saw a gnome. You told your father, and he made fun of you, and you forced yourself to forget all about it. If you just really think and try and remember it will all come back to you," said Sarah.

113

Chapter 19
No Place Like Home

Zepadoodle transported Ifffer to the underground base camp beneath the Pyramids' in Egypt. The trip was rough on the old gnome, and he rested for several days after he arrived but he became increasingly ill as each day passed. The aliens kept assuring the gnome that he would feel well in just a few days, but things only seemed to get worse. They appeared to be genuinely concerned that Ifffer was ill, and fed him fresh fruits and vegetables that they recovered from the earth realm, but nothing seemed to help. The aliens couldn't afford to lose Ifffer, he was a great source of future information, and they needed him well. The gnome knew the true reason that he was sick, in truth, he was aging at a rapid rate, each day he seemed to get years older, and nothing he or the aliens did could stop the degeneration of cells that his body was experiencing.

Ifffer did like this camp better, he felt claustrophobic in the underwater camp. In the other camp everything seemed to be made from metal or unnatural materials, and now in this one, everyone was stone, at least it seemed more earth like and natural to him.

Ifffer was still missing the most important part of his diet, the water he drank from the gnome realm. This was something that had never occurred to him when he left there, or he would have brought hoards of water with him when he made the decision to leave. He would have plotted and planned his departure, knowing that he needed to have water. The water from the realms came directly from the springs of the foundation of youth, this was the very reason that all the realm inhabitants lived so long, thousands of years old. Now without this special water, his body was beginning the break down and age and it was happening at an unbelievably rapid rate. The water saved him from the normal aging process, or at least delayed it, but now, without it, his body seemed to almost be attacking itself. His body had become weak and fragile, he could no longer stand straight instead he was hunched over, and needed the assistance of a walking stick.

Ifffer was scared for one of the first times in his life, seriously afraid. He knew that he needed to get this water, he couldn't live without it, but could he risk telling the aliens the truth. Telling these outer space beings about the power of the water in the realms could be a dangerous thing. If they knew the nutrient's that it contained, they would certainly want to drink from it, and then possibly even drain the spring wells, taking all the water for themselves and their own kind.

This water had been safeguarded for thousands and thousands of years. Humans had gotten a few sips from it from time to time, and it did slow their aging process down, but none ever truly knew the real reason why. The realms never shared the secrets of this water with the humans either, because they knew that the humans would also drain the realms of it. The realms not only had the concerns to keep their own kind going for many centuries, they worried about other civilizations', because in many ways, the realms served as a balance of life for the human world. There were things that the human world simply couldn't handle, because many of them tended to be selfish. Now with the aliens from Kaboris stepping into the mix, things could truly get out of hand quickly. It is natural instinct to want to protect your own people, and desire to have the best supplies, food, medications, and shelter for them, and to not really want to share these things with other societies. Everyone watched out in the end for their own, but it could just be the end of all of it for all of them, if someone didn't protect what everyone assumed was a natural balance.

Ifffer knew that he needed to be clever if he was going to get water from the realms. Zepadoodle would visit him several times a day, making it seem that he was checking in on him, concerned for his health but he always managed to get in several questions. Zepadoodle hoped to gain more valuable information about the realms. Ifffer had come to realize that Zepadoodle was nothing more than a lower pawn for the high up aliens. While he had discovered the realms, it happened by accident, and it was clear that he was rewarded for his great find with absolutely nothing. Ifffer remembered when he first met the alien, he gave the grand illusion that he was one in charge, a man of power, but Ifffer was able to witness first hand, that Zepadoodle's superiors treated him poorly, almost to the point of being a slave.

Zepadoodle worked hard, going over and above everything and anything that was ever requested of him. He wanted to please Zoop, wanted so much to be given a higher position, and it was starting to become clear to him, that this may never happen. Ifffer could see that the young alien increasingly was becoming discouraged, and this was the only weakness in the alien community that he had observed. The aliens worked as one, seemed to be team players, banning together for the best of the entire community, very similar to some of the systems used by the whosawhachits. Ifffer certainly knew that this wasn't full proof, because every once in a while, someone with a strong mind, decided to choose free will, and go against the others, when they deemed something to be best just for them. He would need to think about all of this, and how he could manipulate Zepadoodle to his own advantage.

Ifffer decided to make an attempt to sneak back into the realms, if only he could just manage to get a few sips of the precious water. He was outraged when he realized that he had been banned from entering. He knew that a spell had been put on the realm entrances, after he made several failed attempts to get inside. It was clear to him that no matter what he tried, he would never again be able to gain access to the secret realms. He had no way of even contacting any of its inhabitants; none of them would even know that he was dying.

The gnome returned back to his new room in the alien camp and rested on his bed, he fell asleep and dreamt of being outside breathing in fresh air, deep down into his lungs. He woke to find Zepadoodle standing in his doorway, staring at him.

"You could knock before entering, where I come from, it's considered rude to just open someone's door and come in without being invited," said Ifffer grouchier than he would have preferred.

"I have been banging on your door for 5 minutes," insisted Zepadoodle with no apologetic tone to his voice.

"Well, I was napping," snapped Ifffer.

"You look terrible; do you want me to take you to our laboratory? I think some of our doctors might be able to help you," said Zepadoodle.

"I do not wish for them to do any of their medical experiments on me, no thank you," said Ifffer annoyed.

"Not for experiments, to see if they can give you medical help, medicine," said Zepadoodle sincerely.

"No, I don't believe that they can help me. I'm simply suffering from…being homesick," said Ifffer.

"What is homesick?" Zepadoodle asked having never heard this term used before.

"I miss being in my own home, perhaps I would feel better if I had some of my old things from my house there, to make this place feel more like home to me….I'm wondering, since you do go to the realms, if you would get me a few things," said Ifffer cleverly.

"Well…I don't know…I mean…I have tried to take things out of there before, and they just…disappear," said Zepadoodle, hoping to hear the secrets of how he could remove items from the realms.

"Some things can be removed, others can't. If you attempted to take gemstones with you, they would disappear, only some have the power to leave with them," said Ifffer.

"Do you have the power to leave with them?" asked Zepadoodle.

Ifffer wasn't quite sure how to answer this question. He did have that power, at one time, but not now; he couldn't even get into the realms. He knew that telling that to the aliens would be a big mistake, because they may view him as being useless to them now, and do away with him.

"I do, however, I am much too weak to do so right now. I must get better first," answered Ifffer hoping to buy himself a little more time.

"I remember you talking about a special substance that the realms contained. You promised that all the user had to do was wish for something and it would appear.. What exactly is this substance you spoke about?" asked Zepadoodle tired that it was taking so long to get valuable information from the gnome.

"Oh, it is much more than that, it can also give the power of invisibility," said Ifffer.

"I will go into the realms, and get you a few things from your home, however, in return, I want you to tell me what this special substance is, so that I may bring some of that back here," said Zepadoodle.

Zepadoodle hoped that if he could push the gnome for this powerful substance that he claimed existed; it would be enough for him to be promoted. He knew that he would never see a high position such as general, but at this point, he would be happy for even some small title. Zoop would have to be very pleased with him, if he could produce such a thing, if it truly existed and the gnome wasn't lying.

Ifffer picked up a glass of water that had been sitting on a small table next to his bed. He slowly sipped it while thinking, and then made a face as if he had just drunk poison.

"This water is terrible, just horrible. My water at home always tasted good, probably because I had a glass I used that I really liked. The glass is green, and has gold leaves painted on it, it always makes me smile. Maybe, you could bring me that glass, a few clean shirts, a few books and....I don't know...perhaps...even a few small bottles of drinking water from there," said Ifffer trying not to be obvious with his requests.

"Like, I already said, I will bring you a few things, but...you need to tell me what the substance is, because you're not getting anything, unless I get that," demanded Zepadoodle firmly.

Ifffer carefully considered his options. If he didn't get water soon from the foundation of youth, he was going to die. He had no way of getting into the realms himself to get any, and no way of contacting anyone inside of the realms, to tell them, that they handed him a death sentence. He wondered, if when they banned him from the realms, had Jerry or Gatsby considered that he would age and die without the realm water. Perhaps that thought had never even entered their small minds. Would they have locked him out, knowing in their hearts that they had just killed him? He couldn't picture Gatsby being so cruel in his mind, and wished he had a way of making contact with him, because in his heart, he knew Gatsby would at least provide him drinking water. He was now on his own, with no one to look out for him, except himself, he no longer belonged to a society or group. If he saved himself, and once again sold out the realms, and offered up the information about the fairy dust, then didn't they all deserve what he gave them back for locking him out of the realms? He quickly thought about how much power the aliens could get using fairy dust, it could be dangerous; it could even be the end to everyone's existence. He needed to make a quick decision, either he save himself or he saved the realms, and perhaps the entire world.

A loud alarm began to shriek, and Zepadoodle seemed panicked and turned to exit the room.

"What does this alarm mean?" demanded Ifffer struggling to stand on his own two feet.

"Someone has entered the camp here, someone that doesn't have authorization to do so, we are being infiltrated," yelled Zepadoodle as he left the room.

Chapter 20
Overstaying Your Welcome

This would be a big day for Eric, except he had no idea just how big. Both of his parents were coming to visit, and they all had an appointment with his new doctor, Dr. Booker. Eric tried to make progress, he worked hard on not doing things he knew were bad, but no matter how well he did, it just didn't seem to be enough anymore. He had done so many bad things in the past that no one truly believed he was changing; it was as if, they just didn't or couldn't see any of it. This frustrated him, but still he kept telling himself, that he could do better, and soon they would all just have to see that he wasn't the bad behaved child that he had been labeled. A few times things happened that he was blamed for, and it really bothered him. When he insisted that he was an innocent party, the nurse's only laughed at him, sure that he was guilty, and then he would get punished with either missing out on a special activity, or television time. It almost seemed that some of the other kids were determined to pay him back for things that he had done to them in the past, and were sabotaging him, setting him up or outright framing him for their own crimes. While it was certainly true that he deserved the payouts the others were now giving him, he didn't like it, not one bit.

In the past, if Eric was blamed for something he really didn't do, he was more than happy to take the fall for it, it only added to the character he created, the tough bad guy he wanted to be. The boy was quickly finding out, that once you have a reputation for being something or someone, it would be very hard to change everyone's opinions about you., if not outright impossible.

Eric was thrilled to see his parents, and sat and talked with them several minutes before his doctor finally entered the room. They laughed and chatted like they were sitting around the kitchen table at home, and not visiting in a mental ward. This gave the boy hope, and he was happy for the first time in many weeks. He really missed his parents, and wanted to go home, he hoped that would be the doctor's recommendation. He didn't really like his sessions with this doctor, the man always seemed to get the upper hand, and Eric found no amusement to their appointments, not like he did when Dr. Hammer treated him. Eric had enjoyed tormenting everyone at the hospital in the past but he now knew that he never wanted to come back here, it was no longer any fun. For the first time, he just wanted to have a normal life. He decided that he just needed to be a regular kid, make his parents proud of him, go to school, play baseball, and have real friends, true friends. The kind of friends, that could and would really care about him.

He was aware that he hadn't always done the right thing by Kyle, but deep down, he liked the boy, and thought that they could build a real friendship this time around. Kyle had been a giving, trusting friend, and Eric was determined that this time, he would give the boy the same thing in return, if he was just given the chance.

"Thank you for coming in today. As you know I have been working with Eric on his behaviors, and I believe I have a devised a good plan of action that can really help your son," said Dr. Booker with confidence.

"Please tell us your opinion for treatment, we only want the very best for our son," said Evelyn.

"First off, I would like to remove Eric from all of his medications. He of course he will need to be weaned off of them for a few weeks," said Dr. Booker.

"That's a great idea, because I don't need them anymore, I'm cured," said Eric.

"Second, I think it's time that we discharged him from the hospital," said Dr. Booker.

"Yup, I totally agree, smart doctor, I'm ready go home," said Eric happy.

"I didn't say that I think you should go home," said Dr. Booker.

"What do you mean I shouldn't go home?" asked Eric.

"Where do you think he belongs then," said Evelyn confused.

"The hospital isn't the place for your son. I truly don't feel that Eric belongs here at all, probably never really did," said Dr. Booker.

"I don't think I understand," said Evelyn with a puzzled look on her face.

"What's to understand, I'm ready to go home, I'm fine," said Eric.

"This hospital is a place for children that are truly suffering from mental disorders. Your son seems mentally fit to me, in fact, I would say that he is an overachiever, quite brilliant actually," said Dr. Booker.

"Yeah, I am pretty smart," said Eric pushing out his chest proudly.

"An overachiever? He doesn't do most of his school work, and is failing nearly half of his classes, he looks for every opportunity he can to goof off," said Evelyn.

"That is by choice that he fails. I gave your son an IQ test; he did rather well on it. I believe he doesn't do well in school, because it bores him, and he lacks structure," said Dr. Booker.

"Yeah, it does bore me, probably because I'm so smart," said Eric pleased with most of how the conversation was going.

"Well, if he is so smart, than can you explain to me why he continues to get into trouble," asked Eric's father.

"Yes, I can....again, this is by choice. Your son doesn't have a mental problem, he has a behavioral problem," said Dr. Booker.

"What you really mean is that I DID have a behavioral problem, because now I'm being really good, right," said Eric.

"What about all the lies he tells?" asked Evelyn.

"He is a habitual fibber, but that really just ties in with his behavioral problems. He tells lies to cover his poor behaviors, in order to avoid getting into trouble. It's not a mental issue that makes him lie, he chooses to lie, and there is a big difference. I believe he does much of it for entertainment purposes, again because he isn't being mentally stimulated," said Dr. Booker.

"What exactly do you recommend?" questioned Evelyn.

"Well, just for the record, I think I should go home, and try really hard, just like I have been doing. I haven't even gotten into any trouble lately," said Eric dreading what the doctor would say next and hoping to delay his answer.

"I think the best course of action for Eric would be to go into military school, a boot camp type place. This would offer him the structure that he is missing, while giving him strict discipline, and guidelines that he would have to follow," said Dr. Booker.

"Oh, I don't think that is a good idea at all," said Eric turning towards his mother.

"You mean like a tough love type place?" said Evelyn.

"Yes, that is exactly what I mean. They will teach him to follow directions, rules, so that he can learn to self disciple himself from making poor choices and decisions in life. He needs to learn that there are consequences' for not follows rules. The school work will be more challenging, therefore his mind will be occupied," said Dr. Booker.

"Well, I think I should get a say on where I go, it's my life and I say it should be home. I don't want to go to a boarding school. My teacher likes me so much that he even came here to visit me, I just want to go back to that school," said Eric in a panic.

Eric was sent back to his room, while his parents stayed and spoke with the doctor. The boy was steaming mad when he left the office, but controlled himself from slamming the door on the way out. As he headed down towards the end of the hallway he couldn't help but notice two open pale yellow fresh cans of paint sitting on newspapers on the floor against the wall. Next to them sat a paint roller, paint pan and several brushes, he swore the items called to him. His very first thought was to grab the paint, and run down the hallway, splashing and dripping it everywhere he could. He raced over to the paint, scooped down to pick one of the cans up, but then stopped. Normally he would have done something extra bad, to act out, to get attention, and maybe even to release some of the tension that he was feeling. Once again, he was able to control these urges, and knew that if he had any chance of showing that he could change and behave it was now. He couldn't help but feel that he was being tested, perhaps the whole thing was a complete set up, and he refused to fall for it. He turned the corner, and gave a large smile to the nurse sitting at her desk. He only stopped before entering his room, when he heard the nurse call his name, and he turned around to face her.

"Eric," called out the nurse.

"Yes...what?" said Eric confused that she was calling out to him.

"What did you just do?" demanded the nurse.

"I didn't do anything, why?" insisted Eric innocent.

"I'm sure you did something, just from the way you smiled at me. You do know that it's just a matter of time before we find out what it is, so you might as well fess up now," said the nurse, confident that he did something.

"Well, I did nothing, not one damn thing," said Eric as he turned and entered his bedroom annoyed.

Eric sat quietly on his bed, waiting for his parents to come to his door and tell him what decision they had made. He needed to plead his case with them, make any promise that he could, but somehow he needed to get thru to them. His mother usually did listen to him, but he also knew that he had pushed her buttons, perhaps too far this time, when he damaged his teacher's car. He knew that had to cost his parents a decent amount of money to have repaired. In the office, his father didn't even look at him when they spoke, that couldn't be a good sign of things to come.

The wait seemed like hours, when it really was only 15 minutes. Evelyn finally came to her son's room alone; his father was apparently getting more information regarding the military boot camp boarding school. The doctor had several different pamphlets available from a few different places, and he wanted them to take all the literature home and read it, so they could make what he felt was the best decision for Eric's well being. Leave it to the good Dr. Booker to be well prepared with all the info his parents would require.

"Your father and I have much to talk about tonight. We aren't going to make a quick decision about this," said Evelyn.

"Mom, please, I'm begging you. I know that I have made promises in the past, and that I never kept any of them, but this time it's different," said Eric.

"Why should I believe you now?" said Evelyn tired and drained.

Chapter 21
A Whole New World

Annastarlis, Nerby, Optical and Elise had finally entered the secret underground alien base camp. At first glance the place wasn't much different from being inside the pyramids. All the walls were made from cut stone, and the temperature was slightly cooler than they had all expected. Elise immediately began to complain that she was cold. Annastarlis rolled her eyes in annoyance, especially since Elise had been grumbling that she was hot and sweaty inside of the pyramids. Being around Elise made Annastarlis almost ashamed to be a girl, if that meant she had ever acted and complained as much as the whosawhachette.

Elise had envisioned a magical, fun filled adventure into the human realm, but so far, it all had turned out to be quite boring. She hadn't gotten to see more than two or three humans, and that was only quickly in passing. Her brother Elvin always told her how much fun it was to observe people, and mess with them, and she started to feel sorry for herself that she didn't get to do any of those things, at least not yet. If going on mission's into the human realm consisted of doing things like this, than she had already made up her mind, she was no longer interested, it seemed like all work and no play.

"It's so cold, I don't like it here," grumbled Elise.

"Well, you can turn around and go back home if you want, but the rest of us are going forward," said Annastarlis.

"I'm so not going back all that way by myself, what if I got lost," said Elise.

"Then take the hint and stop complaining, we are here on a mission, this is not a sightseeing vacation," said Optical.

The one thing that they all had found truly amazing was the sheer size of the place. From where they stood, it gave them an overview from up above. Now none of them went in with any preconceived idea of how large or small it would be, but nothing could have prepared them for such a sight. What they discovered was the place was massive, and in fact it actually contained an entire inner working city of sorts. Rooms were separated by six foot high stone walls, with no ceilings, which allowed them to see into many of them. Obviously privacy wasn't high on the alien's priority list, because their environment provided next to none. Aliens seemed to be everywhere, each going about their own business, working in certain rooms or laboratories, and some were studying books in an area that appeared to be like a library. Classrooms were set up, with alien students sitting at desks being taught lessons.

Before they could begin to descend down a long staircase to the floor below them, in order to begin exploring all of it, a loud blaring alarm shrieked. Clearly they had been discovered, how, they didn't know. The one thing they had to their advantage was that they were invisible and their exact position in the camp would be difficult to determine. Annastarlis ordered the group to move quickly into the camp, there was no point in turning back now. They had little information to offer the gnomes upon their return, therefore she insisted that they press forward and complete their task. As they all raced down the stairs Optical insisted that they would have a better chance of not being detected if they split up. Annastarlis yelled in agreement that they should all go in different directions once they reached the ground floor area.

Elise began to cry and panic, instead of going off in her own direction; she grabbed hold of Nerby's arm, and went along with him. Nerby practicality had to drag her along with him as she rested upon his heels, all the time whining in his ear, which slowed him down. This made Annastarlis quite angry, and she watched them over her shoulder as she ran the opposite way, which caused her to crash directly into a large cabinet, knocking her down to her feet. She jumped right up and brushed herself off. Being invisible only meant she couldn't be seen, but she could still come into contact with solid objects, and people. She was grateful that her collision was with a cabinet, and not with one of the aliens, that would have been very bad. She knew that she needed to put Elise out of her mind for the moment. Annastarlis was smart enough to know that deep down it truly bothered her more that she grabbed Nerby, then the fact that the whosawhachette had defied a direct order. In a way it was a good thing, because later on when they returned to the gnome realm, she would be able to use this against her, and Elise would not be allowed to go on anymore missions, or at least that was the outcome that she hoped for. She would certainly press the issue with Jerry that Elise not only didn't help, but got in the way.

"They know we are here, we so should have went back into the pyramids and then home," said Elise.

"We would have accomplished nothing, we didn't come all this way to take a two second peek into this place," said Nerby.

"What will they so do to us, if we get caught," shrieked Elise.

"You can't do anything to someone you can't see, now stop it, and look around, and try and remember everything you see," said Nerby calmly.

"I so don't like this, I'm afraid, look at all of them, they're everywhere," screamed Elise in a panic.

"Stop screaming, we are fine, just do your job," said Nerby determined.

Perhaps for the first time Elise finally realized that they could be in real danger going into the alien camp. If she had not been allowed to go on this mission, she would have certainly pouted and resented it, thinking that she had missed out on fun and adventure. This was not the human world that she had conjured up in her mind; of course she wasn't truly experiencing the human realm. The little bit of the human world that she had seen, the sand that made her sink, the deathly hot stifling heat of the desert, and then the claustrophobic feeling inside of the pyramids just didn't impress her, she wanted to go back home to her pink realm. She hoped that Annastarlis would order that they leave the base camp quickly. Instead of observing different things around her, she spent the time holding onto Nerby, almost making him fall twice.

A pack of approximately 30 aliens, dressed in some sort of military gear, ran past them in a marching type army fashion. Nerby had to pull Elise against the wall with him, so that they wouldn't crash into them. He reminded her that the aliens would feel her should she make the mistake of making physical contact with them. The army looking group of aliens was carrying weapons, which kind of resembled guns, but nothing like anything that Nerby had ever seen before. The guns were lightweight, not made of heavy metal; they seemed to be made from a plastic type of material that shined in an iridescent way. The special military forces had been ordered in by Zoop himself, to do an entire search of the base camp, and to inspect the entrance for any signs that they had been infiltrated. Zoop didn't hesitate when he included the order that they should shoot to kill if someone was located.

Optical went into one of the classrooms; he was especially interested to find out what the students were being taught. He was shocked when he overheard the alien teacher telling the class that soon, the aliens would rule the planet. He talked about the total takeover date, and explained that everyone needed to be ready and prepared. He told the class about the many spaceships that had already left planet Kaboris and were now on route to this planet which would be joining all of them. He said that these ships were only a few days away, and that everything would have to be prepared for their arrival. They would need places to live and work, and it was their jobs to prepare and set up for them. He further spoke about the total disposal of the useless human race, and the entire group all laughed together. The teacher explained to the alien class, that their time living underground was almost over. They would each be rewarded for their service during this time with a beautiful home of their own choosing on the planet earth. The human's would be removed from their homes, leaving them vacant and ready to move into. Naturally they would have some cleanup work to do, removing all of the human's useless nonsense of outdated cooking appliances, electronics and personal items. Once they completed the removal, the house would be theirs to decorate and live in. Optical listened carefully to everything that was being said; clearly everyone in the room knew the exact date of this takeover, which seemed to be only a few days away. He hoped that the date or day would be stated; because that would be the best information he could return with. Many wars are won because of the element of surprise, if the realms knew the time and date, it would at least give them some time to prepare. He didn't know how they would manage to save the realms or for that matter the entire human population, but they were going to try.

Meanwhile Annastarlis went down a long hallway and she managed to pop her head into each of the different rooms, making mental notes of everything that she saw. Since most of the doors were left wide open, it really was making her job much easier. She attempted to count aliens, but after reaching over two hundred, she stopped counting, because she was simply losing track of which ones she had counted and which she had not. She estimated that at least 1,500 aliens were living full time in the place. She entered an area which appeared to be basic living quarters. Most of the rooms were tiny, and considered of nothing more than a bed, and in some cases two or three beds. Every room in that area was unoccupied, probably because the aliens weren't at rest; they were busy at work, preparing for their war on the humans. She started to turn back down the hallway, not wanting to waste any time on empty rooms that were giving her no new information. Just as she was turning around, she thought she heard the sound of a low moaning coming from one of the rooms at the very end of the hallway. She decided to quickly investigate the source of the noise.

Annastarlis flew down the hallway, and to the last room, she was shocked when she poked her head inside of it. There she saw Ifffer lying on a small bed. The gnome looked terrible, sickly, almost deathly, and she gasped at the very sight of him.

She carefully walked closer to his bedside to get a better look, hoping that she wasn't falling into some kind of a trap. She knew that Ifffer had been banned from the realms, because he had joined forces with the aliens, and betrayed the realms over and over again. He was no longer a friend, if he had ever truly been one; he was now considered an outright enemy of the realms.

She couldn't help but wonder, if this was some kind of an act, but it soon became clear to her that it wasn't. Annastarlis watched him hold his chest, and then she noticed his labored breathing. The gnome's skin had paled; his long beard had turned pure white. Ifffer managed to turn from his back to his side and his head fell to the floor. Annastarlis couldn't help but notice that his bald head no longer had a high shine, it appeared scaled and flakey, and now she was sure that this was no act. He was frail, and wore many new wrinkles on his face; there was no mistaking that the gnome was truly ill.

The fairy couldn't help but feel sorry for the old gnome; he was in trouble and needed help. This caused quite a dilemma in her mind. As a fairy, it was listed in the fairy creed that she was to aid anyone in trouble or suffering if it was at all possible. The fairy creed stated that any realm creature should always have absolute assistance, under any circumstances without question, but Ifffer really wasn't an inhabitant of the gnome realm anymore. Then she thought about the fact that he had been a high ranking council member, at one time. She never really liked Ifffer very much, and in fact she truly had feared him many times. He had always treated her poorly, and she knew that he pushed for the toughest punishments he could get the council to approve for her and Nerby.

The problem was that now he seemed like someone different, someone who was quite old, weak, powerless and vulnerable. She never thought she would see Ifffer like this, and didn't quite know what to do about it. Should she help someone that the realms now considered an enemy? Did she even have the ability to heal him?

Could she just walk away and forget about what she had just seen? Walking away from him went against everything that she had ever been taught, yet, how could she possibly help someone that could destroy the realms? She wished that she could instantly ask Jerry or Gatsby a question, but it just wasn't possible. She didn't have the time to go back into the realms, and tell them of the situation. It was clear to her that Ifffer was dying, he had little time, and if she was going to save him it needed to be right now. She had to make a decision on her own, and she knew that it might turn out to be one the hardest choices she would ever have to make. It would be something she would have to live with for the rest of her life, with no regrets. If she helped Ifffer, his death would not be on her hands, but he could go on to help destroy the world and the realms. She wished she could at least talk to Nerby; perhaps he could help her make the decision. Then it occurred to her that she wasn't here in the camp alone, she didn't need to make this choice by herself. She would gather Optical a council member, Nerby, and Elise, and they could vote on what to do. She couldn't bear to have all of this rest on her shoulders.

Chapter 22

A Warning Not Heard

Kyle managed to get his mother to stop her ranting talk about the existence of the realms to Joe. Kyle simply would not cooperate with her to tell Joe about any of it, besides Joe's mind was closed, it wasn't logical. She had insisted that she herself had seen the fairies, and that as a child he too, saw a gnome. They had been down this road before, and Kyle had no desire to go back down it again. He remembered what it was like to be admitted into the mental ward, along with Eric, and he certainly didn't want to go back there ever again. Besides Kyle had also made a promise to Gatsby that he would never reveal any information about the realms to anyone, and he wouldn't go back on his word. The only exception was his mother, after they had made the decision to show themselves to her. He felt bad that he didn't back his mom up, but he just couldn't, and finally she gave up frustrated and exhausted.

The boy was happy that Joe chalked all of Sarah's comments up to stress; because of everything that he had just told her about Aimee Lynn and her birth parents. He insisted that she take a few headache pills, at least that is what he called them and he tucked her into bed. She still mumbled a few things about gnomes, fairies, trolls and even whosawhachits to Joe, but finally the pills her husband gave her worked and she fell asleep.

Joe left their bedroom after she had settled down and closed the door behind him. He allowed his wife complete peace and quiet, something he felt that she truly needed right now, he could see how stressed and tired she was. He was surprised to find Kyle still sitting on the living room couch, as if he were waiting for him. The boy rarely looked to have any conversation with his stepfather, in fact, it seemed at many times that he truly went out of his way to avoid it.

"Your mother is fine, she just needs to get some sleep," said Joe.

"Yeah...I ah...was thinking the same thing," said Kyle relieved.

"It's almost time for you to go to bed too, you've got school tomorrow," said Joe in his usual bossy tone of voice.

"Yes...I was going to work on a plane for an hour and then go to sleep, I'm not really very tired," said Kyle hoping to hold his ground about being told to go to bed.

"That's fine, just make sure you don't keep your sister awake, she needs to go to sleep now. Tell her that I will be in to tuck her in," said Joe as he sat down on the couch and clicked on the TV.

Kyle headed for his bedroom as quickly as he could, relieved that his parents fight was over, and that Joe never mentioned anything his mother said about the realms. He found Aimee Lynn still watching TV in his room. He quickly grabbed the remote and turned her show off, getting quite the dirty look from the little girl.

"Mom, went to bed, she's...not feeling well...so Joe said you have to go to sleep now, c'mon I'll turn your bed down for you," said Kyle delivering the message.

Once Kyle had Aimee Lynn settled in her bed for the night, he went back to his room and sat at his desk determined to put together a plastic model airplane. He had this one sitting for quite a long time; it had been a gift from his real father. Although, he had really outgrown putting models together, for some reason, he felt that he needed to do it. His friend Eric rather enjoyed doing this, and his room had many of them, some Kyle rather admired.

Mystic and Elvin popped into Kyle's bedroom unannounced,

almost making him glue his fingers together instead of the plane pieces. They had been sent to the earth realm by Jerry on official realm business. The realms were in deep trouble this time, and needed the help of humans.

"Yikes, you scared me," said Kyle startled by their sudden appearance, especially the sight of Elvin grinning.

"Things are really bad," said Mystic with a serious face, one that she rarely wore.

"What's wrong?" asked Kyle concerned, directing his question towards Mystic and not Elvin.

"It's the aliens from planet Kaboris," said Elvin proudly responding, even though it was clear the question wasn't for him.

"I kinda figured that. What are they doing?" asked Kyle curious.

"They are determined to wipe out all mankind, and completely take over the planet," gasped Mystic, who now seemed to be almost out of breath.

"We already knew that, and I know that we have to stop them, but what can I do?" asked Kyle.

"We need humans to help us. Jerry and Gatsby had a long meeting, and for the first time in realm history they have decided that we must expose ourselves to people who can help us in this secret war, or none of us will survive," said Elvin.

"Ah...okay...but what people?" asked Kyle uncomfortable.

"We are going to need the FBI, you must tell Joe what is going on," said Mystic.

"Oh, no...have you gone totally mad. He's not going to believe me. I'll end up getting locked up in the mental hospital again along with Eric. I don't think so. Go tell Jerry and Gatsby to come up with another plan," said Kyle folding his arms across his chest angry and defiant. Perhaps if they had showed up while his mother was ranting, he might have considered it, but not now.

"There is no other choice, we are desperate and must have Joe," said Mystic.

"Well that's not going to happen, I refuse," said Kyle completely annoyed.

"Kyle, please, we need you. We can't fight these aliens," said Mystic almost pleading.

"Why does it have to be Joe? We already have my mother on our side, and I can talk to my school teacher. He's a pretty cool guy, and he already believes in aliens, plus he's into all this space stuff. I really think he could help us, he's smart," said Kyle.

"I don't know....Jerry said he wanted Joe because of where he works, but I could go back and ask him," said Mystic.

"Sure, you go back and ask them, meanwhile I'm going to have a little visit with Aimee Lynn," said Elvin with his usual broad smile.

"Elvin, I'm going to trust you for a few minutes, don't disappoint me," scolded Mystic.

Elvin's visits with Aimee Lynn made Kyle uncomfortable. He resented the fact that his little sister liked the whosawhachit. She showed no fear at all towards him, and it made Kyle feel wimpy for being afraid of Elvin. He sat in his room and listened to the soft whispers of Aimee Lynn and Elvin, and he almost felt jealous of their relationship. He heard his sister giggle and laugh several times, clearly having a great time. Kyle was determined that if his sister could be friends with Elvin, than so could he, and he headed to his sister's bedroom.

Mystic took a quick look in the house for Joe before heading back to the realms. She spotted the man laying down on the couch, already asleep and snoring softly. This was a perfect opportunity, and she took it, in order to place a few thoughts into his head. She wanted to take him away, not to the realms, but back in time. She took him deep into his childhood, back to memories that he filed away somewhere in his brain.

Sleeping is quite similar to being in a hypnotic state, allowing one's mind to grab hold of suggestions easier, and bringing repressed memories forward. The fairy made the man dream of the day, when he was a young boy, the day that he encountered a gnome in his grandmother's rose garden. The gnome was taking a nap under a large oak tree, and he seemed just as surprised to see the human boy. Joe never spoke to the gnome, because he immediately jumped up when he was spotted, and ran thru a knothole at the bottom of the tree, disappearing forever.

Mystic sprinkled fairy dust on Joe's forehead, and wished that he would dream this dream over and over again for the evening. She hoped that this dream memory would stir something from within him, or at least, open his mind slightly. This day needed to come back to him, because it had changed him profoundly, and made him the man that he was today, a true doubter in anything unknown or unseen. He had been excited and delighted when he first saw the gnome, but when he told his stern father about the encounter, everything changed. Joe's father was a military man, always played by the rules, and he made the young boy feel foolish when he told his gnome tale. His father gave him a spanking for telling a tale, warning him that lying would get him a severe punishment if he ever did it again. Joe had decided that day, that he would never be made into a fool again, he would always have concrete evidence to prove anything he had to say. As the years passed, he forgot about the gnome, and he stopped believing in anything that the real world didn't believe in.

Pleased with the job she had just done, Mystic finally whispered the word "believe" into his ear, and then she went to the astral plane.

Kyle was uncomfortable as he quietly entered his sister's pink bedroom. Although she was happy to see him, the look Elvin gave him, seemed unwelcoming.

"Hey....I thought I would hang out with both of you until Mystic gets back," said Kyle as he edged his way into the room.

"Dude, did wing lady tell you to come in here and keep an eye on me, because I don't need no babysitter," Elvin said annoyed by the intrusion.

"Oh...no, she didn't say anything. I just...well...I heard Aimee Lynn laughing and stuff, and it...ah....sounded like you two were having a good time," said Kyle as casual as he could.

"Fine, but don't be a buzz kill, if you want to hang with us, we like to have fun," said Elvin winking at Aimee Lynn.

"Yeah, don't be buzzy kill," said Aimee Lynn, followed by a giggle.

Kyle was stunned by his sister's attempt to repeat what Elvin had said. This was one of the first complete sentences that he had heard her say. It was clear to Kyle that Elvin had a positive impact on his little sister.

"So...ah...what game are you playing?" asked Kyle.

"We are playing, flying saucer," said Elvin, as he placed three of Aimee Lynn's dolls on a pillow and made it fly around the room.

"No...make it go up, not around, it doesn't fly like that," said Aimee Lynn.

"Show me how you saw it fly," said Elvin handing the little girl the pillow.

"It go...whoosh, like this, and then UP," said Aimee Lynn excited. Then she took one of the small dolls, and threw it to the ground.

"Is that what happened to you? Did the spacecraft take your parents, and not you?" asked Kyle.

"Yes...they...started to take me...but one green man said no, and they put me back on the ground," said Aimee Lynn.

Kyle was pleased that his sister replied to his question. This showed him that she was willing to talk to him and not just Elvin.

"Well, don't worry about the aliens, you will never see them again," said Kyle attempting to protect her.

"But, I have seen them...they come visit me...here," said Aimee Lynn.

"You mean, the aliens have come to this house," said Kyle shocked and scared.

Aimee Lynn didn't answer him this time; she just looked down at her dolls, and nodded her head, yes.

Chapter 23
Too Little Too Late

Annastarlis flew down the long hallway, she needed to find the others as quickly as possible. She found Optical in a classroom listening intently to the lesson being given. He put his hand up when she began to speak, attempting to silence her, more interested in what the alien teacher had to say, rather than her. She became quite annoyed with his attitude, and ignored his request to stop speaking.

"You have to listen to me now, there is no time to waste," demanded Annastarlis.

"What it is, I'm getting a lot of information here," said Optical still annoyed that he had been interrupted by her.

"I found Ifffer here....he is down that hallway, where all of the aliens private living quarters are...he's sick...I...I...think he might seriously be dying," said Annastarlis.

"What do you want from me?" asked Optical still half listening to her, and half listening to what the alien was saying about the day of doom.

"Well...you are on the council, and I don't know what to do," said Annastarlis.

"What does the fairy creed tell you to do?" asked Optical.

"To heal...but...isn't Ifffer....well our enemy now," asked Annastarlis surprised at the gnomes calm automatic response.

"Remember...first to do no harm, than to heal when you are able. We have no right to decide who we heal and who we do not. This doesn't change because the person you are healing has hurt you or he has a cold heart," said Optical.

"Ok...I understand that...but if I help him, and he goes on to help the aliens destroy us all, won't that make me responsible for the end of the realms," huffed Annastarlis.

"That would make him responsible. You are only responsible for your own actions or lack of your own actions. We never have any control on how other people behave. You must understand that if you decide not to help him, and he dies, his blood will be on your hands," said Optical.

"Well...he's in really bad shape, I don't know if I even have enough fairy dust to help him, I think he needs a gnome for healing," said Annastarlis.

"Show me where he is...we will work together and let us hope that we can also heal his heart too," said Optical.

Annastarlis led the way and took the gnome directly to Ifffer's room. He was still lying in the same position on the tiny bed, holding his belly, and softly moaning. Optical went over to his bedside, and looked down at his old friend, his facial expression upon seeing him told the story. He couldn't attempt to heal Ifffer without leaving his invisible state. This would be a dangerous thing to do, because the room had no ceiling. If just one of the military aliens that were above guarding the entrance to the camp happened to glance down into this room, they would be discovered.

Optical and Annastarlis popped out of their invisibly, and Ifffer opened his eyes to find them standing by his bedside. He was weak, but managed to muster one or two words to them.

"Help me...I need...water," said Ifffer faintly.

Optical ignored what his old friend had to say. He was already busy attempting to heal him. He placed his hands on the old gnome's belly, and seemed to go deep into a trance. Meanwhile Annastarlis was sprinkling fairy dust on his forehead.

"Water...need water...from fountain...of youth...aging quickly," said Ifffer in barely a whisper.

"Are you carrying any water with you?" asked Optical to Annastarlis.

"I had some, but I got thirsty and drank it all," said Annastarlis.

"Mine is empty too, go see if you can find Elise and Nerby, check their water containers, and bring them back here to me," said Optical.

Annastarlis popped back invisible and flew from the room. Optical sat on the side of the bed and softly spoke to Ifffer. Even though, Ifffer had done wrong by the realms this didn't change the fact that the two gnomes had been friends for hundreds of years. He remembered fondly when Ifffer had a kind and caring soul; when he worked hard to get a seat on the council, and started that position with only the purest of intentions. Ifffer had lived most of his life, as a good gnome, It was his jealousy for Gatsby that largely caused his personality and agenda's to change.

Gatsby and Ifffer ran against each other in a vote for Key Holder of the Realms hundreds of years ago. Ifffer had been quite confident that he would win the position, truly because at the time he was the best man for the job. When Gatsby won the election by just one vote, Ifffer sat back, and tried to hold in all of his disappointment. Over the years, as he watched Gatsby control and run the council, and the realms, he had different opinions about how things were being done. Many times he couldn't help but feel that Gatsby wasn't doing as good a job as he would have, and he grew stronger with resentment. While it was true that Gatsby had made some mistakes, every single Key Holder of the Realms had goofed from time to time. None were ever perfect, none could ever be perfect. Mistakes weren't always a bad thing; they needed to be viewed as learned experiences, not only for the leader of that time, but for the future generations to come.

Ifffer would have been an excellent Key Holder of the Realms, had he won the vote for the position many years ago, before his heart had changed from caring about the realms, to just caring about himself. Optical truly wanted to help Ifffer, but he feared that it might be too late. He had seen several older gnomes die over the years, and he knew the look of death, all he could really do, was hold Ifffer's hand, attempt to restore peace, love and joy into his cold heart and wait for Annastarlis to return. He wished so much that not only would they be able to save his life, but change him, and bring him back to being who and what he was, years ago.

Annastarlis found Nerby and Elise wandering around the laboratory, where a few grey aliens had several humans hooked up to different machines. Wires came from their heads, and from their bodies. Each wire was taking different kinds of readings, and a large computer was gathering all the information. The aliens wanted to get just the last bit of data that they could, before exterminating the entire human race. They had abducted dozens of humans during this last week, taking care to pick ones that they felt no one would miss, at least not for several days. The big plan was to operate on them, except this time, they wouldn't worry about leaving behind any evidence on their bodies. Once anyone reported these people missing, it would be too late, because the alien's would already have control of the entire planet.

It was possible that they would keep a few humans captive just to use them as test subjects, medically, if needed to diagnose future disease's, but Zoop hadn't issued any of the official orders about the final decision on that.

The aliens had a list of what kind of people they were seeking in equal amounts. They took two males and two females from different age groups, from children to seniors. Aimee Lynn had been on the list of possible abductees', however they deemed that with her new living arrangements, and adopted parents, she could not be taken, because her disappearance would be noticed immediately.

Aliens also had people that they had tagged with micro chips. Some they had never taken, they just installed the chips while the person slept in their own house, usually unaware of the visitation. Aimee Lynn had one of these chips behind her neck, something she had no memory of because it was implanted quickly in the field she had been found in. At this point, over 500,000 humans were walking around with these chips in them, all the time sending information back to planet Kaboris, and none of them ever had a clue. The chips transmitted all different kinds of information, from that person's health, and location, to things like weather conditions.

"I'm glad I found you, do either one of you have any water from home with you?" asked Annastarlis almost out of breath.

"Not me, I drank all of mine already," said Nerby.

"I so have a little bit, do you need it?" said Elise offering it.

"It's not for me. I found Ifffer, he is dying, he needs this water now," said Annastarlis.

"I'm glad you sooo said that, because in that case...," said Elise.

Elise pulled her hand back, she opened her water container, and took a large swig, drinking from it until it was empty. Annastarlis screamed for her to stop, but it was too late. The whosawhachette only seemed proud of her deed, and stood smiling.

"Why...why did you just do that?" screamed Annastarlis.

"I was so not giving him my water. If he dies, then we have a chance to save ourselves and the world," said Elise.

"But...we had an obligation to save him that was wrong; it's against everything the realms stand for," said Annastarlis.

"Under the circumstances...I so think that some of the rules have changed," said Elise.

"Perhaps she is right," said Nerby.

"No, she isn't right, and you know better. Now I need to go back and tell Optical what she has done," said Annastarlis angry and hurt.

"No, you don't, we must keep what happened here between the three of us," insisted Nerby, fearful that they would all be in trouble.

"I don't know that I can do that," said Annastarlis disappointed in Elise, but more so at Nerby and his attitude.

Annastarlis headed back down the hall to tell Optical and Ifffer the news, that no water was available. Nerby and Elise followed at her heels, all the time pleading with her to keep a secret pact between them about what happened to the last few drops of water. She was torn and confused about where her loyalties should be, and about the proper thing to do. Sometimes the line between right and wrong gets blurred, and she thought about all of it. Her very first reaction to Ifffer was the same as Elise's, that he shouldn't be saved. She had questioned it herself, and didn't even want to make a decision without speaking with Optical first. She fully understood the arguments that Elise and Nerby gave her, as to why Ifffer should be left to die. They both made very good points, ones that she already thought of herself, when she first encountered him in the camp, so how could she be a hypocrite. Perhaps she should have explained to Elise first about what Optical had to say before telling her that the water was for Ifffer. The whosawhachette drank the water in an instant; maybe if she had heard what the gnome had said, she wouldn't have slugged it down in one big gulp. Maybe if she hadn't told Elise who the water was for, and allowed her to hand the canister over to her, and then tell her it was for Ifffer, she would still be able to save him. She couldn't help but feel that if she had handled the situation better, it would not have happened.

The three entered Ifffer's room, and found Optical still sitting on the edge of the bed attempting to do a healing. Elise gasped when she realized that Optical was no longer invisible, after she saw his stone sitting on the small table.

"He's not invisible; they are so all going to see him. We are going to get caught here by those green creatures, and who knows what they will so do to us," shrieked Elise in a panic.

"All you ever worry about is yourself," said Annastarlis popping back out of being invisible.

"Ifffer, I'm sorry, none of us have any water," said Annastarlis as she walked over to his bedside.

The fairy looked into Ifffer's eyes, and she felt terrible. She couldn't help but feel guilty about what Elise had done, and how she wasn't able to stop her. It was clear to her that the gnome was going to die, and she knew that she would feel guilty about it for the rest of her life.

"Can't we take him back with us….home?" asked Annastarlis.

"He is too weak to make the trip, but we must try," said Optical.

"Well...Jerry isn't going to let him back into the realms," said Elise smartly.

"We will get him to the astral plane, and then I will get Jerry to come with water," said Annastarlis giving the whosawhachette a dirty look.

Once again a loud alarm blared in the air. The group stopped and looked up, to see that they had been spotted by the military aliens. This was immediately followed by the sound of aliens charging down the hallway towards them.

Chapter 24
Over the Limit

Jerry was surprised to see Mystic back from the human realm so quickly and he was eager to hear what she had to say. She found him in his office, sitting at the gem covered desk. He was looking thru old books, as if he were searching for something important. She explained Kyle's request to go to his school teacher for help instead of his stepfather Joe.

Jerry told her that if Kyle felt more comfortable going to his school teacher, he could do that. However, he also explained to her that she shouldn't make him any promises about Joe, because things could take a turn when Annastarlis and the group return from the pyramid camp. As of this time, he still had not heard from the group, and was starting to become concerned. Then he spoke about a surprise visit that he just had from the alien Zepadoodle. His stress level was clear, and his voice cracked slightly when he talked about his conversation with the alien.

"Zepadoodle stopped by, he wanted to make a deal. He told me that there is no hope of saving the humans, but he may be able to spare the realms...if we provide the aliens with something that he referred to as "special substance"," said Jerry.

"Special substance...what?" said Mystical bewildered.

"Well, from what I gathered from our brief meeting, he got some information from Ifffer about a substance that is found only in the realms…one that has magical properties, that will allow the user of it to become invisible," said Jerry.

"Sounds like Ifffer is trying to make some kind of a deal with the aliens, trading fairy dust," said Mystic.

"That is what I believe, and now Zepadoodle thinks he can blackmail me," said Jerry sadly.

"Did you tell him you would think about making a deal with him to buy us more time?" asked Mystic already knowing what he would answer.

"I denied any knowledge of a special substance, but I fear that could have been a mistake on my part. Zepadoodle was angry when he left here, and he threatened me that the realms only have days left. I have the feeling that he wasn't bluffing either," said Jerry concerned.

"Well…we have been in tough times before and we will do whatever it takes," said Mystic being her usual positive self.

"Speaking of trouble….where is Elvin?" asked Jerry.

"Yikes, I left him in the human realm, with the little girl Aimee Lynn, I need to go back now," said Mystic.

"Go back, Aimee Lynn, can help us too. She has no problems speaking; if Kyle talks to Joe he will believe everything, especially if he also hears it from Aimee Lynn too. She has never uttered one word to her adopted father before, it will have an impact," said Jerry.

"I will do my very best. Wow, was this a really a bad time for us to hit our limit for the decade, we needed this one badly," said Mystic.

"Yes, I know. Gatsby is pouring thru all the record books to see if he can find a loophole to the law, and I'm doing the same," said Jerry.

"What if we just broke the law?" asked Mystic.

"Nope, already thought about that, and apparently so did our elders. They have a spell at the realm door, so that it can't ever happen," said Jerry sadly.

Mystic returned to find Elvin, Kyle and Aimee Lynn together in the pink bedroom talking and laughing. Aimee Lynn was busy fastening dozens of hair bows onto Elvin's horns, and giggled louder as she attached each one. He looked quite silly, and played along with her, by wiggling his horns to make the bows shake wildly.

"Ok, I'm back. Go to your teacher, but time is running short, you have just one day," said Mystic.

"Geez...one day," said Kyle.

"Kyle, this could very well be the end of the world, we need help now. I wish you would reconsider and just go directly to Joe right now and not waste anymore time. Your sister and mother can back up your story," said Mystic.'

"Why can't you just show yourself to Joe, and ask him for help yourself? Why do I have to be involved?" questioned Kyle stressed.

"I thought you would eventually ask me that question. If I could just go to him myself, I would have already. The realms have a pre-determined human limit. A fairy, gnome or troll can only materialize to a new human that has never seen one of us before, three times a decade. We have checked and double checked all the official records, everyone has hit limit," said Mystic.

"Ok, let me get this straight, you want me to tell Joe, that all of you exist, and that aliens are coming to take over the world, and no one is ever going to show up to back me up," said Kyle.

"I'm sorry, but....yes," said Mystic.

Gatsby popped into the pink bedroom to join them. For an old gnome, that usually moved slowly, he seemed to have a sudden burst of energy. He was carrying an old tattered leather bound book with him, and had a new twinkle in his eye.

"I found a way around our over the limit problem," said Gatsby proudly.

"Do tell," said Mystic smiling.

"We can all show ourselves to Joe, but he has to be inside of one of the realms. Keep in mind, not even inside the astral plane will work, but in a realm itself," said Gatsby.

"Ok, but how are you going to get him inside one of the realms?" asked Kyle.

"That will be your job," said Gatsby.

"Yeah, ok...I knew that...but...well....I don't really see Joe heaping around and spinning inside of a fairy mushroom ring, without me giving him some kind of proof of something," said Kyle.

"You can do it, I have faith in you. I should also tell you that there is just one more small little, teeny tiny catch," said Gatsby.

"Of course there is...ok, what is it," said Kyle almost afraid to hear what Gatsby was going to say.

"In order for Joe to gain entrance into the realms, he not only needs to jump, spin and twirl inside the fairy mushroom ring, he has to truly believe. Deep down inside, he must believe that he will end up in the realms, or nothing will happen," said Gatsby.

"You have to be kidding me. I need to get him into the realms, so that he will believe, but in order for me to get him into the realms, he has to already believe," said Kyle.

"I wish I were kidding," said Gatsby.

"I know that this seems impossible to you, but everything is possible, sometimes it just takes a little bit of magic. You truly aren't on your own," said Mystic.

"Well, it sure feels like I'm on my own right now," said Kyle.

"I have started putting memories into Joe's head. He did see a gnome as a young child, and tonight that is all he will dream about, over and over again," said Mystic.

That night Joe did dream about that day. He woke in the morning, almost haunted by the memories. He skipped his normal breakfast, unable to eat, and left early for work. Sarah had little conversation with him; after he refused to eat the pancakes she had prepared for him. He never remembered his dreams, and this was slightly troubling to him. The dream disturbed him deeply, not so much because he clearly remembered every detail of it, but because he knew deep down that it wasn't just a dream. He was flooded by the memories he had of that day, and the ones that followed after it. He now remembered seeing the gnome, almost as if it had happened yesterday. He couldn't help but wonder how Sarah knew about the occurrence. It was only last night, during their argument that she spoke about it.

Kyle woke early, and waited for Joe to leave for work, before approaching his mother. He told her all about the alien invasion, and how he needed to help the realms, not only to save them, but to save the entire planet. Sarah believed everything her son told her; she didn't question it for one second. Mother and son sat at the kitchen table eating breakfast devising their plan. Aimee Lynn joined them; she never spoke a word, but listened intently to their conversation, until it was almost over.

"I'm sure your teacher could help, he would know which departments of government to get in touch with, and he would seem quite credible...but, we have Joe, and he could cut thru all the red tape immediately, and do something to get them to take action," said Sarah.

"I know...but he has to believe, and he doesn't," said Kyle.

"We just might need both of them," said Sarah thinking.

They threw different ideas back and forth, almost forgetting the time, and both of the kids were going to be late for school. Finally Sarah looked at the clock on the kitchen wall.

"You are going to skip school today; we have lots of work to do, because there is no time to waste. I will drop your sister off, and you and I will get busy," said Sarah to Kyle.

"Skip school? Well...ok...what kind of work?" said Kyle.

"You are going to run away from home, right now in fact. Hurry up and go shower and get dressed for a day in the woods. Meanwhile, I will pack you a nice picnic lunch," said Sarah.

Aimee Lynn understood everything that had been said, and she wasn't willing to be left behind.

"I go....I goes with Kyle," said Aimee Lynn.

Sarah smiled at the little girl, so happy to even hear the child utter the few words.

"Ok, you understand everything that we need to do?" asked Sarah.

"Yes...and I help," said Aimee Lynn.

"Then I guess I'm packing lunch for two," said Sarah hugging the small girl.

Chapter 25
Making the Big Move

The decision had been made; Eric's parents were finally persuaded by Dr. Booker that the best place for their son was military school. Today would be the boy's last day in the hospital. It was a place that had become so familiar and comfortable to him that it almost seemed like a second home to the boy. As he packed his clothes and personal items into a small suitcase, for one of the first times in his life, the boy was truly worried about his future. He knew this wasn't going to be a fun place, and that things were going to be tough.

Eric finished packing and walked down the hall, this time he wasn't looking for something naughty to do, he was actually headed for the payphones. He needed to make a last ditch attempt to plead his case to his mother; hopefully he could talk her out of making him go to this school. He said everything he could think of to get thru to her, things he knew he had broken her down with, in the past. Evelyn was firm, and absolutely refused to change her mind. She told him over and over, that Dr. Booker warned her, that her son would say all these things, and that they shouldn't change anything she had decided. The doctor had instructed the woman on tough love parenting, telling her that because she usually gave in to what the boy wanted, or demanded, she had caused some of his behavior problems.

Dr. Booker almost made her feel like she had been a bad mother, because she would believe her son's promises, and lies, making her feel foolish and embarrassed. The woman had been intimidated in a way by the doctor, and knew that she couldn't change her mind about Eric going to this boarding school, no matter what. She signed the papers in his office, and quickly left. She cried on the drive home, feeling like she had failed her own child. In a way she felt good that the doctor had put her in a situation where there would be no turning back. Deep down she knew that Eric had tested everyone, and hoped that this would finally be the right place for her son to get the help he needed. The doctor warned her several times, that if Eric wasn't straightened out now, he would most likely end up in jail as an adult, and she certainly didn't want that for him.

Evelyn didn't really know all the answers to what was best anymore. Parents don't always have the right answers; they are only human, they just do their best, and hope that the small mistakes they make don't have a major negative impact on their children. Perhaps she had made some mistakes raising Eric; maybe he did need a firmer hand, more rules, and some discipline. She was guilty of spoiling him; buying him just about anything he wanted, whether or not he really needed it. She had taken the boy to so many doctors and therapists over the past few years, and made sure that he took all the medications they prescribed. She had tried everything they suggested, and nothing ever seemed to work. This was truly her very last resort, it just had to work.

Eric hung up the phone disappointed, but he wasn't angry with his mother. He didn't feel the urge to act out, because he hadn't gotten his way, instead, he simply just accepted it. He understood that he had just pushed her too far, everyone has their limit. He really wasn't even surprised that his begging and pleading didn't work this time; the woman had just reached her final breaking point. He headed back down the hall towards his room, to gather up the last of his belongings. As he strolled around the hospital it hit him that this would most likely be the last time he would ever be here. He actually had some fond memories of this place and all the time that he had spent there. He thought about some of the tricks he had played on people who worked or lived in the hospital, and it did put a small smile on his face.

The boy rounded the corner of the hallway, and almost bumped directly into Dr. Melanie Hammer. The two immediately stopped in their tracks, and stood just staring at each other for a second, startled by their almost head on collision.

"Eric...how are you. You really need to slow down in the hallway, no running...you should know the rules," said Dr. Hammer.

"I wasn't running....I was....just walking a little fast," said Eric truthfully.

"So, I understand that you are leaving us today," said Dr. Hammer with a satisfied look on her face.

"I am, I was just going to my room to get my stuff, it's all good," said Eric attempting to hide from her his true feelings about being relocated.

"Think of it as a new adventure," said Dr. Hammer.

Dr. Hammer could see thru Eric's tough exterior, she knew him too well. She felt a tad guilty that she had been secretly happy that morning when she heard that he would be going to the boot camp boarding school. Now, as she stood looking down at the boy and into his deep soft brown eyes, something made her feel bad. Eric had lied to her, many times, he was a terrific storyteller, but still she had to admit that his ghost tales, may have had just a little bit of truth to them. She couldn't deny the things that had happened in her own home. She even needed to take 6 months off from work, relaxing in the sun on the beach, to get over all of it. She knew that while some of it, could have been sheer exhaustion, something did occur that evening to her. The boy insisted that he was seeing ghosts, and who really could say that he wasn't, many people believed in paranormal things, and claimed to have such experiences. She felt that she been thru a true ghost encounter, although, she would never admit that to anyone, she had finally come to terms with it. At that exact moment, she allowed herself to finally admit it but just to herself, that she truly had experienced something paranormal. Maybe she needed some closure, or maybe something about the boy's sad eyes, touched something deep down inside of her, but whatever the reason, she decided to reach out to him.

"Why don't you come down to my office and talk for a few minutes," said Dr. Hammer.

"Ok," said Eric, thinking that certainly a short visit with her would have to be better than rushing off to leave for his new home.

Eric and Dr. Hammer walked together down the hall, neither one said a word, they just walked quietly side by side. It almost seemed like they had reached some kind of mutual understanding, yet, nothing had been spoken. When they finally reached her office, she unlocked the door and the two quietly entered. Eric took his old seat, facing her desk, and all the memories of being in her office flooded back to him. He fondly thought of all the times, he had given the good doctor a hard time. He remembered all the stories that he made up for his own amusement, and how he could get under her skin. For some strange reason, he felt the need to apologize to her, and even he was shocked to hear the words come from his mouth.

"I...I...guess I should tell you that I'm sorry. I did a lot of stuff to you, and I really do feel bad about it," said Eric.

"You know Eric...right now I really do believe you're sorry," said Dr. Hammer.

"You do...but you never believed anything I ever said to you," said Eric.

"Most of the stuff...nope, I didn't...but you have to admit, you did make up some pretty good stories for me," said Dr. Hammer with a laugh.

Eric and his old doctor sat in her office, casually chatting, and laughing. They had bonded, not as doctor and patient, but as friends. They each had finally reached an understanding of what the other was about, and seemed to find a newfound respect for the other. They talked for over an hour, and then they heard Eric's name over the loudspeaker being paged. It was time for him to leave, and start his new school.

"They are looking for me....I've got to go....how do you think this new military school is going to be?" asked Eric sincerely.

"It's going to be tough in the beginning, but I think you're going to be just fine," said Dr. Hammer giving the boy a hug.

"Yeah, I'm just like a cat, I always manage to land on my feet," said Eric forcing a small smile.

Eric went directly to his room, and grabbed his bags. He was slightly disappointed that his parents weren't there to say goodbye, but he already knew that they wouldn't be. Dr. Booker felt it would be best for everyone, if Eric didn't drag out the goodbye's, and that in the end it would be easier on him and his parents.

Eric found himself on a bus, headed to his military boarding school. He put on a brave face, but inside he wanted to die. His parents loved him very much, and the doctor's idea of tough love probably wasn't going to kill him, but he would without a doubt suffer a little. He had learned so much the last few weeks, unfortunately for him, he had learned his lessons a little too late. He was sorry that it all had to come to this point, but he brought it all upon himself, and deserved exactly what he was getting. He sat quietly in the last seat, looking out the window, watching everything go by. There was one older woman who sat all the way up in the second seat from the front; her face was buried in a hardcover book intently reading, but other than that, the bus was empty with the exception of the driver.

When he had first gotten on the bus, the driver gave him a glary look, as if to say, don't give me any problems or else. The man was in his early sixties, gray hair, and carried at least an extra 60 pounds of fat, which seemed to sit dead in his middle section. The man had a half smoked cigar hanging from the side of his mouth, it wasn't lit, and he almost seemed to be chewing on it, making the end of it wet and soggy. He seemed like a no nonsense tough guy, just the kind of person, Eric would have normally enjoyed messing with. Right now, this was the last thing on his mind. He wondered what everything would be like when he got to his new school. He wasn't worried about the other kids, because he could always hold his own against them. He was fully aware that everyone attending this special school, was there for the same reason he was, they had been repeatedly in trouble, and this was the last ditch attempt to straighten them out.

It was a three hour bus ride to the school. The bus stopped at the large metal gates, waiting for someone to buzz them in. Eric overheard the bus driver speaking to someone on the intercom, and then he saw the electronic gates open allowing them in. He wished that the other person would have said, nope, sorry you can't come in, we don't have that name on the list, but he knew that wouldn't ever happen.

The driveway was long, in fact it measured over a mile; it was lined with large trees on each side. The tree's had grown tall and thick, and the branches managed to grow together over the top of the road, making the entrance almost appear more like a tree tunnel, rather than a long driveway. It was more of a creepy feeling than a welcoming one, the tree's made things seem dark and cold, and the boy's stomach began to churn.

He saw the 4 story brick building in the distance, and immediately noticed that all the windows were covered with metal bars, giving it more of a prison appearance rather than a school. Eric could see a field to the right side of the building, and spotted about twenty boys out there in two straight lines, all dressed in matching blue gym uniforms, doing exercises. The boys looked exhausted, as if they had been out there for hours, doing pushups, jumping jacks, and jogging in place.

Finally the bus came to a stop in front of the building, and the driver turned around in his seat, and called out to the boy to exit the bus. He had a smug look on his face, pleased that the trip was uneventful, and that Eric would be going to a horrible place where he would be punished for any bad behavior. The boy thought to himself, that this man most likely never had any children of his own, and probably didn't even like kids, whether they were well behaved or not. Eric rose from his seat, and grabbed his bags which he had placed on the seat directly across from him. He was determined not to show any fear, he needed to pull himself together, because he was going to have no choice but to get thru all of it.

He calmly walked down the aisle of the bus, and looked at the woman in the front seat. She never looked up from the book she had been reading, and he wondered what she could possibly be reading that kept her attention for so long. He turned his neck as he walked by her, attempting to see her book cover, but had no luck. For some reason, as he exited the bus, he stopped and turned to the driver and uttered a few words, things that he would have never thought would exit his own mouth.

"Thank you for the ride, sir" said Eric as he stepped down the stairs.

Chapter 26
Escape to the Realms

Annastarlis sprinkled Ifffer with fairy dust, wishing for him to turn invisible, so that the group could take him along with them, back to the realms. While it wasn't clear on whether or not they would be able to get him inside of the realms, or the astral plane , the least they could do was get him out of the alien camp, and then bring him survival water. Annastarlis didn't have much dust left, in fact, she had but just a few grains, because she had used everything in her bag to try and heal Ifffer. Her magic spell didn't work to hide him. The gnomes head turned invisible but his entire body still showed, which kind of looked funny, however at the time, no one saw any humor in it. With the gnome's body still in full view of the aliens, time was running out. They had no chance of making it out of the alien camp, without everyone being invisible.

Annastarlis looked and motioned towards Nerby, she would need all the dust he carried. Nerby hadn't realized that he dropped his small bag of fairy dust somewhere in the pyramids, and dug thru all of his pockets looking for it. He seemed to always have a bad habit of losing things, and this would most likely never change, even as he matured. Ifffer had told him once that if his head wasn't attached to his body, he would surely have lost it by now. The gnome was so ill at this point, that he failed to even realize what was going on, which was a good thing for Nerby. Even though Ifffer had no power or control over the fairies anymore, something about him still seemed intimidating, even on his death bed. Perhaps it was because of the position he once held, and how he seemed stern, even on his best days.

Annastarlis gave Nerby a glare; as she watched him fumbling for the dust that he was missing. She had no need to ask if he had lost it, she already knew from his facial expression, and so did everyone else in their group. Annastarlis didn't scold him, probably because she simply didn't have the time at the moment, but they certainly would argue about it later. Annastarlis did have a tendency to be somewhat of a nag, she rarely allowed Nerby to get away with anything. Nerby, on the other hand, needed someone to make him more responsible, and he had a way of making her see the lighter side of things, so they were a very good pairing for each other.

Optical, took his own invisibility stone, and pressed his hand hard against Ifffer's, allowing the stone to work for the both of them. They would have to maintain, a strong handhold, or one, perhaps both of them would be exposed, calling attention to the entire gang. The group, helped Ifffer from his bed, the gnome was weak, and barely able to walk. They would not be able to move quickly with him, the old gnome was going to slow them all down quite a bit. Then they heard the loud footsteps of the troops of aliens, marching down the hallway towards them quickly.

"We are trapped in this room, they will feel us, what are we so going to do?" cried Elise in her usual panic.

They had only seconds to act, and Annastarlis instantly took control and screamed out orders. She usually had logical solutions to most problems, and everyone listened and followed her lead.

"Hurry, everyone hold hands, we can't go by them, so we are going to fly above them," yelled Annastarlis.

The room was the last one in the hallway; so in essence, they were all trapped at a dead end. They couldn't stay in Ifffer's tiny room; there would be no room for anyone to stand, even if they pressed themselves up against the wall. Once the aliens would enter the room, they would bump directly into them. The aliens had already seen them in this room, so their position had been exposed. The only place they could go was up, but there was a problem with doing this. Optical, Ifffer and Elise didn't have the ability to fly, only Annastarlis and Nerby did. The two tiny fairies would have to use all of their strength, muscle and powers to fly, carrying the weight of the others. This would be the first time that something like this was ever attempted, but it was the only hope that they had to escape.

The five joined hands in a circle, and Annastarlis and Nerby took flight. They struggled to get the group up in the air, but only managed to get 5 foot from the ground. The aliens entered the room, shocked to find it empty. They began searching every inch of the room, confused about how the fairies, gnomes, and whosawhachette could have just vanished instantly. Annastarlis and Nerby began to fly the group down the hall, all the time looking down to see more and more aliens running towards the room they were just in, only inches below them. The strain of pulling the extra three bodies was just too much for them, but neither gave up. The two fairies put all of their efforts into the escape, and made it all the way down the hallway, out into the main area of the camp. They were exhausted, and weren't able to maintain the full five foot off the ground, and the group started to get lower and lower, sinking a few inches for every few feet they went forward. Elise's foot ended up kicking one of the aliens in the head, as they passed over him, almost knocking him out cold. The collision made the fairies also lose control, and the five ended up tumbling to the ground, hitting it hard. It was bad enough that Optical and Ifffer's hands were not only separated by the fall, but Optical also lost his grasp on the magical stone. This made them both visible, but only for a few seconds. Optical seemed to move like lightening, survival instinct just took over. He found his stone on the ground only inches away from where he had landed; he grabbed it, and then turned and reached out for Ifffer. The fall wasn't good for Ifffer; he injured his leg, perhaps even breaking it but he somehow managed to take hold of the other gnome's hand. As quickly as it all had happened, it was still long enough for three aliens to spot them.

"They have the power to be invisible," screamed one of the aliens pointing in their direction.

"Block off the exit, we will trap them, and hunt them down," called another alien.

"We can't see them, but we can feel them, everyone reach out your arms, and start searching for them," yelled the alien that had gotten kicked in the head.

Aliens began to rush the area where they had last seen Ifffer appear. Annastarlis, Nerby, and Elise ran in one direction, and Optical and Ifffer ran into another. Being separated would make it harder for them to communicate with each other, but it would also make it a little harder for the aliens too.

Annastarlis and Nerby took Elise by the hand, once again working together, they took flight. This time only carrying one extra person gave them more than enough height. They easily reached 15 foot up in the air.

"We have to help Optical; he's not going to get very far. He almost has to carry Ifffer, I don't think he is able to walk anymore," said Annastarlis about as calmly as she could, under the circumstances.

"No, I think we need to just worry about ourselves, let's so get out of here," cried Elise.

"No, that's not going to happen. We aren't leaving here without them. We wouldn't leave you behind, and we're not leaving them behind either," said Nerby.

Annastarlis was proud of her Nerby. Elise on the other hand was not happy. She didn't feel that they should have any loyalty to Ifffer, and also thought that if Optical wanted to make the choice to risk his own life, that should be his own problem, not theirs. The fairies ignored the whosawhachette's constant whining, and instead continued to fly around the alien camp to find the gnomes. Nerby spotted them, kneeling down on the floor by a large wooden desk, hoping it would provide them enough cover for the time being, so that Ifffer could take a few minutes to rest before continuing on. Every step that Ifffer took exhausted him more and more, and he was at the point of giving up.

"You need to leave me behind. I chose my own undoing, go with the others," insisted Ifffer to Optical.

"Never, I will get you out of here," said Optical determined.

Nerby saw that a group of 5 aliens were approaching the area where the gnomes were hiding. Each of them, had their arms stretched out wide, wildly flinging them in the air, feeling for any sense of the intruders. The aliens looked silly, flailing their arms in the air blindly, and it almost made him laugh, certainly if Elvin were here, he would have appreciated it. Nerby, thinking quickly, let go of Annastarlis's hand, flew down, and grabbed a stack of papers that sat on another desk behind them. He took the desk chair, and threw it directly at them, so that they turned and changed their direction. Then he flew around throwing papers down below him, as if it were raining. The aliens, jumped and reached into the air, hoping to grab someone, or something, but Nerby was way too high and far out of their reach.

Annastarlis liked Nerby's idea, but she couldn't join him, without putting Elise back down on the ground. They needed to cause complete chaos and keep the aliens going in the opposite direction of the gnomes. She flew down, and placed Elise on the ground, directly beside Optical and Ifffer.

"Oh, no...you so don't, I'm not staying here on the ground. I so demand that you so fly me back up there," said Elise with an attitude.

"I'm giving the orders right now. I want you to help Optical get Ifffer to the exit, meanwhile, we will get the aliens off your tracks, GO," said Annastarlis.

Elise continued to hold on to Annastarlis and the fairy finally had to peel her off, so that she could get back up off from the ground. The one thing that Elise was happy about was the direct order to head towards the exit, she wanted out of here, and she wanted back into her own realm. She begrudgingly helped Optical stand Ifffer up, so that each of them supported one side of him, helping the old gnome walk towards the stairs to the camp exit. If she had to assist Ifffer, and it meant that she would be leaving here and going home, then she would do it.

Nerby and Annastarlis split up in the air, they took turns scooping down, and grabbing different items, throwing them at the aliens. They managed to make direct contact with them, injuring several of them. The aliens didn't know which direction to run into, and or what they would encounter when they did; many took cover under desks and tables.

The group of aliens, who had been ordered to block the main exit out, abandoned their post when Nerby cleverly bombarded them, by throwing heavy books he had stolen from the alien library. The aliens were more in a panic about what would come next, rather than the pain they were suffering from being hit with objects from above.

Upon seeing the wonderful opportunity, Optical, Ifffer and Elise headed for the stairs. They struggled with Ifffer, and each step seemed like it took forever. Finally they reached the top, and found the exit out. Elise wasted no time leaving the alien camp, the three entered into the pyramids and walked two rooms before they sat down in a corner so that Ifffer could rest.

"We will sit and wait here for Annastarlis and Nerby," said Optical.

"You can so sit here and wait, I'm leaving," said Elise.

"You can't leave, we must stay together, besides, I need help with Ifffer," said Optical.

"So not my problem, it's every man for himself," said Elise as she headed out the door of that room, to find the way out of the pyramids on her own.

Optical called after Elise but she never answered him back, she was determined to get away from the situation. He had no choice but to sit invisible and wait for the fairies. He wiped the sweat from Ifffer's brow, the old gnome looked terrible, and he worried that they wouldn't get him back to the realms in time.

Annastarlis and Nerby continued to taunt the aliens by throwing objects from above, hoping to buy enough time to give them some distance to escape.

"I think we have given them enough time to get ahead, let's get out of here," said Annastarlis to Nerby.

The two fairies left, and hoped that the aliens would still believe they were in their camp somewhere. They knew it would be only a matter of minutes before any of them entered the pyramids and began searching for them there. They quickly located Ifffer and Optical, but were disappointed to see that they hadn't gotten very far. Ifffer had reached the point where he was unable to walk on his own any longer. The only way out was going to be by the fairies picking him up and flying with him.

"Where is Elise?" asked Annastarlis to Optical.

"She abandoned us, and took off in a panic," said Optical angry.

Chapter 27
Searching for Runaways

Kyle wrote the note word for word, as his mother dictated it to him. He would leave the note behind, lying on his bedroom desk, where it would be conveniently found. Then Sarah insisted that Kyle and Aimee Lynn take warm jackets, and wear comfortable clothes and sneakers. She packed them several sandwiches, and a few small snacks, including pieces of fruit, and fruit juice boxes.

"Mom, why so much food, don't you think this is a little overkill?" questioned Kyle.

"Better safe than sorry," said Sarah.

"I want you to promise me that you will take care of your sister. Make sure you hold her by the hand. Remember she's little," said Sarah.

"I promise, don't worry," said Kyle as he gave her a hug.

"You remember our plan? Do you have any last minute questions or anything you want to go over before you go?" asked Sarah handing him the cell phone.

"Nope...got it under control," said Kyle with confidence.

Aimee Lynn turned from the living room and ran into her bedroom. Kyle and Sarah at first thought that she had changed her mind. She was young and perhaps they were placing too much on her small shoulders. It would certainly be understandable if she were afraid, and didn't want to go. Within a few seconds, the child returned wearing a bright smile and carrying her favorite doll.

"She wants to go too," said Aimee Lynn proudly.

"Ok, be careful, I will see you soon, I love you," said Sarah hugging them.

"Love you too," said Kyle.

"Me love you too," said Aimee Lynn.

Just as Kyle was about to open the door, he noticed a man, wearing a suit walking up their driveway. He turned to his mother, and she instructed him to take his sister and hide. Sarah opened the door before the man could knock, she was suspicious of him immediately, and somehow knew that he was going to bring bad news. The man served Sarah with legal papers; she would have to appear in court in a few days. Aimee Lynn's biological parents were seeking to have her adoption overturned, and demanding custody of their daughter. This didn't come as a surprise, she knew it was going to happen, but reading the words on the paper, brought tears to her eyes.

"What is it Mom?" asked Kyle when the man left.

Sarah didn't want to speak about it in front of Aimee Lynn. The child was far too young to understand legal matters, and this one was quite complicated. She hesitated and then showed the papers to Kyle, directing him not to speak about what he was reading. When he was finished, he handed the papers back to his mother, fighting back the tears in his eyes.

"Everything will work out, it will be ok, you just wait and see," said Sarah to her son.

Kyle and Aimee Lynn headed out the door. They would need to leave on foot; because they couldn't take the chance that anyone would spot Sarah dropping them off by the woods. Sarah had to claim that her children had left for school, just like any other day, and that she was unaware of their current whereabouts. Depending on the time, or weather some days Sarah would normally drive them to school, and other days, they would just walk together. Nothing would seem out of the ordinary, although, they did get a late start. If they really were going to school today, they would have been late.

Sarah never called the school to inform them that both of her children would be absent. The school had a new strict rule about this, and by ten o'clock, just as she had predicted, the attendance secretary from the front office called her house. In the student's handbook, it stated the reason for these phone calls, was to make sure that kids didn't play hooky. Eric was the reason this rule was created, because he would forge his mother's signature on a sick note upon returning the next day, therefore, the school now wanted to speak with a parent on the phone to confirm an absence. She had practiced several times in her mind, what she would say when the call came. This would be her chance to put their plan into full swing. Sarah told the school that her kids left two hours earlier, walking to school together, just like they normally did. She acted like she was in a panic, to hear the news that they never arrived. The school informed her that they would call the police, and suggested that she do the same thing.

Sarah didn't call the police, she wasn't about to file a false police report, instead she picked up the phone and did what she knew she would have really done under the circumstances. She called Joe at work, and tried to sound extremely upset.

"Joe…the kids never showed up at school this morning, I just got a phone call, asking if they were going to be out sick," said Sarah doing her best to sound like she was in a panic.

"What? I want you to call the police right now. This might have something to do with Aimee Lynn's biological parents. It's possible that they have kidnapped her, and Kyle got in the way, so they had to take him too," said Joe.

"I doubt that very much. In fact, I was served with papers that they are taking us to court next week. I got the papers right before the kids left for school. These people went thru the trouble and expense of hiring an attorney, I doubt that they would break the law now, and kidnap the kids," said Sarah.

"Get in the car, and drive the exact route that the kids normally walk. Drive really slow, and make sure you look into all of the yards as you go by. I'm leaving work, right now, and I will meet you at home," said Joe.

Sarah didn't leave the house, instead she poured herself another cup of coffee, and sipped on it as she looked out the window of the kitchen. She remembered the day that Kyle really disappeared, and how she felt. She thought about Aimee Lynn's parents, and wondered what they were going thru. She knew deep down, that the little girl would have to go back to them; it was the right thing to do. She had become extremely attached to the child, and hoped that they would somehow be able to work something out, so that she could still be a part of her life.

Twenty minutes later, Joe's car pulled in the driveway. He got out and quickly ran up the walkway. As soon as Sarah saw his car, she went into motion and ran directly into Kyle's bedroom as planned, and waited.

"Sarah...where are you, I'm home," called Joe impatiently.

"I'm in Kyle's bedroom, I found a note that he wrote," said Sarah.

Joe headed for the bedroom, eager to see what the note said. Sarah handed it to him, acting as if she had just read it for the first time.

Dear Mom and Joe,

I'm sorry that I ran away from home, please don't be mad. Aimee Lynn went with me, because I don't want her to go back to her real parents.

Don't call the cops, and don't send anyone looking for me, you won't find me, because I have a secret hiding place.

Other stuff is going on, things that I need to take care of, but no one would ever believe me. I'm not coming back until I can get Joe to really listen to what I have to say. Only he and my teacher Mr. Koza can help me now.

I stole Mom's cell phone (sorry Mom, but I really needed

to use it). I will call you sometime today. Don't worry
about us, we are safe.
Love
Kyle & Aimee Lynn

"Well, at least he has your cell phone," said Joe.

"Yes, I'm glad that he took it," said Sarah.

"Let's give him a call, he needs to know that he can't just cut school and run away. This is unacceptable as far as I'm concerned, and I'm very upset that he took his little sister. This is a very serious thing to do, and when it's all over, he really should be punished," said Joe in his usual official tone.

"I don't think that is taking the right attitude. He's upset, we are all upset. If you are going to call him, and get him to come home, you can't be talking about disciplining him," said Sarah.

"I may not be a parent very long, but I think I'm smart enough to know that," said Joe annoyed.

Joe was surprised at what Kyle had to say on the phone. The boy refused to back down, insisting that he had his own demands. Kyle informed Joe that he and Aimee Lynn had no intentions on returning, unless, their demands were followed exactly.

"Kyle, do you realize that technically this is kidnapping. It's one thing for you to run away from home, but it's another for you to take your sister against her own will," said Joe angry.

What happened next was the biggest shock to Joe. Aimee Lynn got on the phone with him. She spoke, not using too many words, but just enough to get his attention.

"I with Kyle and I want to be here with him. I run away from home too. You and teacher come here now, and listen," said Aimee Lynn.

"What....Where are you?" asked Joe.

"By the time you get my teacher, Mom will have figured out where we are hiding. I want you to come here with him," said Kyle taking the phone from his little sister.

"Aimee Lynn talked to me, clear as day, she talked. She had such a sweet little voice," said Joe.

"Then I guess she is doing just fine with Kyle, that's a big step for her to talk," said Sarah.

"Yeah, but Kyle hung up on me, now that's just downright disrespectful. He needs to learn a lesson. We can't just give in to his demands. You do realize that he's also breaking the law," said Joe.

"Can you ever just think like a stepfather, and not like you are upholding the entire country's laws," said Sarah angry.

"I'm sorry, but we can't allow him to call the shots, and we're not calling the school for his teacher either," said Joe.

"What are you really afraid of...that the school will see that Kyle has to go to extreme measures in order to get your attention? That he has to run away to get you to listen to him?" asked Sarah firmly.

"So...you seriously want to call the school, and go on a hunt for him with his teacher?" asked Joe shocked.

"What choice do we really have right now?" asked Sarah.

Chapter 28
Surprise Inspection

The timing just couldn't have been any worse for the aliens that lived and operated the pyramid base camp. Zoop and Krempie arrived for an unannounced inspection and under normal circumstances they were usually quite critical. The leaders had routinely conducted surprise inspections, and nitpicked any tiny little problem discovered. Everyone dreaded it when they would arrive, afraid of the consequences that would be bestowed upon them. They would bark orders, and punish anyone with jail time, if they thought they weren't doing their job. Naturally, the leaders had expected everything to be running smoothly, and all to be working on the final preparations for the takeover of the planet.

The two leaders discovered many of the aliens, hiding under desks and furniture, cowering like small frightened children. Some were still running around wildly with their arms flying in the arm, hoping to capture or at least touch one of the invisible beings. Although, humorous to perhaps to someone just entering, Zoop and Krempie found nothing funny about the sight. The base camp was far from being orderly; in fact it was complete chaos, with papers, books, chairs, lab equipment, maps and other items littering the floors.

They were only two days away from the scheduled master plan, the complete and total takeover of planet Earth. At this point, everything should have been checked and double checked. Things should have been prepared and ready, with everyone knowing exactly what they needed to do. Zoop was very angry, and he looked around, seeking the target to attack with his anger.

Zepadoodle picked the wrong place and the wrong time to materialize. He had just returned from the realms, after speaking with Jerry. He had no "special substance" with him, and still no more information to provide about what it was. He was just as surprised as his own superiors to see the condition of the base camp, and slightly relieved that he hadn't been a part of what had happened there. His first thoughts were for himself, wrongfully thinking that at least he couldn't or wouldn't be blamed for anything that had occurred there.

"I demand to know what happened here," said Zoop directly towards Zepadoodle.

"I....I....don't know. I wasn't here," said Zepadoodle.

"Why weren't you here?" demanded Zoop.

"I...I...was....in the realms," answered Zepadoodle.

"What reason did you have to go there?" asked Krempie.

"I was...there...to find out...about...the special substance Ifffer talked about," said Zepadoodle nervously.

"Did you bring us any of it?" asked Zoop.

"Well....ah...no...but I'm still working on it," said Zepadoodle not quite sure how to answer the question.

"How does it work? What does it do?" fired out Zoop.

"I...didn't...I don't...I'm not sure," said Zepadoodle.

"You are useless, completely useless. We have wasted enough time on you," said Zoop.

"I will work harder," said Zepadoodle graveling.

"It's too late for that; we are almost out of time. You have failed your mission. You are to get on a ship, and go directly back to planet Kaboris," ordered Krempie.

"But...our planet will only be in existence for a few more days, I will...expire there," said Zepadoodle.

"You have brought that fate upon yourself, now off with you, before I kill you myself," said Zoop.

Zepadoodle left the base camp and went straight back to the underwater camp in the Bermuda Triangle. He began to prepare one of the ships to travel. He went to the tiny room that he shared with three other comrades, and retrieved his personal belongings. Then he packed the ship with extra nutrients and water, and other things that he felt he would need not only for the trip itself, but for survival for a long time. Basically the leaders had given him a death sentence. At this time, there would be no signs of life left on planet Kaboris, everyone who was living there, had no doubt evacuated to a camp on planet Earth. If they hadn't arrived on Earth yet, they would be in transport on the way. The only beings he would find on planet Kaboris would be a few humans who had been purposely left behind to die, having no further use for them.

As he packed the space ship, he wondered what would become of him. If he followed orders and went back to his own planet, he would surely die. If he defied orders, he would have a chance at living, that was unless, his leaders found him. His mind began to race with thoughts of other planets he had visited over the years, and he wondered where else he could go to live. Many of these planets had harsh weather conditions, they weren't deemed livable, which is why his nation had abandoned any thoughts of using them. He kept telling himself that one of these other planets had to have shelter for him to hide, should he decide to make a go of it on his own. He tried to list each and every place he had visited, and the reasons why the planet had been rejected. One by one, he attempted to see himself inhabiting each location. One was worse than the other, and then there was the other issue of being alone. While, he would still be alive, the thoughts of never having another to speak to, eat with, or any other kind of companionship would drive him crazy.

He wondered if he should make just one last ditch to plead with Zoop, offering something of use to him. Perhaps the old gnome Ifffer had said something to him,, anything that he could use to show he had value , and was worth keeping alive. He thought about every single conversation he had with the old gnome, going over every detail. He remembered the items that the gnome requested, especially his drinking cup, he seemed rather insistent about it. Then he thought, and thought, just maybe the gnome was after a liquid that he would put into that cup. Maybe the cup had a secret compartment that contained this special substance. He needed to return to the realms, he had to locate the things the gnome wanted. If these things were so important to him that he would request them, then perhaps they could be important to the aliens too.

Zepadoodle took his ship and flew off with it, but he didn't take it out into space. Instead, he located an area out in the desert, a place in Arizona, where he felt he could hide, at least for a while. The aliens had an underground base camp there, many years ago, in the 1940's. They had abandoned it, after one of them accidently had a crash landing, and the human's discovered the wreckage. People began speaking about this UFO crash, causing too much attention in that location, therefore the aliens built a camp in the Bermuda Triangle and moved there.

Chances were that Zepadoodle's ship had been spotted by some humans when he flew in, but he wasn't worried about that. In that area, the United States military often tested different kinds of strange prototype planes and people were used to seeing these things flying in the sky. The calls and reports of these incidents were so common, that no one would ever pay any attention to his arrival, at least he hoped not.

The alien flew his craft directly into the old camp, deep under the ground. The entrance opened perfectly for him, and then closed behind him. The earth outside would appear to be untouched, therefore, he would not be detected should someone decide to investigate the area they thought they had seen a UFO land.

Although no one had lived here in many years, the camp was still in fairly good condition. Everything was dirty and dusty, but much equipment had been hastily left behind, things that he would be able to use to survive. He located beds, blankets, medical supplies, and many other things, and he was quite pleased. Some of the items were extremely outdated, but he could still manage to get along just find using them. He made the decision that he could use this place as his new home, and no one would hopefully ever discover him.

Zepadoodle walked around the camp savaging everything that he could find, and bringing these items back to just one of the buildings. He had been living in a tiny room for many years now, sharing the cramped space with at least 2 others, sometimes even more. For the first time in many years, he stood, looked around and smiled. The entire camp was his, all his, and he could arrange things anyway he wanted. He was the boss, the ruler of his own camp, and he would do what pleased him.

He walked down one of the hallways, and located a small bedroom, very similar to the one he last had. He removed all three beds, and dragged them out into the main room. He had decided that this main working room would now be his new bedroom. The room was massive, although nearly empty now; it had originally housed at least 50 desks, chairs, and file cabinets in it. He pushed all three beds together, now deciding that he should sleep across all of them, spreading out, and enjoying the luxury of it all. He spent the next few hours, removing unwanted items and storing them into other areas, so that his main living quarters was spacious and offered complete comfort.

Zepadoodle had no form of entertainment there, at least not yet. He would have to make trips out in the night, to steal items from human homes in order to finish decorating his new residence. He would also need to find things to bring back there to keep him happy and occupied. He decided that being alone might not be such a bad thing, he no longer had to share anything, it was all his.

He located the office, where the head superiors would have worked. It had a huge desk, and a padded comfortable chair. He removed both of these items, and dragged them back down, to his massive living quarters. Why should he settle for using a common small desk, when this one was available, because as he now saw it, he was the leader in this camp.

He sat smugly in the large chair, spinning around and around in its wheels, proud to be behind the leader's desk. He began opening all of the drawers, and sifting thru the items he found inside of them. Many of the things he deemed to be garbage, and he tossed them directly into the trash pail. He had no books to read, and decided that maybe some of the papers; the reports stored in this desk could pass some time. They were old documents, so some might even be entertaining.

Each file had a sticker posted on it, stating that it was top secret confidential information, this made him smile. The files were now his, and therefore he had every right to read them. One file caught his attention. It had a red label on it, and written in block letters were the words "SAVING PLANET KABORIS."

He sat back in his chair, and flipped thru all of the papers. Some had different official looking stamps on them, showing which important officials had read them. He even saw several which had gold leaf embossed seals, this was quite exciting. On one of those papers, he spotted Krempie's signature, larger than most of the others, as if to call attention to his own importance. Zepadoodle never had the privilege of seeing documents like this, although many were quite old and outdated. He handled them carefully with the respect that they desired, taking care with the ones that had yellowed over time, which seemed more brittle. The most current paper he had seen was from 1947, most were far older than that. He thought about how Zoop or Krempie would be, if they could see him now, lounging behind a leader's desk, in a fat comfy chair, reading his government's most important secrets.

He read all about the different experiments and tests his predecessors had been diligently working on, in order to save his own planet. Many of the tests had never been completed, due to the aliens having to abandon this particular base camp. He wondered why, they never picked up this important work, and finished it when they moved to the new base camp, unless this paperwork had been lost or forgotten about. Krempie had been there, he knew all about this file, he would not have forgotten about this important work, unless he had another reason to leave it behind. As he continued to read, he realized that maybe there had been other ways of saving his own planet, and that taking over Planet Earth may not have been the only option for them.

He closed the file and began to put it back into the desk drawer, when he noticed a small handwritten piece of paper, attached to the inside back flap of the folder. Curious, he removed the paper and read it. The note said "final formulas for saving Planet Kaboris are hidden in the locked vaults under Stone Hedge. Why would Krempie hide this information? Why would he allow his own Planet to be destroyed? Zepadoodle wondered if Zoop knew of this information too, and he flipped back thru the file, searching for his name, but never found that he had signed any of these documents. Leaders always made secret decisions that their constituents never knew about, clearly this was one of those times. Zepadoodle couldn't help but feel that this should have been put out to a vote, that him and the other aliens should have been made aware of the fact that there was another solution to their problem. The final decision had been made by their leaders, well, at the very least Krempie, and Zepadoodle wanted to know why.

He knew what he had to do. He would go to Stone Hedge tonight. It had been a long time since he had visited there, and he hoped he remember how to unlock the secret codes to get inside.

Chapter 29
I've got to be Me

Eric followed all the rules in his new school. He was exhausted from the amount of school work, and physical labor they made him do. The place consisted of extreme exercise, structure, formation, strict discipline, rules and even marching for hours. Then the drill sergeant added insane amounts of chores, such as cleaning the school, and the living quarters which all the boys shared. Eric was responsible for his own laundry, and even had to shine his shoes. Sneakers were not allowed there, and he had to wear a uniform, which included a tie, and he truly hated it. The boarding rooms were inspected at 5:00 am every morning. If something was out of place, or one bed wasn't made to perfection, added chores were given to everyone who shared that room.

At night, he was so tired; he would crawl into bed and fall asleep immediately, dreading the sound of the rude awakening he received every morning. One of the drill sergeant teachers would open the door, flip on the light switch in his room, and scream; get up. He fondly remembered how sweetly his mother would call into his room in the mornings, and he missed her terribly. Most days he would beg her for 5 more minutes of sleep, and she allowed it, calling him again to get up, 10 minutes later. He was happy that he could talk to her on the phone, but the school only allowed that twice a week.

He never had any time to himself, not even one minute to think. There was no time for recreation or relaxation time. The school had no TV's, but offered plenty of books to read. Every minute of every day, he was ordered to do something, which was the exact idea of the school itself. One of his teachers, Mrs. Sherry would say daily that "idle hands were the devil's tools. When Eric asked her what she meant by that statement, she replied, "Children are more likely to get into trouble when they feel bored and have nothing to do". He didn't appreciate her statement, and thought the woman needed to lighten up. He knew deep down that he often got into trouble because he had been bored, but this place took keeping him busy to the extreme.

Eric had first encountered this woman teacher on the bus when he arrived. She had sat in the front seat reading, completely ignoring him during the long ride, or so he thought. She really had been observing him and his behaviors, taking everything in about him, so that she would know how to handle him later on. Mrs. Sherry was a tough, no nonsense woman, but Eric really didn't mind her all that much. She had been in one of the branches of the military for 20 years, before retiring and taking this job. The woman always looked for ways to make things more difficult. If she could take a 5 minute job and make it into a one hour one, she would do so, to keep the boys "busy". She made Eric realize that the teacher he had last year, Mrs. Edwina wasn't so hard on him. He really missed Mr. Koza, he was probably the best teacher he had ever had, yet, what he had done to the man's car, was purely evil.

The male drill sergeants, all just seemed to enjoy punishment and downright torture. They created ways to make more work for the boys too. Once Eric was finally able to do 30 pushups with ease, and this fact was noticed, the next time he got into trouble, he had to do 50 pushups, and so on. He overheard one boy who had been there for 2 years, being told to do 300 pushups.

Eric wasn't a stupid kid, and if anything he knew how to survive. When his pushups were raised up to 50, then he smartly decided to make it look like he was struggling. The drill sergeant yelled and screamed, but Eric acted as if both his arms would break any second. He received no sympathy, in fact he was screamed at even more. The one thing he felt he had accomplished was keeping his pushup limit strongly at 50, at least for a while. Even if he reached the point, where 50 were easy, he would never let on; he would always act as if he were dying. His thinking was that they could only make him do as many as he was capable of doing.

All the boys were once again outside, ordered to form three straight lines for marching drills. Eric did as he was told, even though he was dying on his feet, hoping for a break. He listened to the orders that the drill sergeant barked at everyone, but something happened to him, deep inside. He realized that he had shut himself down, and had started to become a drone. He started to observe the other boy's there, and they just seemed dead inside, their own personalities had been crushed and destroyed. They had a deep dark look in their eyes, as if they were hollow, and nothing was behind them. They started to appear to be more like robots than even real people. None of them ever laughed or smiled, although it was never said, Eric had the impression that this wasn't allowed here; they didn't want you to be happy.

He thought about the little bit of conversation that he had shared with the other boys, during meals, and before bedtime. Most of them rarely spoke, unless first spoken to, and would reply with a one or two word answers. The conversations were never personal, the words were all meaningless, and lacked any sort of happiness, goals, wishes or desires. They had been deprogrammed and shaped to fit the mold that the school had created. The school seemed intent on telling the boys that one of the only ways they would ever become something, make something out of themselves would be to go directly into the military forces upon graduation, because the real world, would reject them for the outcasts that they were.

Eric began to analyze everything that was being done and said there. Did this mean that none of the boys would even have a choice about what their future would be? Would they not be able to choose even their own career path? Would everything they do in life, be because of the brainwashing techniques that these people were using on them?

Eric obviously hadn't formerly studied psychology, but he certainly knew enough about it, just from working with doctors over the years. At times, he would look different things up on the internet, not because he was interested in learning the medical information, he needed it, to fake different symptoms and diseases.

Today the drill sergeant doing the drills name was Sgt. Anthony Lockwood, he was especially tough, and everyone feared him, just as he wanted.

Suddenly the drill sergeant walked over to Eric, as if he had just noticed a glimmer of life still left inside of the boy. It was clear to Eric as the man pressed his face an inch away from his and screamed that he would not be happy until the boy's emotions and brain were void of any independent thoughts or ideas.

"Are you daydreaming boy," screamed Sgt. Lockwood.

"I was just thinking about stuff," replied Eric casually.

"I didn't tell you to think," screamed the sergeant.

"You can't stop me from thinking my own thoughts," said Eric stunned.

"Ohhhhh, we have a wise guy here," screamed the man even louder.

"I'm doing what I'm told to do, you can't control what I think or feel," said Eric sincerely.

Eric waited for the man's next words, usually they started with something like drop down and give me, followed by the amount of pushups. He was in no mood to do anymore pushups, and he decided right then, that he was going to refuse to do them. What the man did next though surprised him; however he understood what he was attempting to do.

"Because Eric wants to think about stuff, how about everyone here, the entire group, drops down and gives me 150, that's right you all heard me, I said 150 pushups, NOW," yelled the man.

Eric understood this new tactic the drill sergeant was trying to use on him. He would get all the other boys mad at him. All the boys would have to suffer, just because of Eric, and therefore the boys would pressure him to stay in line. It was a form of reverse peer pressure, to the adult's advantage.

Eric watched as the boy's all jumped down to the ground, and began doing the ordered pushups. He stood, amazed at how, they followed the order from the man, even though, it was wrong. They never questioned why they were being punished; they just accepted it, even though they had done nothing to deserve it.

"That's not going to work," I know exactly what you are doing," said Eric.

"You can drop and give me 200 right now, you hear me boy," screamed the man in the boy's face.

"You want to punish everyone else, just because I said I was thinking? I shouldn't even be punished for that, this is just wrong," huffed Eric, crossing his arms across his own chest to show he was protesting.

The man's face turned bright red, and Eric could see the anger in his bloodshot eyes. He moved even closer to the boy, and his nose now touched Eric's nose. He never did quite remember what the man yelled at that point, because it was so loud it hurt his ears. He did notice the spit that came from the man's mouth as he yelled, and some of it splattered into Eric's face. He also noticed that the man's breath was horrible, most likely due to the yellowed stained teeth in his mouth.

"That's gross....you're spitting on me, there has to be a law about that. You can't just spit on people," said Eric turning and walking away in disgust.

The man couldn't believe that the boy disobeyed him, completely defied him, and he seemed shocked as if this could even happen. With each step Eric took away from the man, the man moved in closer, still continuing to scream. The other boys never made it obvious that they were looking; for fear that they would be given even more pushups. Instead they just continued to do their ordered punishment, but Eric could see the some of their eyes dared to move to watch him. Eric even thought, that for one second, he could see that one of the other boys smiled.

"I don't mind being punished if I deserve it, but I refuse to accept this. I will NOT do any pushups, not for thinking, it's not fair," said Eric once again defending himself to the man.

"I don't care if you think it's fair or not. You will do what I told you to do, life isn't fair. Learn that lesson now, because you'll be taking orders from people for the rest of your life. You're nothing but a LOSER," yelled the man, once again, nose to nose with the boy.

"Nope, life isn't always fair, but you have to stand up for what's right and wrong, that much I have learned. You can't stop me from being me; you can't stop me from having my own mind. I have the right to think my own thoughts, I didn't do anything wrong," yelled Eric back at the man.

The man never stopped yelling to even respond to what Eric had to say. He just continued to scream about pushups, adding more of more of them, saying something about 1,000 of them. Eric knew that in reality, it was physically impossible to be able to do that many pushups, even under the best of circumstances, at least it was for him. Then the man turned towards the other boys, and did something shocking.

"If Eric refuses to do his pushups, all of you will do them for him. Do you HEAR me morons, everyone will do 1,200 pushups NOW," hollered drill Sgt. Lockwood.

"Now, that's just ridiculous, don't you think, I mean seriously," said Eric standing his ground.

"You are invisible, I don't see you," said the drill sergeant, which just seemed childish.

The man took a new approach; he was now completely ignoring Eric, determined that he wouldn't lose his power and control. He instead, shifted all of his attention and anger towards the other boys, determined to keep law and order. Screaming that their eyes better be looking up front at him.

"I'm NOT going into the army when I grow up. How sad for

you that the only job you could get was humiliating and degrading children," said Eric wisely.

The man still continued to ignore him, clearly taking pleasure from the pain some of the boys there were starting to feel from doing pushups. He seemed evil and cruel. This made Eric realize a few things, he actually learned something from this man, although it wasn't the lesson being taught. Eric had been mean to people in the past that didn't deserve it. He had good caring parents, teachers and even doctors but he had abused them, for no good reason. This man was using his position to abuse others, just because he enjoyed the power that he felt from doing it.

The man began to taunt the other boy's with humiliating statements, ones that were unnecessary, especially since they were already doing his unreasonable punishment as ordered.

Eric forced the tears that started to well up in his eyes back. He didn't want to cry because his own feelings were hurt, he was angry that the other boys were being tormented for no reason. He knew that crying in front of this man, would only show a sign of weakness, and it would give him pleasure. What was wrongfully happening now was a matter of principle, something he never really cared about. He felt bad for the other boys, and he was determined to do something about it.

Eric ran into the building and found Mrs. Sherry and told her about what was happening outside. He noticed how large her eyes got when he mentioned 1,200 pushups, and at first she didn't believe him. She finally walked over to the window and watched the boys struggling, their arm muscles shaking from the strain and pain. She opened the window and listened to the man screaming at them, calling them terrible degrading names.

Mrs. Sherry ordered Eric to stay inside and she left the building to talk to the sergeant. The boy watched from the same window their heated conversation, and then he heard Mrs. Sherry order all the boys into the building to take showers. A few of them had gotten sick, from pushing their bodies far beyond its limit.

Eric never knew what the woman had said to the man, but he could see that he was quite unhappy. Eric left that room and walked down the hallway. For some reason the glass trophy case in the hall got his attention. He stood looking at the different trophies that school had won in competitions against other schools. The case also displayed black and white pictures of some of the different teams the school had at one time, football, baseball and wrestling. They no longer had any of these teams, because playing sports was considered pleasure, a recreational activity. It was Sergeant Lockwood who had banned all sports at the school, stating they made boys weak. Something caught Eric's eye, and he couldn't believe what he was seeing. It was an old photo from the sixties, which had a trophy next to it for wresting. The photo identified the boys by name, printed under them. He saw the name Anthony Lockwood, and he studied the picture. It was clearly Drill Sgt. Lockwood, when he was about 14 years old. Eric then walked into the classroom that the sergeant usually occupied during classes. The sergeant would be teaching a course in that room later on this afternoon. Eric picked up a piece of chalk and wrote largely on the blackboard.

> I became a drill sergeant because I have low self esteem. I need to make others feel worthless and weak to feel better about myself. I am a loser, and no one likes me. Other kids wouldn't play with me when I was a student here, because I was a bully and still haven't changed. I enjoy making others feel pain, and I have a big butt because I eat cake every night like a pig. I have bad breath, and yellow teeth, and need to go to the dentist, but I'm afraid to go, because I'm a sissy girl wimp.

Eric's mother was called to the school that day. Eric had time to explain to her what had happened, and she listened to him. He told her all about Drill Sergeant Lockwood being a student there, and what he had become. He didn't want to be anything like that man when he grew up. He didn't want to go into the army either. That day made him decide his future. Eric wanted to be a school teacher. He wanted to be more like Mr. Koza, and he begged his mother for a chance to go back to his old school. He now knew that he could still be a cool guy, crack jokes, and maybe even be a little bit of a wise ass, but he would always treat people fairly.

Eric went home that day, his mother saw the positive changes in him. During the car ride home, he thought to himself, I'm back, I like me, and I like who I am. He did make changes, he behaved for his parents and teachers, but when someone needed to be put into their place, he was the one to do it. He learned how to express himself verbally, to stand up for what was right, but he never again, destroyed others property. He did get into some trouble once in a while; after all, he was still Eric.

Chapter 30
Lost and Missing

Annastarlis, Nerby and Optical struggled to carry Ifffer out of the pyramids. They had expected to find Elise at the outside entrance, and were concerned when she was nowhere to be found. They wasted fifteen minutes searching the area for her, but she was missing in action. They were careful to keep an eye out for the aliens, but they had not been followed out into the open.

"I bet she just left us all behind and went back to the realms," said Nerby.

"She would do something selfish like that. The rule was that we all travel together, it was explained to her," said Annastarlis annoyed.

"Can we really expect that she would follow the rules?" asked Optical.

"I'm surprised that she would walk out here thru all the sand by herself. You don't think that...maybe she sank down into it, and now she's disappeared forever," laughed and teased Nerby remembering how Elise was afraid of the sand.

"She couldn't wait to get into the human realm, and then she couldn't wait to get out of it," said Annastarlis.

The group attempted to get back into the astral plane, but they were unable to do so. The ban placed on Ifffer, would not allow any of them to enter as long as they were touching or carrying him.

"We can't just leave Ifffer here, it's just too dangerous and we need to create more distance between us and the aliens, and we have already wasted too much time searching for Elise," said Optical.

"I agree, we need to hide somewhere safe, let's just go to Kyle's house," said Nerby.

Annastarlis was able to transport the group into Kyle's bedroom. They knew the boy would be in school, but could expect his mother to be home. This wasn't a problem; she would help them, perhaps she would even care for Ifffer while they went to retrieve water for him. When they heard Joe's voice, arguing with Sarah, they knew this wasn't going to be a safe place to hide the gnome. Naturally they had assumed Joe would be at work.

"Let's just go to the gnome transport tree in the woods, the one where we first met Kyle," said Annastarlis.

"That's a perfect place," said Optical pleased that she thought of it.

Annastarlis was able to wish the group to the woods by the baseball field. This wooded area was a special place, for many reasons. It held fond memories, of enchanted celebrations and magical fairies dances. It was always quiet and peaceful, with soft sounds of the bubbling brook water, and the smell of sweet pea's always filled the air. It was especially private because humans rarely ever went into the area. The gnomes had placed a transportation tree there, for their own use, which Gatsby had often used to come and go into the human realm.

When they arrived, they were surprised to hear the sounds of humans quietly talking. They carefully placed Ifffer on the ground, with his back sitting up against the transport tree. Optical pressed the invisibility stone into Ifffer's hand to keep him hidden from any danger. When he realized that Ifffer wasn't strong enough to even hold onto the stone, he took it from his hand, and placed it into Ifffer's pocket. The old gnome was quickly fading, and they didn't have much time to save him.

Optical then entered the transport tree to go back into the realms. His plan was to grab some water from the fountain of youth, and return back to the woods hopefully not only with the water, but also with either Jerry or Gatsby. He didn't really know if one of them would agree to lift the spell which was placed on Ifffer, he could only hope they would show compassion. He had already decided that he wanted to be the one who would personally tend to Ifffer's care, because he would need someone to nurse him back to complete health, if the council would allow him to do so.

Meanwhile the fairies investigated the woods to see how many people were there. Annastarlis and Nerby popped out to show themselves almost immediately when they discovered Kyle and his little sister. The two were sitting by the brook, casually eating a picnic lunch packed by their mother, acting as if they didn't have a care in the world. Aimee Lynn seemed content smiling and laughing, and even having conversation with her brother. She had opened up quite a bit, and appeared to be extremely social.

"No school for you today?" asked Annastarlis suspiciously.

"Wow, am I glad to see you. No school today, we cut...but my mom knows," said Kyle.

"We just got back from the alien camp in the pyramids, we messed with them pretty good. Now we're just waiting for Gatsby or Jerry to get here, we have Ifffer with us, he's pretty sick," said Nerby giving a full report.

"Ifffer...but...I thought he was dangerous.... A traitor...," said Kyle before his statement got cut off.

"Kyle, I can't believe you didn't go to school. Didn't we have an agreement that you were going to talk to your teacher today? We need help now, you need to go to Joe, we can't afford to wait any longer," said Annastarlis in a scolding type tone.

Kyle wasted no time explaining the idea that Sarah had come up with. Even Aimee Lynn chimed in with a few details that her brother had left out, to everyone's complete amazement. The little girl was bright, smarter than anyone even knew.

Within a few minutes they could hear the sounds of gnomes

talking not far in the distance by the big oak tree. Optical had returned as promised and he wasn't alone.

"We need to go now, stay here, we will be back," said Annastarlis.

"Ok, we will see you, one way or another," said Kyle giving a wink.

Annastarlis and Nerby ran back to the tree, where Ifffer had been sitting. He was gone, along with whoever came to get him. The two popped into the astral plane, but still saw no signs of anyone; therefore they headed straight for the gnome realm. They needed to report everything back to Jerry about things they had learned inside the pyramid camp, and would be able to get an update about the Ifffer situation at the same time. They could also let the council know what Kyle had planned, so that they would be ready, to assist him when the time was right.

The fairies went straight to the Great Hall of Justice and headed for Jerry's office, but he wasn't there. They waited for several minutes, but the building was quiet.

"Where do you think he went?" asked Nerby getting inpatient.

"Well, somewhere with Ifffer I would guess," said Annastarlis.

"Let's go outside and see if we can find anyone that knows what's going on," said Nerby anxious.

Annastarlis and Nerby walked outside in search of anyone that could give them information about where they would find Jerry or Gatsby. They asked a young gnome who was planting flowers in the garden out front, and he told them to go to Optical's house. The fairies headed down the path running, and then finally both took flight into the air to get there faster. On the way, they had a conversation about what Ifffer's future would be in the realms.

"Do you think that when Ifffer gets better, they will let him become a council member again…if he's going to be a good guy now," asked Nerby curious.

"I have no way of knowing that…but I would guess that they won't. I don't forgive him for what he has done, and I don't really see how anyone else can," said Annastarlis in a stuck up snotty way.

"There is no point in burying the hatchet if you are just going to put up a marker on the site," said Nerby turning into an adult.

"Well, let's be honest, no one really forgets where they buried the hatchet," said Annastarlis in rebuttal.

They finally reached Optical's tree house; it sat on a lower branch in an elm tree. The two stood for a minute or two, trying to decide which one of them would knock on the door. They weren't quite sure if they should interrupt, but at the same time, they did have valuable information for Jerry about the alien's, which needed to be reported immediately. Nerby was just about to knock, when the door opened. Jerry and Gatsby exited, both seemed stressed and upset.

"Sorry, we didn't want to intrude, but we came to give you a full report about the alien's pyramid camp and their plans. I know you would want to know everything right away," said Annastarlis.

"Yes, I need to hear everything you know. Optical did tell me some of it," said Jerry.

"We managed to get lots of information. Elise turned out to be pretty much useless, she got in the way mostly, and I'm sure she didn't have much to report," said Annastarlis, determined that she could make sure that the whosawhachette wouldn't go on any other missions.

"I haven't spoken with Elise yet, I had hoped that she would be with you," said Jerry.

"Ah...no...didn't Optical tell you, she returned back to the realms without all of us. She just went ahead, and just left us behind, carrying Ifffer," said Nerby, hoping to help Annastarlis

"Well, we've got a big problem, because Elise never arrived back here," said Jerry disappointed in the situation.

"We will go back and search for her right now," said Annastarlis upset that they were most likely in trouble.

"We have no time for that right now. I suspect that she's in no danger; she's undoubtedly looking to explore and create trouble. I will send someone else out to look for her," said Jerry.

Jerry called for Elvin, he planned to send him out to look for his sister, hoping that he would be the voice of reason, to convince Elise that she had to return. The last thing he needed right now was the whosawhachette roaming, unsupervised in the human realm. He called for Mystic to escort Elvin, knowing she was responsible enough to handle the situation and both of them.

"Ah...how is Ifffer doing?" asked Annastarlis casually and not truly genuine.

Jerry and Gatsby looked at each other, neither one seemed quick to answer, but finally Gatsby replied softly.

"We will be having a funeral after this alien stuff has been resolved. Ifffer didn't make it, we did everything we could, but he just got water too late. I'm sorry to say that he passed away," said Gatsby sadly.

"I'm sorry...I don't know what to say...I...did try and help him," said Annastarlis flabbergasted.

"I know that your heart is closed to forgive him for what he has done. Our sense of fairness tells us that someone should pay for the wrong that they do. But you will come to learn that forgiving is love's power to break nature's rule because someone who cannot forgive breaks the bridge over which he will someday have to pass himself," said Gatsby wisely.

Chapter 31
Learning to Listen

Sarah called the school and was able to speak to Mr. Koza directly. The teacher was concerned to hear that one of his students had run away from home. She explained that her husband had a brief telephone conversation with Kyle, and told him about her son's request to talk to him.

Joe pressed Sarah to think about where she thought Kyle would be hiding. She of course knew exactly where he would be, but acted as if she didn't have a clue. She knew that if she told him before the teacher arrived at their house; Joe would just go on ahead, which could have a negative outcome on their master plan.

"You have to have some idea about where he would go, what about that kid Eric's house?" asked Joe attempting to help.

"No, Eric isn't there; he would have no reason to go to his house… maybe he would go to the mall. He loves playing all the games in the video arcade," said Sarah hoping to stall for some time.

"Why don't you just stay here, and I'll go over to the mall and take a quick look for them," said Joe.

"Ahhh…well…I'm sure his teacher will be here in a few minutes, there really is no need for us all to go in different directions," said Sarah.

"Actually, that would make more sense, if we spread out, we would find him quicker," said Joe.

"Well...I was thinking, instead of going on a wild goose hunt, that we could just call my cell phone when Mr. Koza gets here, and ask Kyle where he wants us to meet him," said Sarah smarty.

"That gives him power; I think it's better if we find him on our own. He really couldn't get very far on foot, especially with Aimee Lynn. That will send a direct message to him, that we are smarter than he is, and it will put an end to this nonsense," said Joe firmly.

Before Sarah could even respond to him, Mr. Koza's car pulled into the driveway. The teacher quickly walked to the door and began knocking before Sarah could open it.

"Thank you so much for coming. I'm must apologize that I even asked you to go out of your way to do this, I do realize that this is over and above the call of duty," said Sarah with a smile.

"I'm happy to help. I must say I'm surprised that he would run away. It doesn't seem like anything Kyle would do, he's one of my very best students," said Koza concerned.

"Kids...you never know what they are going to do. TV and movies....puts all these crazy idea's into their heads. Makes them think they don't have to listen to adults anymore," said Joe slightly annoyed.

The room had an awkward uncomfortable silence for a minute. Sarah was embarrassed and didn't know how to correctly respond to her husband in front of the teacher, therefore she purposely ignored him. Joe was still new and discovering what it was like to be a parent. He had strong ideas about discipline, raising children and Sarah was working to soften him. The woman then began to fumble in her purse to retrieve her car keys, hoping to hide her flushed face. Mr. Koza was more puzzled by the man's statement and lack of concern for the safety or whereabouts of his two children rather than Sarah's lack of response to it.

As they all piled into Sarah's car, Koza slipped into the back seat and he carefully studied these parents. The entire situation was strange, and he wondered what he had just gotten himself into. Joe seemed more determined to locate the children, so that he could dish out punishment, and lay the law down, rather than to simply bring them home safe. He also noticed something odd about Sarah. She wasn't riddled with worry or fear, she seemed more nervous perhaps even anxious as if she were anticipating something. He found it curious that they hadn't called the police to report their children as runaways, even though, Joe worked for the FBI, he still thought it would have been best to go thru all the proper channels.

"Let's not go to the mall, I think I know where Kyle is. I bet he is in the woods, the one by the baseball field," said Sarah as casually as she could.

"You mean the place where he...well...talked about those mushroom rings...geez...you are making sure that he is taking his medications I hope," said Joe almost sounding annoyed.

Sarah didn't answer him, instead she allowed him to drive over to the wooded area in silence. They parked by the baseball field lot, and got out, headed in the direction of the heavy treed area.

"Just so you know...Kyle hasn't taken his medication in a long time. He doesn't need them," said Sarah borderline angry.

Koza walked along a few steps behind his students parents, observing their movements and listening to their disagreement. He thought about the position that he was in, and secretly wished that he had not been called out of class to take Sarah's phone call.

Sarah seemed to lead the way, it almost appeared that she knew exactly where she would locate her children. After walking down several paths, they spotted Kyle and Aimee Lynn standing by the stream of water. Kyle was teaching Aimee Lynn how to skip rocks into the water and she would giggle when the rocks bounced for him.

"I'm glad that you are having a good time....I can't believe that you have made your mother and I worry like this, you know I had to leave work because of this," huffed Joe.

"I'm sorry you had to leave work, and I'm sorry that you did too Mr. Koza, but this is really important, it could mean the end of the world," said Kyle.

"Oh, here we go," said Joe angry.

"Stop your attitude, and please for once, just listen to him," said Sarah to her husband.

"Mr. Koza…you believe in aliens…they are coming here in two days. They are going to take over our planet. My friends from another dimension told me all about them, they come from planet Kaboris," said Kyle.

"Oh yeah, it was such a good idea, to take him off of his meds, clearly he doesn't need them," said Joe as he started to walk away.

"Where are you going, we need you," said Sarah pleading.

"WE need you? So…you knew what was going on here, this was all just a big scam," said Joe disappointed.

"Yes, I knew…we needed to find a way to make you listen, to show you things," said Sarah.

Joe was angry; his mind was far from open about any thoughts or ideas regarding aliens. He felt deceived by his own wife, and didn't understand why she would do something like this. He noticed a large mushroom ring, and walked over to it, and in anger, he kicked several of the mushrooms, making them fly in the air.

Koza looked at Kyle, the boy always seemed sane and rational to him. He was an above average student, and he clearly had a message that he needed an adult to hear. He knew that Joe would not give the boy a minute of attention, he wouldn't hear what the boy had to say and so he turned to the boy. He could clearly see that the child's stepfather had a closed mind. Perhaps, Koza now partly understood why it was requested that he come along to whatever was going to happen.

"Kyle…slow down, you're talking very fast. Tell me why you brought me out here," said Mr. Koza calmly.

"Because…you will listen…and because you believe….in things," said Kyle.

"Ok…I'm listening," said Koza giving the boy his full attention.

Kyle talked about the realms and his visits there. Then he spoke about the aliens, and talked about things that would happen, if they didn't help the realms save the world. He explained how the fairies and gnomes were over their limit, and that they couldn't show themselves to Joe and Koza in the human world, but they could if the men entered the realms. Then the boy explained that he wanted to take them into the realms but only under one very important condition, they had to believe to make the entrance open. Koza didn't laugh at the boy, he stood stroking his beard, something he usually did when he was deep in thought.

Sarah began to speak about talking to the fairies. She told the story about first seeing them outside of the hospital, and how they would often visit the house. She even explained how they built the swimming pool in their backyard in just one day, as a thank you gift for Kyle, hoping that Joe would realize it was all the truth. She dared to sneak a peek at Joe, and he looked angry, yet she continued to talk, hoping to back up everything that Kyle was saying.

"Listen, I realize that all of this sounds insane to both of you men. We need help, Kyle is telling the truth," said Sarah.

"The fairies are my friends too....but I don't like the aliens...they scare me," added Aimee Lynn.

"See Joe...this is the reason Aimee Lynn never spoke before. She's finally opening up and talking, because I'm listening to what she has to say, you must believe in your children," said Sarah hoping to reason with him.

"What do you want from me? I mean seriously...I just don't have time to play these games. I need to go back to work, my job is very important," said Joe angry.

"Yes, your job is important, but what about your family? Isn't your family important?" said Sarah searching for the right answers in her husband's eyes.

Sarah turned to the teacher who stood there, not knowing what to do or what to say. He was at a loss for words, which was something very rare for the outspoken man.

"You believe in children, don't you Mr. Koza," said Sarah hoping she could get him to assist in convincing her husband to listen.

"Well...I do remember that Lady Bird Johnson once said, that children are likely to live up to what you believe of them," said Koza being his usual history teacher self.

Koza had hoped that his answer would be diplomatic enough. He was feeling uncomfortable being put on the spot. His mind was thinking that the job he had agreed to was done. He helped locate the missing children, and he listened to what the boy had to say, but still, he was curious about the realms, fairies, gnomes, and certainly the aliens.

"Well, will you or won't you enter the realms with me?" asked Kyle seriously.

Chapter 32
Discovering the Past

Zepadoodle waited until the cover of darkness before exiting his new home in the Arizona desert. He flew his ship to England so he could gain entrance into Stonehenge. Stonehenge might just appear to humans to be just large stones standing, because from a distance it gives the feeling that it has no purpose at all, but it really has many. Over the years, from time to time, people began to question it, and started to study it, but they never truly uncovered much about it. People have speculated as to why someone would have built this structure. Most believe that it was created in ancient times for use in different kinds of religious ritual activities. In fact, it had been used for such things by humans once they discovered it there, but that was not the reason the aliens had originally built it.

The monument's mysterious presence created many different tales, legends and theories in folklore, including that a wizard named Merlin had something to do with its creation. The aliens found all of these stories amusing, especially when some of these tales told of the stones magically being transported from Ireland, perhaps that even giants had assembled them. Another human idea was that maybe it was the leftover ruins from a Roman temple. In any event, although different groups had tried to take credit for masterminding its build, the real truth is that the aliens from Kaboris truly designed and built it.

The aliens had built the above ground area of Stonehenge for several reasons; one was to use it for an astronomical observatory. They had purposely laid out the stone pattern, so that the circle was exactly aligned with the midsummer sunrise, the midwinter sunset, and the most southerly rising, and northerly setting of the moon. While the aliens were living underground on earth, they could use Stonehenge's celestial influence because of its planned alignments with certain stars for use not only as a calendar but also to predict a coming solar eclipse. What most humans failed to understand was that the exact ground plan and structural engineering combined sophisticated mathematical and geometrical technology, far beyond what the eye can see and what humans were capable of during its creation. The aliens did in fact also use the outside stones for a sky marker, as a convenient easy identifiable spacecraft landing area.

The bluestones which weigh as much as four tons have mythical powers that the aliens tapped into, for the purpose of energy and other things. The Sarsen stones also had other principles, which were useful to them. The aliens never did anything by chance; they had a clear cut purpose and plan for everything they made on this planet and others. Stonehenge had also originally served as a place where aliens and even people later on could be healed from different diseases. Some of the healings revolved around the power of the smaller bluestones.. The stones at one time were powered naturally by ice age glaciers long ago. Now, the aliens possessed all of these healing powers, having removed them from the stones and the area centuries ago, therefore they no longer needed to use that exact site for such a purpose. They didn't even need it anymore to use as a calendar or even to predict solar storms or other celestial happenings, they had much more modern ways of during so, due to their advancements in technology.

The aliens could have built Stonehenge anywhere, but they picked this location in England for a reason. This area allowed the power from the blue stones to be increased because of the intersecting ley lines it naturally provided. Ley lines are alignments of places in ancient times, to allow direct passing thru natural ridge tops and water fords with ease. Stonehenge has fourteen of these different ley lines that meet in the middle which the aliens felt naturally created more power. The thinking on this is similar to how the Chinese feel about Feng shui, that everything placed properly, will improve life by bringing position energy. Feng shui translated into English means, as wind and water, the wind scatters but is retained when encountered by water.

The ley lines of course are still there at Stonehenge, which might truly have some spiritual power. For this reason today some people believe the area itself is said to hold special psychic and mystical energies, which can allow supernatural forces to become more powerful.

Humans have never discovered the true hidden secrets of Stonehenge, certainly not what is harbored below it. This was the place that Zepadoodle was headed to. It wasn't easy to gain entrance to the underground camp; he needed to remember several different combinations of taps, which had to be executed perfectly or the door would not open. This camp was the very first one that Zepadoodle had ever been to on planet Earth. He hadn't been there since he was a small child, and fumbled with the stones hidden locked combinations. He was denied access four times, before he finally had gotten it correct, and one of the large stones opened. He quickly stepped inside, and descended down a tight spiral stone staircase, which almost seemed like it had no end. The camp was deep down in the ground, and when he finally reached the bottom, he was winded. He stood for a few minutes to catch his breath, and then set out to do the job which he came for.

The camp was extremely dirty; no one had been there in many years. He saw nothing he considered to be useful, because everything there was hundreds, perhaps even thousands of years old. The alien laughed to himself, when he noticed how outdated some of the items were. The foolish humans would have seen many of these things as treasured valuable antiques, but to him, it was all just useless junk. This was the very first camp the aliens had built and although they no longer inhabited it, having abandoned it for more modern facilities, it still had purpose. It contained several large hidden vaults, which were used for storage, containing secret files, formulas, weapons and other things from their history. Many of these things had been transported directly from planet Kaboris for safe keeping, so that their history would always be preserved for future generations to come. The aliens knew that history should never be forgotten, otherwise they wouldn't learn from it.

Zepadoodle had taken the top-secret file he found in the Arizona camp for reference, he needed to find all the other files that it corresponded with. He sifted thru several vaults, having the combinations for all of them; however, he didn't find what he was looking for. He came to the very last vault, and immediately noticed that it had an engraved metal plate attached to the front of it. The plate said "do not open, under penalty of law, this contains Krempie's personal items". This intrigued him, why would Krempie store any of his own personal items in a vault? What did penalty of law really mean? For all intensive purposes, the law no longer applied to Zepadoodle, he had been handed a death sentence by being told to return to Kaboris, so therefore, nothing worse would truly be done to him. He considered himself to be an independent nation, with himself as the leader. He decided he would open this vault and investigate.

It was clear to Zepadoodle, that the combination to this vault had been changed, because the original combination of taps was no longer working. He tried several different ones, but all failed to open it. The alien began to think, he used every combination that seemed possible, including dates that could have been significant to Krempie including his birth date, but none of these worked either. He knew he was wasting valuable time, but still pressed forward, sure that the answers he needed would be found in this locked vault.

He began to search thru all of the prehistoric weaponry, hoping that something there would blow up the door, and just allow him to open the vault, but none of those helped either. The vault was built to be secure, and that it certainly was, without the proper combination, it became clear to him that he would not be able to open and enter it.

Zepadoodle sat down and thought and thought. He needed to get into old grumpy Krempie's mind. What was important to him besides being mean to everyone who held a position below him? He jumped up from the old dilapidated chair, and ran over to the vault. He would try a series of taps that represented the date his nation planned to take over this planet, which was now, only just one day away from happening.

The alien jumped for joy when the vault door swung open, he had finally cracked the elusive combination. Just as he had suspected, the vault didn't seem to contain any personal items. Instead, he found containers loaded with different kinds of old medical potions, chemicals, high tech weapons, Kaboris money currency, gemstones and files. Many of the files had research reports from different laboratories, and even included diagrams or pictures. He was sure that he would locate something in these papers that went along with the file he found in the desert. He grabbed the files and started to leave, but something buried deep in the back of the vault got his attention, probably because it had been carefully covered with a large material tarp of sorts. Perhaps underneath it he would find something that really was Krempie's personal property, or just maybe he was hiding something else of importance.

Zepadoodle quickly removed the tarp, exposing a large piece of machinery, which kind of looked like some kind of a weapon. Not understanding the significance of it at the time, he covered it back up and left the vault. He assumed that this must have been built on site in the laboratory there, and then the project had been abandoned for one reason or another. Since it was quite large, it would most likely not have been very reasonable to remove and take along when they moved, especially if they didn't have an immediate use for the object.

With the files he located in hand, off he went back to the desert. He relaxed in his new home, surrounded by the all the comforts and peace and quiet he needed. Zepadoodle took his time reading the new files he had found. Once again, he discovered that all the top secret documents had Krempie's signature on the bottom of them, as he had been in charge of researching ways to save their planet.

One file was called OPERATION LASER DESTROYER, which he casually flipped thru, at first believing that it would contain little or no information. The file talked about practical experiments with energy laser weapons, including something relating to a giant ray gun of sorts. When he flipped to the next page, he found a complete diagram, which had been hand drawn of this object. There was also a handwritten note in Krempie's writing stating that this object had in fact been built as well as tested. Then he realized that this was what he had found under the large tarp inside the vault. The next paper showed a document that stated, this directed energy weapon, emitted powerful energy in its aimed direction, without the means of using a projectile. It had been tried and tested, and that it hit its targeted area over and over again for the desired effect intended. The laser energy used was made using electromagnetic radiation, particle beams and sonic sound. According to this record, the purpose of this laser was to save planet Kaboris. It was documented that it would be able to avoid the catastrophic collision expected with his planet, because it was capable of destroying all the embryos currently in orbit, which the aliens felt would shatter their planet in a expected collision, only a few days from now.

Zepadoodle was confused, and wondered why this weapon had never been used, when it clearly was the answer to all of their problems. He noticed that this report had been signed by one of the highest scientists who worked in that lab, but he had suddenly disappeared many years ago, never to be heard from again. Zepadoodle fondly remembered him, and often wondered what happened to him.

The last page in the file shocked him. It was a report, which talked about this laser, but said just the opposite of what the previous report said. This one stated that the laser had been tested, and failed miserably. The item was deemed completely useless, and stated that the lead scientist, disappeared to hide in shame when his project was found to be a waste of time, effort and money. Naturally, this last report had just one signature signing off on it, Krempie's. The last line of the report was the one that really got his attention. It stated in capital letters, that the laser weapon had been destroyed, and used as scrap.

He instantly knew what he had to do, he needed to get this massive weapon, and save his planet. The problem was, it had to weigh, far more than what he could possibly lift, and he would need help. He needed extreme manpower, or at least the use of some kind of magic, perhaps the magic that the realms possessed. He made a decision that he would enter the realms, because they were his only hope. He would have to make them listen; it was their only chance to save themselves and all the people on the planet Earth too.

If he could pull all of this off, he would go down in history as a hero with his own people. He knew that Krempie was not looking out for the best interest of his nation, for some reason, he wanted to take over this planet, even though it wasn't truly necessary.

Zepadoodle needed to be careful, because if any of the other aliens spotted him, they would now deem him as an enemy because he had been told to go back to Kaboris, and he defied a direct order from his leaders. He went straight to the tree, which in the past had given him access into the realms, and hoped that the gnomes hadn't closed it on him.

He gained entrance into the astral plane, and went directly to the green door and knocked loudly, hoping that one of the gnomes would answer.

Chapter 33
When Magic Happens

Kyle convinced his teacher to attempt to enter the realms with him. He explained in detail how the mushroom circle worked, and what they needed to do. The man stepped into the circle, although, feeling slightly foolish he pressed on, with his student at his side. He told himself that he really didn't have anything to lose, except perhaps his pride should they not be transported anywhere. He didn't just have Kyle's word, the words his mother spoke seemed quite convincing that this place existed. The last voice Koza heard was Kyle's, repeating to him over and over again in a faint whisper, you must believe, you must believe.

Joe stood in the distance, still arguing with Sarah about how ridiculous the entire situation was, annoyed that his time had been wasted. He was still quite angry that she had any part in all of this, and wondered about her mental health at this point. He questioned whether or not, she had problems, which she passed on to her own son, which hadn't been diagnosed yet.

Aimee Lynn stood outside the mushroom circle, not quite sure if she wanted to join her brother or her arguing parents. Standing alone, she felt out of place, feeling no security whatsoever. She turned her head back and forth from the circle to her parents trying to make a decision which ones she wanted to join.

Kyle and his teacher, jumped spinning in the air, but nothing happened. They weren't transported into the astral plane, and they both finally stopped jumping.

"I don't understand why it didn't work. You have to keep thinking that you believe, and really really believe," said Kyle.

"I am, believe me, I am," said Mr. Koza feeling flushed and looking in Joe's direction nervously.

"I bet I know what happened. The mushroom ring got broken; half of them are missing, because Joe just had to kick them. Maybe that broke some of the spell," said Kyle.

"Yeah…ah…maybe that's what happened," said the teacher feeling uncomfortable and wishing that he were back in his classroom teaching.

"I'm going to call my fairy friends, they can fix the circle. I have a stone to call them. You won't be able to see them, but I will. It will look like I'm talking to no one, but I will be talking to them. You just have to believe me, and believe in them," said Kyle.

Kyle used his magic stone and called upon Annastarlis and Nerby. They appeared almost instantly to him, pleased that he had come thru and gotten everyone to the magic circle. They too, believed the problem was undoubtedly the missing mushrooms and told him that they would just create a new circle for him.

Mr. Koza stood watching Kyle as he spoke to thin air. He began to question his own sanity for being in this position. Yet part of him deep down, his child side truly wanted to believe in all of it.

Aimee Lynn ran over to the area where Kyle stood talking, she seemed excited as if she too, had seen the fairies. She whispered softly and laughed, joining in on their conversation.

Sarah turned from Joe, and saw Annastarlis and Nerby. She could also see them, because they had appeared to her before.

"There they are, the fairies, they are here right now," screamed Sarah as she pointed towards her children.

Joe's face turned red, partly from the anger building inside of him, but more so, because he found himself in a situation that he saw as being out of control. All of it was beyond any normal reasoning, and he didn't know how much more of it he could possibly stand.

Koza never took his eyes off of Kyle and Aimee Lynn. He carefully studied the air that they spoke to, and he wondered if it could all just be possible. Right before his eyes he saw a mushroom ring appear. It wasn't there a few seconds ago, and right there is was, beckoning him to enter it. Deep inside he believed, he believed in things that he couldn't see, perhaps he always did.

"C'mon, it's time to go," called Kyle.

Koza quickly entered the new circle, he had no doubt left, he had been convinced. Where they would be going exactly, he really didn't know, but he was willing to take on the magical adventure.

Aimee Lynn had made up her mind that she didn't want to stay behind. She ran and jumped into the circle, joining her brother and his teacher. The three jumped and span together in the air, wishing and thinking that they truly wanted to go to the realms.

Joe stood in the distance still arguing with his wife and thinking how foolish all of this appeared. He was determined that he would get help for his wife, and his stepson, and certainly demand a new teacher for Kyle, because Koza was off his rocker. He had entertained all of this long enough, and now he was going to put a stop to it. He walked away from Sarah, realizing that anything he was saying to her had fallen upon deaf ears. Sarah followed behind him, still pleading her case, that the realms did exist. As they neared the circle area, suddenly right before them, Mr. Koza, Kyle and Aimee Lynn simply vanished.

"What....what happened? What kind of trick is this now," demanded Joe.

"It's not a trick, don't you get it...they went to the realms, just like Kyle said they would," said Sarah thrilled with the sight of it.

"That's just ridiculous; he learned some kind of magic trick, where are all of them hiding. I have had just about enough of all of this," sniped Joe.

"You have seen it all with your own eyes, and you still don't believe.

What is it going to take for you to realize that we are all telling you the truth," screamed Sarah in frustration.

"Well, I certainly have no intentions in making a fool out of myself, and jumping and leaping in the air, so don't even ask me," said Joe sternly.

"I didn't think that you would. The fact of this is that I don't believe in you. Kyle didn't believe in you either, he trusted in his teacher, before his own stepfather," said Sarah.

Kyle, Koza, and Aimee Lynn had been transported directly into the astral plane, much to the teacher's delight. He walked thru the foggy mist with his student, and sister, and listened as Kyle explained the different color doors, and where each one of them would take them. Just as they were about to enter the green door, Zepadoodle appeared from the mist, startled to run directly into humans there.

"What are you doing here? You aren't going to take over our planet, because we are going to stop you," said Kyle showing no fear.

"I don't want your planet. I need to talk to the gnomes right away because I believe I have a way of saving your planet and my own, but I need help," said Zepadoodle.

Koza stood in complete amazement, standing in front of him was a real live green alien. He had dreamt about this day for many years, and he strangely felt at home. He had no fear of the alien, he was curious, and thought about many questions he had, determined that before all of this was over, he would ask them. Deep down, he always knew that humans on the planet earth were not the only intelligent beings that somewhere out there, something else just had to exist.

Aimee Lynn had seen the aliens many times before, and she didn't like them, not one little bit. She looked up at Kyle's teacher, and grabbed his hand to hold it. As soon as he squeezed her hand tightly, the little girl relaxed, she knew that this man would protect her.

No one in the group opened the green door; instead, it swung open from the inside before any of them could touch it. Standing in the open doorway was Gatsby; he smiled broadly when he saw that Kyle had brought help. He was slightly disappointed that Joe wasn't in attendance, but he also knew that the man wouldn't enter the realms easily, he was far too stubborn, but he had a plan.

He invited Kyle, Aimee Lynn inside, directing them to go straight to Jerry's office. Gatsby asked Koza to stay behind with him, because he felt that the only chance they had of getting Joe to enter, was to send Mr. Koza back for him. Joe would never listen to his children, but perhaps this adult teacher could get thru to him. Koza left the astral plane half heartedly; he had just gotten there, and certainly didn't want to leave. The man understood the importance of bringing Joe back with him and therefore did as requested. He would return back to realms with or without Joe because his adventure was just beginning and he didn't want to miss one minute of it. Gatsby assured him, that he would leave a troll at the door, so that when he returned he could take him straight to the Great Hall of Justice.

Zepadoodle stood at a distance, slowly approaching the old gnome, not wanting to seem intimidating or threatening. He wanted to talk to the gnomes, wanted to make a deal, except this time they would all be working together for the same common goal. Zepadoodle needed to make the gnomes listen to him, and he understood that this wasn't going to be an easy task, as they viewed him to be their enemy after all the threats that he had made. He really didn't have anything against the inhabitants of the realms, at least not personally, it was just that they possibly stood in the way of his own people's existence; at least they did when he first met them.

Gatsby stood in the astral plane entertaining everything that the alien was telling him about this massive laser weapon. He didn't know what to believe, was the alien playing games or truly telling the truth? He decided to keep him in the astral plane, denying him access to the realms, at least for the moment. Gatsby told the alien, there was no reason they couldn't speak freely right where they stood. Besides, this would give Koza extra time to talk Joe into the realms.

Kyle lead the way thru the gnome realm, directly to the Great Hall of Justice. Aimee Lynn was happy to finally be in the realms, she loved everything about the place, the trees, flower gardens, and of course seeing the beautiful gem lined streets. She was delighted at the sight of the groups of gnomes, casually strolling around, young and old. This was the first time the child had seen gnomes, and she giggled at the very sight of them.

Koza popped back into the mushroom circle. He found Joe and Sarah still arguing. Joe was insisting that Kyle had learned to perform some kind of a mirror magic trick, sure that everyone was simply hiding somewhere in the woods. He jumped when Koza suddenly appeared before him, in the center of the mushroom ring.

"Well...I know you probably think everyone is crazy, but I have news for you. I not only have already seen and talked to a gnome, I also spoke to a real live little green alien," said Koza with a huge smile on his face.

Joe stood silent; he didn't know what to say at this point. He was feeling more frustrated than anything else. He listened to Koza talk, and heard his wife continuing to nag him about doing the right thing.

"Listen, what do you really have to lose by going with him? If you are just so sure that this place doesn't exist, and that gnomes, trolls, fairy's, whosawhachits, and aliens are just a child's fantasy world, then why are you so afraid to go?" asked Sarah.

"You want me to jump around and spin like a fool in the circle, fine, if that will make you happy, I'll do it...I'm just sick and tired of all of this already," said Joe angry.

"You will not make entrance into the realms, not unless you really believe you will end up there. I'm serious...it's an amazing place, and I can't wait to get back. You must think in your mind, that you are going there, because you believe in it," warned Koza.

Sarah, Joe and Koza entered the mushroom circle together. The three adults were quite a sight, jumping and leaping in the air. Koza was the first one to enter the astral plane, and then Sarah, however Joe didn't transport. Sarah stood in the fog, and spotted the different colored doors and then the gnome speaking to a green alien in the distance of the mist. All of it was exactly how her son had originally described it. She never doubted for one minute, that she would arrive here, and she was disappointed that her husband didn't arrive along with her to experience all of it. She knew that he couldn't or wouldn't allow himself to believe. He needed to see something with his own eyes, before his heart would allow him to truly believe. All she could think about was how if only he could believe for a minute, he could get here, and see it all for himself.

Just as Sarah and Koza decided to enter the gnome realm green door, they heard Joe's voice. He had made it into the realms. It was against everything he had always stood for, but for some reason, he pulled down deep inside of himself, and he remembered, he remembered the gnome he saw as a young boy.

Chapter 34
Worlds Come Together

There they were everyone together in the gnome realm, humans, gnomes, fairies, and an alien. Gathered in a meeting to save the world from the disaster that would occur just one day away, they calmly spoke about what each and every one of them needed to do.

Zepadoodle showed them all the files he had found, even the one with the diagram of this massive laser. He explained how they could use it to save his own planet. He sincerely felt that with everyone's help, it could all be done in time. Then he would go into the underwater camp in the pyramids and tell his peers that they could all just return back home. It all seemed like it would work, but still Joe had his reservations about all of it. First off, he was shocked to hear about all of these alien camps that had existed on the planet for thousands of years. He didn't truly understand how, the FBI couldn't have been aware of them, especially since national security was at stake, it almost made him feel like a failure in his position at the bureau.

Now the man knew the truth that everything Kyle spoke about really existed. Things he always doubted, completely dismissed as fairytale folklore, things that were beyond reason, it was all true. All of it made him question who he was, and how he had been living his entire life. He wondered about so many different things that people had claimed to him over the years, and how he ridiculed them, perhaps wrongfully now. If he could help the alien save the world, he would still be changed forever. He thought about all the training he had, and how he was taught to base everything on concrete facts. He didn't even know if he would be able to stay at the same job he had, because he would be a different man. He remembered all the jokes and laughs that happened around the water cooler at work, how they would all make fun of people who made such claims.

His mind was now open to new possibilities; never again, would he be quick to dismiss anything that someone said. He certainly owed Kyle and his wife apologies, and he would humbly give them, even though, that was something he wasn't very good at, and never did. Joe always thought he was right, admitting he was wrong about something was one of the hardest things he ever had to do.

He recalled the interview he had with Aimee Lynn's parents. The mother cried for her child, and pleaded with him to believe her alien story. He treated the parents on an official level, and wrote in the final report that they either had severe mental issues or that they were on drugs. He had been wrong about these people. In another week, Sarah and Joe would be in court, to begin the custody battle for the little girl. He knew now that there would be no fight, her natural parents deserved to have her back. Aimee Lynn did witness her parent's alien abduction, he truly believed that. She had been traumatized enough; she needed to be with them, it was where she belonged. Clearly these people loved their daughter, and wanted her more than anything. They risked their own reputations, their jobs, by telling the abduction story, insisting that it was all the truth, even though they had been laughed at and called liars. Now they were paying good money for an attorney to fight it all in court, even though they couldn't truly afford it financially. Joe knew that Sarah was right, they would have to sign Aimee Lynn back over to her parents, he only hoped that her parents would be understanding and still allow Sarah and Joe to be a small part of her life, and allow her to visit them. He reached out for his wife's hand, and squeezed it gently, perhaps he wasn't saying much in words, but she knew from his gesture that he was sorry.

The gnomes insisted that Joe could contact the right people in the government, so that they could get a hold of this wonderful futuristic weapon and use it to save the world. The problem was that Joe simply didn't think he could help; he spoke about all the red tape that he would have to go thru to make this happen. He clearly explained to all of them, how he had been trained to dispute all of this, and that he would most likely never be able to get anyone to believe him. His own superiors would most likely believe that he had been working too hard, and obviously needed a leave of absence, for a mental rest vacation. The government didn't move quickly on anything, they wouldn't go into action, until some kind of an attack had begun, and then it would be too late.

What Joe did do, was take over the situation, he started to do what he did best. He started a full investigation, and asked questions, he needed facts and details. He would put a plan into action; however the army he would use, would be one that he put together from the realm habitants, not humans.

"You can obviously transport yourselves all over the world, but can you take humans with you when you do this?" asked Joe seriously.

"Yes, I can," said Zepadoodle.

"Yes, I can take humans with me too," answered Annastarlis.

"Well, than I guess the best thing we can do right now, is for you to take me to see this weapon, let's see what we have to use, where is it stored?" asked Joe sincerely.

"It's in the vault, in the camp below Stonehenge," said Zepadoodle.

"Stonehenge…ah….ok….well, then, I guess we are off to England," said Joe surprised to even hear those words come out of his mouth, however he now knew that just maybe all things were possible.

Jerry called in Hubert, requesting for him to join the group. They might need the help of the troll, because from the description of the weapon, it would be very heavy. Joe, Koza and Sarah were shocked at the sight of a troll, and Sarah couldn't help but notice the smell that lingered around him. Kyle stood proudly, and every once in a while, he would just give Sarah a smile.

Gatsby dished out invisibility stones to everyone who didn't have that normal capability, including the humans there. He explained how they worked, and his reasoning that they could be seen by humans making a pilgrimage to Stonehenge. They would have to be as discrete as possible, and this was their best chance at doing that. Kyle was thrilled that Joe took the stone without even questioning it, he just seemed to accept the fact that it would work the magic the gnome claimed it would.

Once they arrived, Zepadoodle led the way, opening the vault and uncovering the weapon. The trolls and humans struggled, but managed to push the massive laser weapon from the vault.

"Understand that no one from the realms can use a weapon that has the capabilities of killing another, even if it's just being used to destroy items floating in space," said Jerry.

"I guess for you, it's a good thing that I have found a way for us to save my planet, because without weapons, we would have crushed you," said Zepadoodle.

"That isn't true, we have the power of magic, you would be very surprised on how we can protect ourselves. We have gotten quite creative in the past," said Gatsby in response.

"Well, since you have the power of magic, isn't there anyway you can just transport this huge weapon along with us, somewhere else, so that we don't have to keep moving it," said Joe.

Zepadoodle handed over all the laboratory documents which explained how this large laser worked. Between the teacher and Joe, they were able to figure out how to use it, collaborating together. They carefully calculated the specifications written down for Planet Kaboris, and the area where the upcoming colliding space debris objects were expected to be right now. Joe was more cautious about sending the laser rays out, but Koza reasoned that since it was only going out into space, whatever they hit, if anything, would have to result in little or no damage to anyone or anything.

Everyone held their breath, as if they were all afraid to even breathe, as everyone took their assigned positions. No one knew for sure that this laser would even work. They had no backup plan, nothing to go to, if this didn't work, therefore it just had to. Annastarlis suggested sprinkling the weapon with fairy dust, if not for anything, but perhaps good luck, but Jerry refused her request, insisting magic and weapons didn't mix.

This weapon needed to be fired from three different places, all at the same exact time, assuring that it could never be used by just one being, or even two. It was all part of a security system to make sure that when it was used, it was done properly and hopefully for the right reasons.

Joe, Koza and Zepadoodle each took their position around the massive machine. They would all activate the buttons in front of them, on the count of three.

"I'll do the countdown, are you both ready," said Joe taking charge.

"I'm ready," said Zepadoodle.

"As am I, let's rock," said Mr. Koza.

One, two, three, and off the large laser went, shooting out a massive green beam, which was nearly blinding. Zepadoodle, quickly checked all of his astronomical gadgets, which showed him, that the laser had in fact worked. His planet was no longer in any jeopardy, and the survival of his people was assured.

He needed to transport to the main camp, the one under the Bermuda Triangle. He hoped that the guards would allow him to pass, so that he could have a word with Zoop, to tell him the good news. He would bring all the files he had found, which would make Krempie angry, but they showed all the proof that he needed. He guessed that Krempie would get into some kind of trouble for hiding all this information and the laser itself.

Zepadoodle would no doubt also be in a little trouble for disobeying direct orders, because he didn't return to planet Kaboris as told. Then there were the issues of breaking and entering into the old abandoned camps and snooping in top secret files, plus opening Krempie's personal vault, that certainly wouldn't go over big.

The alien returned to the underwater camp, and hoped for the best, his stomach churned, and his hands trembled with fear. He entered as a grey, which stressed him even further. Krempie was one of the first to greet him, but not with a smile, nor with congratulations. The older alien was angry, and instantly demanded that Zepadoodle hand over all of his old personal files.

"This is all I have to prove what happened. I'm not giving these to anyone except Zoop, get out of my way," said Zepadoodle bravely.

"You were ordered to return to Kaboris; in essence you were sentenced to death. I have no problems killing you right now. No one would ever question me," snickered Krempie.

Around the hall corner came Zoop, it had already been reported to him that all threats to planet Kaboris had been vaporized by something or someone.

"Allow him to speak," said Zoop.

Zepadoodle quickly explained everything that happened to Zoop and the alien listened to him. He produced all the old files, showing the evidence that Krempie not only knew about this laser, but that he went as far as to hide the weapon in a locked vault. Naturally Krempie insisted that all the documents were falsified, and he was being framed but Zoop knew it was a lie.

Zoop ordered most of the aliens to return to their planet, along with Krempie who had been placed in some kind of magnetic energy shackles. He would be held accountable for his actions later on and face a trial in front of a panel of his peers.

Zepadoodle would be honored as a hero, although, he never did get the promotion that he so desperately wanted, he did receive several decorated metals of honor, which pleased him.

The aliens didn't completely leave planet Earth, they still to this day, maintain several camps, and continue to study humans.

Chapter 35
It's a World of Magic

Back in the realms, Kyle, Sarah, Aimee Lynn, and Mr. Koza sat with the gnomes and fairies. Jerry explained to them about how the realms have secretly protected the humans over the years from many threats. He naturally requested that they return to their own world, never to speak of anything they had learned.

Joe would return to work at the FBI with a new enlightened, open attitude. Mr. Koza would return back to school to teach for many years. He never stopped talking about the space shows that he watched, and he still continued to collect different kinds of space items, in fact, his collection only got bigger and better. Both of the men, held to their word, and never told anyone about their experiences with any of the realm inhabitants. From time to time, the realms would visit all of them; sometimes it was just to say hello, and other times to make small requests of assistance, or to offer their help during difficult times.

Kyle truly built a lifelong relationship with not only Mr. Koza, but he finally bonded with Joe.

Elvin and Mystic had been everywhere in Egypt searching for Elise. They had found some evidence that she had been possibly visiting several open air market areas. They overheard people in several shops speaking about invisible strange forces, claiming they witnessed objects flying thru the air, leaving a wake of destruction in its path. This even included a large pink carpet, which acted as if someone were riding on it, causing it to soar around in the air over people's heads. More alarming were the angry jewelry vendors, screaming to the police that much of their precious gems, necklaces, bracelets, and rings vanished right before their very eyes. Several shops down, Mystic heard a woman claiming that rolls of beautiful silk fabric just disappeared from inventory, but the odd thing was it was only the pink material, every other color remained untouched. Even being outside, the bazaar shopping area reeked of strong perfumes, as most of the fragrant bottles had been mysteriously emptied, which made many people cough and choke because the odor was so strong.

Now Elvin certainly understood how his sister Elise felt in the human world. She was excited and was unsupervised which was like locking a child in a candy or toy store, she was just out of control. He had the same feelings, the sudden freedom to do as he pleased, having no one to answer to, messing with humans was just plain fun, especially when they couldn't see you. High on discovering different things, places, and observing people, it was all new to her, and she had no intentions of stopping. To be fair, when she went out on her first mission, she didn't get to do or see anything fun; it was all work, some of which she found outright frightening.

Mystic insisted that they continue to follow the path which Elise had most likely taken. As they rounded each and every corner, they found more people clearly upset about something that had happened. The leader of the fairies was determined to locate Elise, and insisted that they move along faster.

Elvin understood that his sister would be in big trouble when she finally returned to the realms. Even though, this was the first time that she truly had defied direct orders, the gnomes would not go lightly on her. He hoped that she wouldn't find herself locked up as a prisoner in her own realm, as punishment, especially because this would most likely mean even he would not be able to see her. He loved his sister, and he had warned her about doing these kinds of things.

Still, even he had to admit to himself, that he would have enjoyed joining in on all the fun. He knew that she was having the time of her life, and as he imagined the expressions on people's faces as all of these things happened, it did make him want to laugh. Mystic, would always seem more like a mother figure to most in the realms, picked up on Elvin's attitude.

"I guess you think that all of this is funny?" asked Mystic in more of a stern tone than usual.

"Nope dude-ette, I know it's not...well...it is a little funny," said Elvin honestly.

"Really? A little funny? We could be facing the end of the realms, the end of planet Earth as we know it...and your sister is running around causing havoc. We should be helping the others, not out looking for her right now. I see no humor in any of it," said Mystic angry.

Elvin thought about the statement the fairy just made. It was certainly possible that the world as he knew it would end within a day. He had no idea that the crisis was over. In his mind he began to think about things like what was the point of working anymore, being serious, when it could all just be over. Maybe his sister did have the right idea. Perhaps Elise really was smarter than him. Maybe he should also be spending the last of his time alive, having fun, just like she was. If he had to die, he wanted to go with a bang.

The whosawhachit made a snap decision, and he would never turn back from it. Since Mystic had taken the lead, and he followed closely behind, he could easily take off from her sight and disappear. Mystic was looking straight ahead, and side to side viewing all the damage, and searching for Elise, she never turned around to look behind her. She wouldn't know if Elvin had accidently gotten lost from her because he wasn't paying attention or if he just took off on his own.

Elvin went in the opposite direction, as quickly as he could, determined that he would lose the fairy leader. He thought about how angry she would be, just flying along talking to him, not even realizing for a while, that he wasn't there listening to her. He didn't care anymore; none of it really would matter anymore, because the world was, coming to an end. He wanted to do two things, one find his sister, and the other, to outdo her.

Elvin found a museum down one of the streets and entered it. He looked at all the different artifacts, mummies and other things that had been carefully removed from several tombs. The museum had high security with several guards posted in different areas watching every move people made. They naturally couldn't see Elvin because he was invisible, so off to work he went. He carefully looked at the face on a large Sphinx statue, which resembled a lion to him and changed it immediately to a unicorn head. The whosawhachit was able to use some of his own magic, however as much as he tried; he wasn't able to turn items purple, much to his own displeasure. He had to settle for altering items in design, which still rather amused him. He noticed several other statues, all which had strange animal heads or were of humans, who were highly painted, many decorated in pure gold. He decided that the image of his own face would look much better on them, horns and all. Right before people's eye's he was changing Egyptian history and it delighted him. He was especially proud of one of the largest statues, which depicted a Pharaoh that now sported his own huge grin.

He only wished the he could materialize and show himself to everyone. Oh how scared all the people would be, but the realms were over their limit, it just couldn't be done.

Elvin headed out towards the desert, he didn't want to take any chances that Mystic could spot him. While he could hide from humans, he wasn't able to hide from her. He saw several men riding on camels, and he thought they just looked silly. These camels all had one hump, and the whosawhachit knew that some breeds of this animal could have two humps; he wondered how the men would react, if their camels instantly had three humps. The men were frightened by the sudden deformity of their camels, and leaped from them down into the sand in fear.

The whosawhachit decided to head in the direction of the Nile River, because it was clear to him, that he wouldn't find much to do in the deep desert. In the distance he saw something. He was sure that he spotted a quick flash of pink, and his eyes focused on it, before it diminished. Elvin was positive that this pink movement was his sister. She was probably attempting to flee from him, most likely seeing him before he saw her. Since she had no place to hide, Elise had decided to dig herself down into the sand, hoping her brother would never find her.

She hated the feeling of the hot sand on her body, but dreaded going back to the realms even more. She poked a hole up thru the sand around her face, with one of her fingers, just enough for her to breath, but small enough to keep her hidden, at least she hoped so.

Elvin scanned the area where he had been certain he had seen her. He walked thru the sand, kicking it with his feet, and calling his sister's name. He told her over and over again, that he had no intentions of bringing her back to the realms, because he wasn't going back either. She didn't respond to him, most likely afraid that her brother was tricking her. She stubbornly held her position, hoping that he would give up shortly, because she couldn't stay under the sand much longer. She had wrapped herself in beautiful fabrics, and weighed her entire body down with as much jewelry as her body could possibly carry, which now made her extra uncomfortable considering her hiding position.

Elise thought she felt something with one of her feet, not sure what the item was, she wiggled her toes. She was relieved that it wasn't any type of live creature, because just the thought of something crawling on her, almost made her scream. The object was solid, felt smooth, and held the heat from the sand. She moved her foot over it and thought it was some kind of metal. Her mind raced with ideas of what she had found buried down deep in the desert, maybe it was some kind of hidden treasure. She reasoned that it could be something from ancient Egyptian kings or queens, hidden away for centuries, hopefully even jewelry. She began to wiggle more in the sand, hoping to pull this hidden object up by just using her foot. She was sure that if she could just get it by the area of her hand, her fingers could tell her more about it. Elise was always curious; she needed to know what she had found right now, the suspense was just killing her. She just didn't have the patience to wait until Elvin moved on, therefore she moved around under the sand more and more, determined to grab this object, wrongfully believing that her brother would not find her.

Nothing ever got pass Elvin, he saw the sand moving around as if it had just come alive. He was sure that something was under it, disturbing the sands usual calm flat lifeless existence. Elvin saw one of Elise's horns carelessly peep out from under the surface, he had her now. She would have no place to run no place and hide, and once he explained his new attitude to her, she would have no need to flee from him.

"I see you under the sand, so you might as well just come out," said Elvin.

The sand stopped moving, Elise stayed as still as possible. She had her toes curled around the object determined not to lose it.

"Listen, I'm not going back to the realms. If the world is going to be over in another day, than I want to have fun too. Just come out, and let's see what kind of fun we can get into," said Elvin.

Elise listened to every word her brother said, from the tone of his voice, he certainly sounded sincere. Elvin had never lied to her, and the things that he was saying made sense. He had no reason to return back either, besides when she saw him, he had been alone. She knew that the realms would have never allowed him to enter the human realm alone therefore; he must have run away too.

Elise popped out of the sand, but the object she had held so long in her toes fell from her grasp slipping back down into the sand. She stood in the sand talking to her brother, and knew that he was telling her the truth. He discussed different things they could go and do together. He suggested that they leave the desert, and head to a more populated area, where they would find people to mess with. Right before they left, Elise remembered the object in the sand, and told her brother about it. The two of them got on their hands and knees and began digging in the sand hoping to locate it again.

Elise's hand finally reached it. It was a metal object, gold in color.

It looked like some kind of a small teapot, or oil can, maybe even an old type lamp.

"I know what that thing is, it's a magic lamp, put your hand on it and rub it," said Elvin.

Elise did as her brother instructed and to her amazement, a genie flew out of the lamp.

"Yes, master, I am here to grant you three wishes, anything your heart desires," said the genie.

Elise and Elvin looked at each in delight, this just had so many wonderful possibilities.

BOOKS AVAILABLE BY THIS AUTHOR

Woofing it Down
The Quick & Easy Guide to Making Healthy Dog Food At Home
Lapping It up
The Quick & East Guide to Making Healthy Cat Food At Home
The Ultimate Yorkshire Terrier Book
Guide to Caring, Raising, Training, Breeding, Whelping, Feeding and
Loving a Yorkie
The Ultimate Dachshund Hound Book
Guide to Caring, Raising, Training, Breeding, Whelping, Feeding and
Loving a Doxie.
Tales of the Whosawhachits
Key Holders of the Realm (Book 1 of series)
Young Adult Novel
(YABI Award Winner)
Tales of the Whosawhachits
Enter the 5th Realm (Book 2 of series)
Mirror Mirror
Seven Years Bad Luck
Adult Paranormal Fantasy Novel
(Covey Award Winner)

COMING SOON

True Encounters with Imaginary Friends
Young Adult Novel
The Ultimate Dachshund Hound Book

For more information about this author please view Patricia's
website at
www.patriciaogrady.com